Pr... ...quartet

'O... ...he weaker, but Julia
Golding has surpassed herself here by delivering a
... good vers...

evil is the underlying... ...to get the
better of a shapeshifter as well as someone who can
kill just by looking. Awesome stuff with an ecological
twist and completely unputdownable.'

Lovereading4kids.co.uk

'absolutely great and keeps you hooked'

Ambika, age 12

'Crackles with tension'   *Times Educational Supplement*

'5/5 … so brilliant you simply have to read it.'

Jenii, age 10

'This has all the ingredients of a must-read series'
Publishing News

'This is a brilliant book … It is amazing how authors
invent totally new things and all the details about them'
Lilliane, age 11

The
GORGON'S GAZE

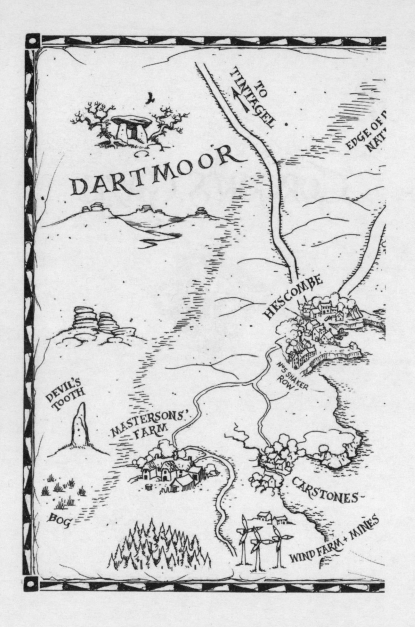

TO TINTAGEL

DARTMOOR

EDGE OF NAT...

HESCOMBE

N°5 SHAKER ROW

DEVIL'S TOOTH

MASTERSONS' FARM

BOG

CARSTONES-

WIND FARM + MINES

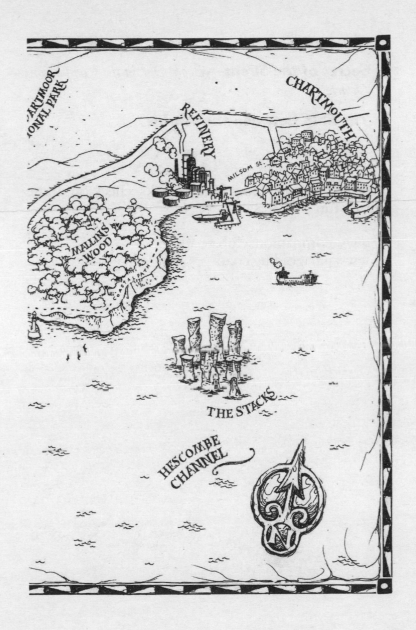

Also by Julia Golding

Secret of the Sirens—*Book One in the Companions Quartet*

The Ship Between the Worlds

If you enjoy reading Julia's books, check out these two fun websites:

www.companionsclub.co.uk
www.juliagolding.co.uk

BOOK TWO
THE COMPANIONS QUARTET

The GORGON'S GAZE

JULIA GOLDING

OXFORD
UNIVERSITY PRESS

For Joss

OXFORD
UNIVERSITY PRESS

Great Clarendon Street, Oxford OX2 6DP

Oxford University Press is a department of the University of Oxford.
It furthers the University's objective of excellence in research, scholarship,
and education by publishing worldwide in

Oxford New York

Auckland Cape Town Dar es Salaam Hong Kong Karachi
Kuala Lumpur Madrid Melbourne Mexico City Nairobi
New Delhi Shanghai Taipei Toronto

With offices in

Argentina Austria Brazil Chile Czech Republic France Greece
Guatemala Hungary Italy Japan Poland Portugal Singapore
South Korea Switzerland Thailand Turkey Ukraine Vietnam

Oxford is a registered trade mark of Oxford University Press
in the UK and in certain other countries

First published 2006
First published in paperback 2007

British Library Cataloguing in Publication Data
Data available

ISBN 978-0-19-275457-8 (hardback)
ISBN 978-0-19-275461-5 (paperback)

Typeset by Newgen Imaging Systems (P) Ltd., Chennai, India
Printed in Great Britain by Cox & Wyman Ltd, Reading, Berkshire

3 5 7 9 10 8 6 4 2

Contents

1
Gold

'You're going to get us both killed!' shrieked Connie. She was torn between terror and delight as Col nudged the winged horse into a heart-stopping dive through a wet, grey cloud.

Col laughed back over his shoulder, his flying helmet and goggles sparing him the worst of the weather. 'You don't fool us, Connie Lionheart— you're loving every minute of the ride.'

'Am not!' she shouted crossly in his ear. 'Aargh! Look out!'

The pegasus plummeted to his left. Thud, thud: Skylark's hoofs hit turf, almost jolting her off his back.

'Nice landing.' Connie slid thankfully to the ground.

1

'What d'you mean? That was a perfect Athenian dive, followed by a Thessalonian Roll!' Col's eyes, an odd pair—one green, one brown—shone with indignation as he met her gaze. He was looking into eyes that were a mirror image of his own.

Connie stroked Skylark's nose. 'So now we've got here, will you tell me what's going on?'

They were standing at twilight on top of a hill in the middle of Dartmoor. For miles around there was nothing but grass rippling in the breeze. All was silent, except for the snake-like hiss of the wind in her ears.

'Ask Dr Brock.'

'What? Why?' Connie was completely confused now. Col grinned. He could be so infuriating. 'You'll tell me what's going on, won't you, Skylark?' she appealed to the pegasus. Skylark shook his mane and shifted his feet evasively. Connie was beginning to feel angry: what was the point of dragging her to the middle of a moor when Dr Brock was probably miles away sitting comfortably in his garden in Hescombe right now? 'Oh, come on, Col! You can't bring me all the way out here for nothing!'

'Not for nothing, Universal,' came a voice behind her. Connie spun round: there was Dr Brock, his ginger-streaked white hair flapping

2

untidily in the wind. Where had he come from? He seemed to have sprung out of the ground itself.

'What are you doing here?' she asked in surprise.

'We have something special to show you. Follow me.' Dr Brock, a companion to dragons and leader of the local chapter of the Society for the Protection of Mythical Creatures, turned and led Connie, Col, and Skylark to a steep path leading away from the brow of the hill. The track ended at a brook trickling through marshy ground. Undeterred, Dr Brock picked his way upstream, splashing in the ankle-deep water. It gave off a gassy reek as he disturbed it. Connie wrinkled her nose but did not hesitate to follow him. The rivulet issued from a dark gully that fractured the hillside. As they got deeper, the roof of stunted oak trees and lime green ferns shut out the little daylight that was left. Skylark's hoofs clattered on the stones, sending echoes ricocheting off the walls. The hair on the back of Connie's neck prickled. She had a growing sense of a presence— there was a creature, or creatures, ahead.

'I think we need some light, my friends,' called Dr Brock, taking a torch from his belt. 'Do I have your permission?' The last comment was addressed not to Connie and Col, but to the dragon-shaped shadow crouched in front of Dr Brock, dwarfing the humans. Permission must have been granted for a beam of white light sprang into life, rippling its way over the uneven rock walls.

'There!' Dr Brock exclaimed hoarsely.

Caught by the beam was a second dragon, slightly smaller than the first, curled up in the far corner of the crevice. It was lying on the ground bent round so that its tail cradled its head. A pair of emerald eyes watched them steadily. The dragon's hide shone in the light with the pristine tones of a chestnut fresh from its husk. Dr Brock bowed solemnly, a gesture copied swiftly by Connie. Col and Skylark backed off, knowing better than to approach dragons, or any other mythical creature, unless you were their companion. The chestnut dragon lifted its head briefly, its tongue flickering out to scent the air, before bowing its snout in response.

'This is Castanea,' Dr Brock said in a low voice to Connie, 'Argot's mate. Come closer—there's something we want you to see.'

Connie followed him carefully over the stony stream bed to Castanea. Argot shifted his tail to one side to let them pass, observing them with what Connie sensed to be suppressed excitement.

'Go on,' urged Dr Brock, ushering her past him.

Connie moved forward into the pool of light until she was in reach of the outer edge of the circle made by the dragon's tail. She wondered what she was expected to do: did they want her to encounter Castanea? Share her dreams as was the practice between dragons and their companions? Neither the dragon nor Dr Brock gave her a hint so she edged forward a few more steps and stretched out her hand.

Then she heard it: a squeaking, snuffling noise coming from directly in front of her. She pulled her hand back quickly and glanced up into Castanea's shining eyes. She was so close now she could smell the sulphurous aroma of dragon-breath warm on the damp air. Lids closed briefly over green eyes: she had been given consent to continue. Leaning over Castanea's tail, Connie looked down into the hollow ring formed by the curled body. Dr Brock came to her side and lifted the torch high so it shone down into the dark cavity. There lay a twisted mass of legs and tails—crimson and brown shot through with gold—amid fragments of creamy white shell. Connie finally understood: she was looking into the dragons' nest at their new family.

'Wow!' breathed Connie. Argot ruffled his wings, near bursting with pride. 'How many are there?' she asked, turning to Dr Brock.

'Ah, that's the really exciting thing,' he replied. 'May I?' he deferred to Castanea. The dragon nodded. Passing the torch to Connie, Dr Brock reached down into the nest and lifted out a single scarlet dragon, which squealed a protest at being separated from its warm bed of siblings. He scooped up another with his free hand—this one a chocolate brown with a long thrashing tail. Connie peered down to count how many remained. There were two still curled around each other—one ruby-red and the other . . .

'Gold!' Connie exclaimed as the torchlight glanced off the scales of the smallest of the dragon brood.

'Pick her up,' Dr Brock told Connie. 'This is what we wanted you to see.'

Connie gently untwisted the golden dragon and lifted it out. Dr Brock returned his two charges to the nest and took back the torch so she could cradle the dragonet in her arms. It did not protest but snuggled down against Connie's chest—the size and weight of a cat. She ran her index finger down its neck and felt it shiver with pleasure. A tiny connection was established between Connie, the universal companion—the only living person who could communicate with all creatures—and the dragonet. She could sense that its thoughts were unformed, running in her

6

mind as a succession of fierce needs. It wanted its mother. It wanted its father. It wanted Connie. Suddenly, as if a match had been put to gunpowder, Connie felt the fire ignite in its belly for the first time. Sparks issued from its tiny jaws like needle-sharp stars pricking her fingers. Argot and Castanea rumbled proudly at their child's swift progress.

'Are gold dragons rare?' Connie whispered.

'Indeed they are,' Dr Brock replied. 'Dragons are having fewer broods—dragonets of any hue are rare—but as for gold, it can lie dormant for many generations and only come to light once in a millennium. Argand here is the first pure gold dragon I've ever seen.'

Castanea blinked her emerald eyes once and Connie realized reluctantly that she must try the mother's patience no further. Placing the little dragon back in its nest, Connie gave all four young a swift stroke and stood up.

'I am honoured—thank you for letting me see your new family,' Connie said, looking over to Argot.

'Universal, Argand's companion,' Argot said in a subterranean growl of a voice.

'Me?'

'If you wish, that is,' added Dr Brock. 'Argot, Castanea, and I, we thought . . . well, we thought

7

what would be more fitting than our only univer-sal being matched with our only golden dragon?'

Flying back to Hescombe on Skylark, Col and Connie were by common consent silent, thinking over what they had been privileged to see.

'How long does it take for dragons to grow up?' Col asked at last. 'Do you know?'

'No,' Connie replied, 'I only know that drag-ons live for centuries.'

'I was hoping we'd be able to fly together but it sounds as if we might be past it by the time that golden one gets off the ground.'

'Oh, shut up, Col.' Connie gave him a poke in the ribs. She knew him well enough to realize that he enjoyed teasing her, not only to keep her from inflated ideas about her special role as a universal companion, but also because he was jealous of his identity as the rider in their friend-ship. Col said no more but Connie would have sworn that he was smiling even though she couldn't see his face.

They were now flying over the outskirts of the little fishing port of Hescombe—tonight a snakes-and-ladders board of lights bitten into at the south-eastern corner by the sea. Connie looked down to see if she could spot the roof of her home, Number Five Shaker Row, from up here.

'Hey, what's going on?' she wondered out loud.

Col glanced down and saw what had caught Connie's interest: a trail of red brake-lights wound its way out of Hescombe towards the nearby town of Chartmouth.

'That's weird,' Col said. 'Perhaps there's been a crash. Let's go and see what's up.'

'Should we? I mean, what if we're spotted?'

Connie wished she hadn't said anything as she felt Col's vague interest harden to determination once she had questioned his wisdom.

'We'll be fine,' Col replied airily, directing Skylark on a new course.

The chain of lights led over the hill behind Hescombe and across open countryside before stopping abruptly at the edge of Mallins Wood. This ancient, magical woodland was the largest forested area in the district. Even from up here, Connie could feel the presence of thousands of creatures in the trees and ground below, living secret lives hidden from humans. At the moment, the road had to loop a long way inland round the edge before it was able to descend steeply into Chartmouth. To Connie, Mallins Wood appeared a precious but endangered island as people got closer and closer. From her vantage point above the trees, she could see the lights of the Axoil refinery on the industrial outskirts of Chartmouth eating up the horizon with an angry orange glare.

'So that's it!' Col pointed ahead and down. 'They've arrived.'

At the head of the queue of cars, a convoy of battered old buses and caravans was slowly pulling off the road into a picnic spot on the fringe of the woodland. One bus appeared to have broken down—they could see figures flitting in and out of the headlamps as well as hear the angry hooting of cars stuck behind the blockage.

'Who are they?' Connie asked.

'The protestors—the ecowarriors. They're here because of the road.'

Now Connie understood. There had been a local campaign against plans to build a new road to the refinery at Chartmouth, but it had failed to stop the project going ahead. She was still furious that planning permission had been granted to broaden and straighten the existing road, cutting a great swathe through Mallins Wood, making countless animals homeless. Tree-murder, Connie considered it—and so apparently did these ecowarriors.

'Are they Society members?' Connie asked Col as they turned for home.

Col laughed. 'No—or only one or two are. Dad

hangs out with them—he says they're even weirder than we are.'

'I find that hard to believe.' Her short time as a member of the Society for the Protection of Mythical Creatures had proved to her that it comprised the oddest people she had ever met.

'We'll just have to go and visit them to find out, won't we?' Col replied, turning Skylark for home.

2
Family

Col and Skylark left Connie in a secluded bay not far from her house. As she crunched her way along the high-tide mark, she savoured the prospect of the summer holidays ahead. The people in charge of the Society for the Protection of Mythical Creatures—the Trustees—had exciting plans for her training and she couldn't wait to get started. She had been a member of the Society for less than a year and much of its work was still a mystery to her. The Society had been established over a thousand years ago to protect the last remaining mythical creatures by hiding their existence from humans. Only those with the gift of companionship with mythical creatures were allowed to join—and only after making a strict vow to keep the Society's true business secret. Usually, humans in the Society had a bond with one species only, but very occasionally a universal companion would turn up—someone who could communicate with all creatures—in short, someone like Connie. Connie was considered all the more remarkable because everyone had believed that the universal gift had died out years ago. For this, and for other, darker reasons, she was regarded as special and her training was of the utmost importance to more than herself.

A cloud shifted from the moon, bathing the beach in silver light. Connie pulled up short by a rock pool, her eye caught by its eerie midnight-blue sheen, two pale anemones floating near the surface like eyes. Involuntarily, it reminded her why else the Society thought her unique. She was hunted by the Society's enemy, Kullervo. The skin of this shapeshifting creature was that shade, no matter what form he adopted.

Her heart beat faster. She looked up and down the deserted strand. He couldn't be here, not now, could he? Hadn't she defeated him last year when he had persuaded the sirens to attack an oil tanker? He'd been attempting the first step towards his goal of ridding the world of humans, but she had beaten him by turning his power on himself. Connie knew Kullervo would be back for her because he had to have a universal companion to complete his mission. Without her as a channel for his enormous destructive powers, he remained confined to working through other creatures.

'Please let it not be now,' she murmured. 'I'm not ready for you yet.'

A cloud passed over the moon and the water returned to harmless black. Her imagination had been running away with her. Kullervo was nowhere near. He was probably still licking his wounds; he might wait years before he confronted her again. She had time—or so she hoped. That was the chief reason why the Trustees wanted her to spend her summer with creatures from all four companies of the Society. By encountering a diverse range of beasts from each grouping—winged creatures, sea creatures and reptiles, elementals, and two- and four-legged creatures—it was hoped that she'd learn enough about her own powers to resist any new attack by Kullervo. If she stuck to that plan, she'd be prepared.

And now she had Argand. Connie could find no words to do justice to her feelings. She had become used to the idea that her gift meant she would never form a bond with any single creature, unlike every other human companion in the Society for the Protection of Mythical Creatures who had one creature to be their life-long friend. As a universal, being able to communicate with all creatures had made her strangely isolated—a friend to all but special to none. Or at least none that she would willingly choose to be linked with: she could not forget that Kullervo, as the creature in the mythical world with powers most like her own, had once claimed that her place was by his side. It seemed good to her to stand up to the shape-shifter in this way and choose another companion. Though a bond with a dragon might never be as strong as that between the universal and Kullervo, over time it might grow into a counterweight to the pull of that dangerous enemy.

Connie bounded up the steps from the beach to Shaker Row, waving to Mew the seagull as the bird circled overhead, and pushed open the gate of Number Five.

She stopped. Two strangers were sitting on the front step waiting for someone to come home.

'Hello, Connie,' said the elderly man. He had hardly any hair—only a fringe like a monk's tonsure round a sunburnt pate. He was sitting on a large trunk covered in stickers from countries all around the world.

'Er, hello,' she replied.

'You probably don't remember us,' he continued. 'You were only little when we last saw you.'

'I was?'

'Yes, about four I think. I'm your great-uncle, Hugh Lionheart. This is my sister, Godiva.'

Connie had a vague memory of her father mentioning these relatives from time to time when another exotic postcard from them landed on the mat. According to him, they were spending their retirement on cruises, barely setting foot on dry land. So what had washed them up on her doorstep?

Great-aunt Godiva was staring at Connie with a far less friendly expression than her brother. An imposing woman, her hair was the silvery colour of beech bark and she appeared to have a nature as prickly as the nut. It was only as Connie approached that she realized that Godiva also had mismatched eyes—in her case, two different greens.

'You see, Hugh: it is as Gordon and Beryl feared,' Great-aunt Godiva said aside to her brother. 'Evelyn's clearly not been taking a blind bit of notice of their messages. Letting her run wild like this! What on earth are you wearing?' Godiva looked back at Connie, regarding the brown leather flying-suit with pursed lips.

'What kind of fashion is that supposed to be?'

Connie was lost for words: she could not explain that it was the suit she had for riding dragons.

The brutal roar of a motorbike prevented her from having to dream up an answer. All three of them looked to the road where a massive motorbike, gleaming with chrome accessories, pulled up abruptly at the gate, peppering the fence with gravel. The rider revved once before turning it off. His passenger dismounted, took off her helmet, and swung her long brown hair free. The driver parked the bike and then swept Evelyn Lionheart into an embrace. Connie watched helplessly as her aunt, not realizing she had a reception committee awaiting her, kissed the dark-haired biker in a lingering farewell and turned to enter her garden. Just as Connie had done a few moments before, she halted on the path to take in her audience. She said something briefly over her shoulder; the motorcyclist followed her in.

'Hello, Hugh, Godiva,' Evelyn said, kissing her uncle on the cheek. She made no move towards her aunt. 'It's been a long time. Satisfied your wanderlust yet?'

'Not quite, my dear,' said Hugh, patting her arm affectionately.

'Sorry I wasn't here to greet you—there was a hold-up on the Chartmouth road—I thought you'd've got caught in it too?'

'We came by train,' said Hugh. 'Our ship docked in Plymouth this morning.'

Godiva Lionheart glared at her niece: she evidently considered not being here to greet them, coupled with the behaviour they had just witnessed, a personal insult. She shot a poisonous look at the man standing with his helmet tucked under his arm. Evelyn misinterpreted the look (wilfully, Connie thought, from the gleam in her eye) and turned to introduce her friend.

'Oh, and this is Mack Clamworthy.'

So this was Col's father! As Mr Clamworthy moved into the porchlight Connie could see his face with its firm jaw and mischievous brown eyes. He had the looks of a movie star just past his prime and moved with the confidence of someone who knew the power of his physical presence. She recognized that swagger: Col acted like that when feeling particularly pleased with himself.

She had heard a lot about Mack—two very different versions from Col's grandmother and Col himself—but she had not thought she would first meet him as the man kissing her aunt.

Uncle Hugh held out a hand but his sister batted it away.

'For heaven's sake, Hugh,' she snapped at him. 'Remember why we're here!'

Mack responded to the snub by turning to Connie.

'Hi, Connie. I've heard a lot about you. It's great to meet you at last.' He seized her hand and pumped it up and down in his firm grip. 'All that stuff you got up to with Col—very cool!'

'What "stuff" is that exactly?' barked Godiva.

'Surely you heard about it, even on your cruise?' Evelyn intervened, stepping between Mack and her aunt. 'Connie's quite a celebrity around here for preventing a tanker wrecking at New Year.'

'Is she indeed?' Godiva did not sound impressed.

'Well I never! How did you do it, lass?' asked Hugh. He at least was brimming over with interest.

'My friends helped me,' said Connie, glancing at Godiva's expression. She looked as if she had just swallowed a pine cone.

'And they saved lots of people as well,' added Evelyn. 'But shall we go in? We could talk more comfortably inside.' She got out a key and opened the front door.

'I'll leave you to it then, shall I, Evie?' Mack asked flatly, picking up the message from

Godiva that he might not be a welcome spectator to the family scene that was brewing. 'See you same time tomorrow?'

He turned on his heel and strode back to his bike, his black leathers gleaming like the skin of a shark in the lamplight. Silently, the Lionhearts watched him go. The eruption of the engine echoed off the houses of Shaker Row, disturbing the peace of the respectable neighbourhood. Mack's parting wheelie as he sped off seemed to be the final insult.

'She's not even twelve yet and you're letting her loose on her own at this time of night!' exclaimed Godiva.

'Connie was with very responsible friends. She was with Dr Brock. I think you remember him, don't you, Aunt?'

'That madman! Still up to his old tricks, is he? Well, if that's your idea of responsible . . .'

Connie sat hugging her knees in the dark hallway listening to the raised voices in the kitchen. She had been sent out and they had been going on like this for at least half an hour. She had learnt quite a lot, like the fact that her parents, who worked in the Philippines, had been leaving Evelyn strict instructions to limit the time Connie spent with Society members, advice her aunt had chosen not to pass on or respect. Despairing of influencing Evelyn from afar, her parents had appealed to what they called 'the sensible Lionhearts'—Godiva and Hugh—begging them to break off their world cruise and make a surprise inspection of the goings-on at Shaker Row. Godiva clearly considered that their reception had confirmed her worst fears.

'Connie's doing very well here. Ask her teacher—ask anyone,' said Evelyn firmly, ignoring her aunt's slur against Dr Brock.

'But look at her clothes, Evelyn. You can't claim that's normal for a girl of her age.' Godiva was struck by a new suspicion. 'You haven't let her ride on the back of that man's bike? You're not turning her into one of those Hell's Angels, are you?'

Evelyn snorted with laughter. 'Don't be ridiculous.'

'And you—out with your biker boyfriend—not knowing what Connie might be getting up to!'

'Connie does not "get up" to anything, Aunt. You've only just met her—and I know a damned sight more about her than you do!'

'Don't you swear at me, Evelyn Lionheart. What would Robin, God rest his soul, say if he could hear his daughter use words like that to me!'

'Well, what do you expect, Aunt? I didn't see you offering to take her last year when I got landed with her. Now you waltz in here, treating us both like criminals! You have some cheek!'

'It's not cheek—I have every right. Her parents have asked me to take appropriate action to ensure you are not corrupting their daughter with all that Society rubbish.'

'It's true, Evelyn,' chipped in Uncle Hugh, his voice placid in contrast to the shrill tones of the women. 'I can't blame them for wanting to make sure that . . . well, you know . . . nothing *happens* to their daughter. I've never heard anything good of people who get messed up in that society of yours—quite the contrary.'

'Have you told Connie what happened?' asked Godiva. 'Did you explain how half of my generation got wiped out in one fell swoop while on a mission for the Society? About my sister's husband?'

'Yes, Connie knows about the dangers.' Evelyn's voice was now subdued. 'If you hadn't turned your back on all that, Aunt, I'd be able to explain to you why she can't avoid them. But you made your choice, didn't you?'

'Yes, I did—and never regretted it for a moment.'

'Never?'

'No. That's all water under the bridge. And soon Connie will be able to say the same. Call her in. I've got something to tell her.'

There was a pause then Evelyn put her head round the door and beckoned to Connie.

'I expect you heard all that,' she whispered, putting a hand on Connie's shoulder. 'It'll be OK. I'll stick up for you.'

Godiva was standing with her back to the kitchen dresser, studiously ignoring the twinkling collection of feathers, shells, and old glass bottles Connie and Evelyn had collected on their walks together on the moor and beach. Among the common finds were some rarer objects: a silver tail hair from a unicorn, a black feather from Storm-Bird, fragments of a dragon egg, and jet mined by a rock dwarf.

'Connie, your parents have decided that it's time to stop this nonsense,' Godiva announced.

'I don't understand.' Connie looked up at Evelyn. Her aunt was white-faced, her lips pressed in a thin line.

'We're taking you with us.'

'No!' Connie burst out. What about her plans? Her training? Her friends?

'We're opening up the old house in Chartmouth.'

'Your parents, Connie, are very worried about you,' said Hugh gently, reaching out to take her hand.

'Quite right too,' added Godiva. 'That's what I would expect of Gordon. He has decided enough is enough.'

'But I don't want to go away. I want to stay here,' Connie protested, her mind struggling to catch up with this disastrous development.

'It's not that they're ungrateful, Evelyn,' said Godiva, ignoring her great-niece's objections, 'but Connie's parents admitted to me that they had made a mistake placing her with you.'

'You must see, Evelyn, that a young girl like Connie is a heavy burden for a single woman in your circumstances,' continued Hugh reasonably.

'Hescombe's the best thing that's ever happened to me.' Connie appealed to her great-uncle, believing him to be the most sympathetic. 'Please don't do this!' She could feel Evelyn's hands gripping her shoulders, shaking with fury.

'We're not thinking of taking you away completely—only as far as Chartmouth. We've got a very nice house there—far too big for two old codgers like us,' said Hugh.

Godiva raised her eyebrows on being called an 'old codger'.

'And we'll be taking charge of her education, of course.'

'You—teach her?' exploded Evelyn.

'Home schooling—that's the answer. I wish someone had beaten the nonsense out of me when I was Connie's age—not let it build to a crisis. Catch them young, that's what I say.'

'Beat it out of her! What on earth do you mean, Godiva?'

'Old-fashioned discipline, that's what the girl needs. It was my saving—and it'll be hers too.'

Hugh looked uncomfortable. 'Not literally beating her, Evelyn. I think my sister just means a strict regime—like good old navy discipline.'

'She's a child—not one of your junior sailors, Hugh!' exclaimed Evelyn. 'You're not taking her away from me. You don't understand. She's not like other people—she needs special care.'

'For once, I agree with you, Evelyn,' said Godiva. 'It's time she outgrew her animal problem. You are just encouraging her. Her parents have decided that Connie is to cut all ties with that madcap Society of yours and behave like a normal teenager with normal friends.'

'But she's not normal, Godiva! Why can't you face the truth for once in your life? You've run away from your own destiny but Connie can't.

She's extraordinarily gifted! She needs the Society and the Society needs her!'

'You're talking nonsense. You're ruining what chance she has to live an ordinary life.'

'What good's an ordinary life when you're a . . . you're Connie? Godiva, you are nothing but a narrow-minded bigot! You always sided with my father about the Society, no matter how much you knew it hurt me and Sybil. I'm not going to let you do the same to Connie!'

'What utter rubbish, Evelyn,' Godiva said, her voice now icy. 'You forget it's Gordon's daughter we're talking about, not yours, and he has given me permission to take all necessary steps to save Connie from you.' She turned to Connie. 'Pack your things. We're leaving.'

3
Rat

The taxi dropped the Lionhearts outside the gates of a large, square house on the Abbey Close in Chartmouth. Connie gazed up at the four storeys to the slate roof outlined against the night sky. The building had the air of a fat, well-fed citizen who had always occupied this privileged spot in the old part of the town and was in no hurry to move.

'Here you are, Connie: this is Lionheart Lodge,' said Godiva. It was the first time Connie had heard her approve of anything. 'There's more to your family than all that Society nonsense: the Lionhearts have a long, respectable history in this town. We were one of the leading mercantile families for centuries. Go in the abbey opposite and you'll find your relatives' names cover the walls. We even paid for the stained-glass window in the south transept.'

Connie made a muted expression of interest. Indeed, she would have liked to know more about this if she hadn't been feeling so depressed about leaving Shaker Row.

Aunt Godiva took out a key and opened the gates.

'Did you phone Mrs Wellborough, Hugh?' she asked.

'Of course. She said she'd have the place ship-shape for us.'

'I don't doubt it. I can see that her husband has kept the garden in check as instructed.' Godiva nodded at the immaculate lawn and well-behaved yew hedge. She bent closer and took out a ruler from her capacious black handbag to measure the border. 'Good, good: nothing over six inches. Perfect.'

Bemused by this precision, Connie picked up her suitcase and followed Godiva up the path; Hugh wheeled the trunk behind. As her feet crunched on the gravel, Connie shivered. There was something wrong here—something sick. The garden felt as if it was trapped in a straitjacket.

Godiva paused on the front step, fumbling in the dark to find the right key. Hugh switched on a light, illuminating the door panels. They were decorated with a very familiar symbol.

'Hey, that's mine!' Connie exclaimed. What was the sign for the universal doing on this front door?

'What's that?' Hugh was now level with her. 'You mean those? Lovely aren't they? They're part of our family coat of arms—the star compass. Shows that you come from a long line of sailors like me, doesn't it?' He rolled up his sleeve and displayed a dark blue tattoo in the same shape. 'Had that done in Singapore in nineteen fifty-eight. The old man who did it nearly fell off his stool when I showed him what I wanted—asked me all sorts of peculiar questions.' Hugh rubbed his forearm thoughtfully. 'In fact, of all my tattoos, it's the one most people are interested in.'

'Do you know what it means?' Connie couldn't stop herself asking.

'Of course. It means north, south, east, and west—surely you know the points of the compass at your age? Never Eat Shredded Wheat—that should help you remember.'

He didn't know it was the Society's symbol for the universal companion—or was he very good at pretending?

Godiva opened the door and led the way into the hall, turning more lights on. Connie was immediately struck by the staircase: it had black wrought-iron banisters and white marble steps. The lobby floor was stone; the only furniture an alabaster vase with dried flowers standing on a metal table in front of a large mirror.

Connie carried the sense of sickness she had felt in the garden with her across the threshold. There was something very wrong with Lionheart Lodge—something missing.

'We start your lessons the day after tomorrow, Connie . . .' announced Godiva.

'But it's the holidays!'

Aunt Godiva raised an eyebrow and continued, '. . . so I suggest you spend tomorrow getting to know your new home.'

It wasn't home, thought Connie sourly. She felt as if she had just been uprooted and re-potted in the wrong soil.

'Your bedroom is next to mine on the first floor. I'll show it to you now so you can spruce yourself up before supper. You'll want to change, of course.'

Connie looked down at her jeans. 'I do?'

'Of course. We'll have no trousers in the dining room in this household. I suppose you possess a dress or skirt?'

'Um . . .'

Godiva gave an irritated tut. 'You can borrow one of mine if you can't find anything suitable.

You are to act like a lady from now on, Connie; not a tomboy.'

'I'm not a tomboy.'

Godiva sniffed as if to say there was no room for two opinions on that subject and set off upstairs. She paused briefly outside a door, hand hovering but not touching the white-painted wood.

'This is my room. And this . . .' She took a few steps down the hall, '. . . is yours.'

Connie walked through the open door and put her case down. A narrow iron-framed bed stood against one wall, a metal table under the window, and a set of coat pegs hung over a big leather trunk like the one with which Uncle Hugh had struggled home. The room had a bleak, cell-like atmosphere. Only the faded wallpaper—pink roses climbing a trellis—made any attempt at softening the impression.

'You're to hang your things on the hooks and put the rest of your belongings in the trunk,' said Godiva. She ran a finger over the surface of the table and gave a pleased smile when it came away with no dust.

'All right.'

'Don't you say "all right" to me in that sulky tone, young lady. You say "yes, Aunt Godiva".'

'Yes, Aunt Godiva.'

'That's better.' Godiva approached her great-niece and, using the finger that had just checked for dust, stroked her under the chin. 'I know it will be hard to start with, Connie, but you have to believe that it's all for the best.' She must have read doubt in Connie's eyes. 'I wish you would trust me. I really do know what you're going through because I went through it myself. First step to your recovery is to recognize that what you feel is unnatural—it's like an illness. If you acknowledge that then you'll be well on the way to recovery. I'll leave you now.'

The moment the door closed, Connie threw herself down on the bed and let the tears that had been building inside her flood out. She'd tried so hard to be brave, not letting Evelyn see her distress as she packed away her things in her beloved attic bedroom in Shaker Row. Now Connie was alone, she gave in to her despair. She already hated her great-aunt. There was something funny about her—she obviously understood more about the Society than she admitted. It was almost as if she knew.

Being taken away from the Society was bad enough, but what was really scaring Connie was the thought of how Kullervo would use her isolation to his advantage. She'd have no chance to learn how to defend herself. And then there was her new companion. When she'd agreed to be Argand's companion, she hadn't realized what difficulties lay just round the corner. For them both to be complete, she'd need to see Argand regularly; if she didn't, they would both suffer. Entering into a bond made them part of each other—that was what was so special about the relationship between companions. As a universal, she could have fleeting encounters with as many creatures as she wished, but to be bound as a companion to a particular one was something else. It was like the difference between friendship and a marriage—she and Argand now belonged together and should not be parted.

There came a gentle tap at the door.

'Yes?' Connie wiped her eyes on the back of her hand.

Hugh put his head round the door.

'I thought you might be a bit upset so I've brought you a present.' He held out a beautiful curved shell. 'If you're anything like me, you'll miss a view of the sea when you're here; but at least with this you'll be able to hear it.'

'Thank you, Uncle Hugh.'

'Don't mention it, my dear.' He placed it on the quilt and left.

* * *

Col was in the paddock behind the cottage grooming his pony, Mags, when his grandmother found him. She leant on the fence to regain her breath, still flustered by the news she had just heard from Evelyn. Col was whistling softly, oblivious to everything else when this near to the eight-year-old chestnut. Mrs Clamworthy didn't want to disturb them but this couldn't wait.

'Col?'

He looked up, stopping mid-stroke, surprised to find her so close. 'What's the matter, Gran?'

'It's Connie.'

'It's not Kullervo, is it?' Col asked quickly. The name tasted foul in his mouth as he said it.

'No, dear. But it's almost as bad.'

Col dropped the brush. 'Tell me.'

'Connie's been taken away from us—away from Evelyn, the Society, everything.' Mrs Clamworthy seemed close to tears. Her hand was quivering as it rested on the top of the fence.

'Who by?'

'Her parents have sent in her great-aunt and uncle. Now Godiva Lionheart's got her claws into Connie, I dread to think what will happen.'

'Connie's left without saying goodbye?' Col couldn't believe it. Only yesterday they had been talking about the summer holidays together, making plans.

'She had no choice. They carted her off to Chartmouth to that house of theirs right after they arrived last night. None of us are allowed to see her.'

Mags nuzzled Col for some attention; he patted the pony distractedly.

'But they can't do that! What about her training? What about Kullervo?'

'That's exactly what we're all thinking. Your father said they wanted nothing to do with him when he dropped Evelyn at home yesterday evening—Godiva is virulently opposed to anything or anyone to do with the Society.'

A new suspicion struck Col. 'What was Dad doing with Evelyn, Gran?'

Mrs Clamworthy blushed slightly. 'That's their business and none of yours. Now hurry up, I want you to take a message to Mack for me. He doesn't yet know how it all ended last night.'

Mags turned off the road and picked up his hoofs, carrying his rider further into Mallins Wood. Even though they were the bearers of bad news, Col couldn't help but feel his spirits lift a little. They both loved riding under the trees. They looked forward to galloping together through the many different parts of the wood:

lofty green halls of beech; dark, mysterious tunnels of oak with acorns crunching underfoot; white-columned cloisters of silver birch on the sandy ground. Not only were the trees so diverse, but they changed so much with the seasons. One visit, Col and Mags would brush through the freshly minted greens of spring, next they were beneath the riotous leaves of summer, wading hock deep in brazen autumn or spooked by skeletal winter. Over the years spent in Mallins Wood, Col had taught himself to ride and jump, climbed trees, made dens—it had always been the most amazing playground. Though he thought he knew it well, he had never lost the sense that it was a place of mystery, somewhere truly wild. He could feel that the wood was alive with creatures, hiding in tree and earth. Connie had often said that it was bursting with life. If she had been here, she could've told him what the creatures were. He pulled Mags to a halt and looked about him. And this was what they wanted to cut down and cover in tarmac—sacrificing Hescombe's last remaining piece of the great forests that had once covered the area. He felt the loss almost like a physical pain.

Who would benefit, he asked the trees angrily? Oh yeah, the Axoil terminal would be able to send its tanker lorries rumbling to the motorway much more efficiently. Col had also heard commuters to Chartmouth complaining about the slow road.

But where are we to go to escape the cars if all of this has been concreted over? he wondered.

The trees rustled as if approving his sentiments.

Mack Clamworthy was sitting outside a tent, his motorbike parked under a sycamore. Mallins Wood was beginning to fill up with other encampments, ranging from tents like Mack's to caravans scattering children, dogs, and deckchairs haphazardly around them. Overhead, two men in brightly-coloured cotton clothes were perched in the treetops stringing bunting through the branches, small bells attached to a line ringing in the breeze. The sound of hammering in the distance betrayed the activities of tree-house builders.

Mags plodded into the clearing and stopped by the campfire.

'Oh, hello, son.' Mack yawned, rubbing his unshaven chin wearily. 'Come to join us, have you? We're already digging in to give the police a hard time shifting us—so the more the merrier.'

Col did not reply but slid from Mags's back and let the pony wander off to graze.

37

'Have you heard about Connie?' he asked his father.

'No, what?' his father asked without much sign of interest, poking the fire with a twig.

'She's been taken away from Evelyn—and her family are refusing to let her have anything to do with the Society.'

Mack shot a surprised look at his son but then continued his probing of the embers. 'That's a shame.'

'It's more than a shame—it's a disaster. What about Kullervo? How can we protect her if no one from the Society's allowed near her?'

Mack frowned. 'What a mess. I bet Evie's upset.'

'Not as much as Connie.' Col paused. 'Are you going to tell me what happened last night?' He slumped down opposite Mack on an upturned bucket.

'Nothing—I had nothing to do with it. I didn't exchange two words with them. Evie's told me how the family's been hassling her about Connie.'

Col scuffed his trainers in the leaf-litter, looking down at the ground.

'So what's this about you and Evelyn, Dad?'

Mack got to his feet and stretched.

'Sleeping outdoors—nothing like it,' he said, yawning again.

'Dad?'

'She's a friend—known her for years. Look, Col, I'm sure Dr Brock and the others will think of something for Connie. Forget about it for the moment—you can't do anything. Why don't you come and meet some of the others here and take your mind off things? I know where we might get a hot drink. Follow me.'

Col trailed after Mack in a dark mood. Forget about it, his father said. But how could he? Mack always seemed so confident, so big—dominating every room, every gathering, brushing obstacles aside as if they didn't matter. Col felt he could not grow in the long shadow his father cast. It was just as well that Mack was usually on the road and left Hescombe well alone. That was until he started going out with Evelyn Lionheart. Col was not sure he welcomed the prospect of seeing more of him.

Mack stopped outside an old white bus decorated with rainbows. He knocked on the door and it was flung open by a wild-eyed woman with a mass of red hair.

'It's you, Mack!' she exclaimed with relief. 'I thought it might be the police again.'

'No, Siobhan, just me—and I've brought my boy this time.'

Col stepped out from behind his father and looked up at the woman with interest: she seemed to him like a dash of red energy in this calm green place.

'He's a rare one,' Siobhan said admiringly, her hands on her wide hips. 'Eyes of one of the little people, he has, but it seems only us Irish talk about them these days.'

Col shot a look at his father to ask if she knew about the Society; Mack gave him a slight shake of his head, before replying:

'Yeah, he looks weird, doesn't he?'

Thanks, Dad, thought Col sourly.

'I wondered if Rat might like to meet him—they must be about the same age,' Mack continued.

Siobhan shouted lustily over her shoulder into the dark confines of the bus: 'Rat! Rat! Where are you, you lazy bit of no good?'

A pale face surrounded by the rumpled hair of someone who had just got up emerged out of the darkness. It was a boy: thin and wiry with light brown hair, blinking at the morning with sleepy eyes. His nose was sprinkled with freckles and his red-tinged ears stuck out prominently either side of his sharp face.

'What's your boy's name?' the Irish woman asked, pushing Rat forward.

'Col,' said Mack, slapping his son hard on the back.

'Well, Col,' she said, 'this is Sean, but everyone

round here calls him Rat 'cause of our name being Ratcliff, you see.'

Col did see—sort of. He and Rat eyed each other warily for a moment like two stranger dogs until Col smiled. Rat grinned back.

'So, Mack, you'll be wanting tea?' Siobhan said, standing aside. 'You two get yourselves off somewhere—but not too far, mind. And don't get into any more trouble, Rat!'

'Ma!' Rat protested.

'Don't think I don't know what you get up to—I wasn't born yesterday.'

Rat pulled on some wellingtons and jumped out of the bus.

'Come on then,' he said with a casual toss of his head at Col. 'Let's go and see the tree-houses.'

Col followed on his heels, fishing around for a safe topic. Football? Would a lad living in a bus follow any clubs? He did not seem the type somehow. Wanting to make a success of their first conversation, Col wondered what they would have in common.

Rat suddenly stopped and put out an arm to hold Col back. Col paused. What was Rat playing at? Then Col saw the reason for himself. They were standing in a grove of beech trees, a light green canopy overhead and a copper floor covered with last year's leaves. There, in the clearing, stood a deer, its front right hoof lifted delicately like a ballerina poised at the barre. The two boys stared for a moment into the liquid brown eyes of the creature, hardly daring to breathe. A wind rustled the leaves above; the deer twitched its tail and was gone in two bounds.

'I like this wood,' Rat said simply, beginning to move again.

'So do I.' Col hurried to fall into step beside him. 'Hey, Rat, if you like animals, do you want to ride my pony?'

4
Cassandra

L ate in the afternoon, the gate bell rang. Connie watched from her window as her aunt, who had been determinedly rooting up seedlings from the flower borders all day, rushed to see who it was. She returned a few minutes later, marching in front of two girls. She was holding her house-keys like a prison warder escorting visitors to see an inmate. Connie's heart lifted: it was Jane and Anneena, her best friends from school. She ran down the stairs two at a time to meet them in the hallway.

'It's so good to see you!' she exclaimed.

'And you.' Anneena hugged Connie and gave a significant look over her shoulder at Godiva. 'What's going on?'

'Oh, this is my great-aunt. Aunt Godiva, this is Anneena Nuruddin and Jane Benedict.'

'Young woman,' rapped out Godiva sharply to Anneena, 'do you have anything to do with the Society?'

'The what? You mean Connie's thing?'

Godiva nodded.

'No, no, I don't.'

'And you?' Godiva rounded on Jane.

'Me neither.' Feeling Godiva's gaze drilling into her, Jane hid shyly behind her shoulder-length blonde hair, letting it flop over her face.

'Good, then I'm pleased to meet you, girls. As Connie will tell you, there have been a few changes to her life recently, but you at least are welcome to continue your friendship with her.'

'Er . . . thanks,' said Anneena, clearly wondering what right Godiva had to say with whom Connie could be friends.

'I expect you'd like to go into the garden?' said Godiva, ushering them out as if trying to tidy up the mess they made of her hall.

'It's OK, I'll take them up to my room,' said Connie.

No sooner had Connie shut the door than Anneena burst out, 'Col said you've been taken away from Evelyn.'

'Yeah, I have.'

'Why?'

'My parents are worried about me. They want my great-aunt and uncle to have a go at making me normal.'

Anneena gave a snort. 'Normal? What's wrong with the way you are?'

Connie shrugged, but silently she agreed with the question.

Jane was examining the shell. 'So you're living here? For how long?'

'I don't know.'

'If you're still here in September, at least you'll be close to Chartmouth Secondary.'

'My aunt plans to home school me.'

'You're joking?' asked Anneena.

'Am not.'

'And she wants to make you normal? She hasn't a hope.'

There was an awkward pause as Connie bit her lip to stop herself crying. Anneena and Jane gave each other a quick look, then together pulled Connie into a hug.

'You two have got to save me, OK? I'm not allowed to see Col or anyone, so it's up to you.'

'Course we will, Connie,' said Anneena returning the squeeze. 'I've got an idea. Why don't you help us with the Hescombe Festival? Dad's

45

organizing it this year. If you say yes, then that'll give you lots of opportunities to get out and about with us.'

'Sounds great,' said Connie, sitting down on the bed next to her friend. Everything always felt full of possibilities when with Anneena. The future seemed less bleak already.

'This year the Festival is going to be really big news—it might not be your sort of thing. We've got *Krafted* coming.'

'Who?'

Anneena rolled her eyes. 'You know, the band—they've only been number one for the last three weeks.'

Jane touched Connie's arm. 'Don't worry, I hadn't heard of them either.'

'Don't you two ever listen to the radio? You can't go five minutes without hearing one of their tracks.'

'A slight exaggeration, Annie?' teased Jane.

'Yeah, well, you get the idea. It's the first time the music festival has managed to attract a real headline name. There'll be loads of other bands as well—it'll be brilliant.'

'Why are they coming here?' asked Connie curiously. She knew about the festival, of course, but it was no way as big as Glastonbury or any of the other summer gigs.

'Because of the campaign. Didn't you realize that the new road passes right by the fields used by festival goers? *Krafted*'s drummer's from Chartmouth and he's dead against it. We're going to use the festival to try and stop the tree-massacring council.'

'Always so balanced, isn't she?' whispered Jane wryly.

Anneena ignored her. 'The tickets were sold out the moment they went on the internet.'

'And what can I do to help?' Connie asked. She was beginning to catch some of Anneena's excitement. Perhaps it really might make a difference? She was desperate to save the wood—now maybe they could.

'Well, it always kicks off with a carnival procession. We haven't picked this year's theme yet, but usually there are animals—horses and so on. You could help keep them under control.'

'You've asked the right person.'

'I thought as much. Shall I ask your great-aunt or do you want to?'

'I think it'd better come from you—you're good at that sort of thing.'

'What sort of thing?'

'Twisting people round your little finger, Annie: you are to people what Connie is to animals,' explained Jane.

Anneena smiled proudly. 'Thanks. OK, I'll tackle her for you. What are her weak spots?'

'I don't think she has any,' said Connie. She thought a moment. 'She likes hard work and order.'

'Right, I'll lay it on thick what slave labour it's all going to be.'

'Don't worry, Connie, your aunt doesn't stand a chance against her,' said Jane as Anneena disappeared downstairs. 'No one's yet got the better of her. I almost feel sorry for your aunt.'

It was a tougher battle than Jane had predicted. Godiva only agreed to allow Connie to work on the festival preparations as long as it was at her house and under her scrutiny. As for going out on site, that was out of the question.

Anneena chewed the end of one long black plait thoughtfully as she reported back from her initial assault.

'Your great-aunt is a funny one, Connie. When I mentioned you coming up to Mallins Wood it was almost as if I'd said some terrible swear word. She'd been coming along nicely until then—I think I almost had her persuaded—but she suddenly backed off and said you weren't to be allowed within a million miles of the place—that she couldn't bear it and that the sooner the whole thing was cut down the better.'

'She didn't!' Connie was outraged. She hadn't liked Godiva before but now she had reason to detest her. How could anyone want to see all those trees felled?

'She did. But anyway, at least she's agreed to us coming to visit you from time to time.'

Connie put her face in her hands. 'This is a nightmare.'

'Isn't there anything you can do?' asked Jane. 'Have you asked your parents?'

'Uh-huh. They said I had to try my great-aunt's regime for at least a few months and I wasn't to expect it to be easy.'

'Wonderful,' said Anneena in a hollow voice.

'Thanks for trying.'

'I'm not beaten yet. Let's hope next time I have more luck.'

A few days later, Col and Rat were lying in the long grass of a woodland clearing, watching a woodpecker hard at work in a nearby chestnut tree. The tree was decked with countless leaves like splayed-fingered hands and hundreds of pale green baubles. Every time the breeze passed across the clearing the leaf-hands rose and fell in a Mexican wave of applause. Col felt it was almost as if Mallins Wood was celebrating the perfect summer's day.

'Look at him go!' Col exclaimed with admiration as the bird rapped his beak so rapidly against the bark, its head became a blur.

'Yeah, bit like my dad at a heavy metal gig,' Rat said. 'Must mess up his brain, don't y'think? Ma's always saying that Dad's never been quite right since he started doing it.'

Col snorted with laughter as Rat grinned broadly back at him. He passed Rat the binoculars and lay on his back, looking up at the blue sky overhead, picking out shapes in the clouds—a face, a ship, now a hawk . . . Swallows swooped, catching insects.

'Hey, here's something worth looking at now,' Rat said with sudden excitement.

'W . . . what?' Col asked, snapped back to the present to see Rat gazing across the clearing with the binoculars.

'Cor! Would you look at that!'

'Here, give me those!' He grabbed the binoculars and focused them in the direction Rat had been staring. It was someone in a white dress—a woman with long golden hair that fell in curling ringlets about her shoulders. Col dropped the binoculars as if they had burnt him.

'What's the matter?' Rat asked, rubbing his nose with the back of his hand. 'Has she gone?'

'No, it's not that.'

'What is it then?'

'It's just that . . . well, she's my mother, if you must know,' Col said more aggressively than he intended.

'Well, are you going to say hello or not?' Rat asked calmly, picking up the binoculars. He looked puzzled as Col stayed rooted to the spot, unaware that his friend was both confused and frightened by the very sight of his mother. 'You'd better hurry.'

Col nodded and began a strangely uncoordinated half-jog to his mother as if his legs could not decide whether they wanted to go forward or not. She was now kneeling, hair in a thick curtain around her face, thumping the ground with her fists as if it were a drum.

'What are you doing?' Col asked.

'Calling the snakes,' she replied in her husky voice that always made Col shiver. She turned her forget-me-not blue eyes on her son. 'Hello, Colin.'

'Oh . . . er . . . hi, Mum,' he replied, fidgeting awkwardly.

She rose in a fluid motion from the grass and came to his side. Taking him by the shoulders, she stared hard into his face.

'You've grown up,' she said with a fierce kind of pride. 'You've known danger and mastered your fear.'

Col would have preferred a more ordinary greeting, but he was pleased that she had noticed him for himself at last.

'Thanks,' he said briefly, pulling away. She continued to gaze into his face, making his insides squirm as if she had drummed up snakes in him. He tried to distract her:

'So why are you calling snakes? Isn't it a bit public here at the moment—against Society rules and all that?' His mother was a companion to the snake-haired gorgon and he was thinking of how Rat had almost seen her in action.

'Ha!' She gave a short derisive laugh. 'When have I ever cared about rules?'

True, thought Col. 'So why are you here?' It would not be to see him, of course.

'To join the protest. This wood is the last home of the gorgons in southern England. It is the place they have returned to for centuries to spawn their young. If it goes, the gorgon's hair will die—she will die.' Col swallowed and glanced behind him: he had not known that gorgons roamed these woods and he certainly did not fancy meeting one just now.

'Oh, that's . . . that's bad,' he replied feebly. 'So where are they now?'

'There's only one and I've got her well hidden,' his mother said. 'She'd be in danger if she's discovered by one of these protesters or the road-builders.'

Yeah, Col thought, to say nothing of the danger the unfortunate person would be in from the gorgon's eyes, which had the power to turn living beings to stone, but he guessed that his mother was not concerned about that.

'Dad's here, did you know?' he asked tentatively as she set off back to the camp, her long white skirt brushing the bracken, picking up burrs by the dozen. She did not reply but from the determined set of her jaw Col knew that this was unwelcome news.

Col followed her to the steps of a pale green campervan parked at the far end of the picnic spot.

'You'd better not come in,' she said. 'Wait here for me—I've got something for you.'

She vanished inside—Col could hear voices and tried not to imagine what she was talking to. He sat down on a picnic bench and ran his hands through his hair: he was feeling terrible, feeling just how he had done when he was five and still living with his mother. He hated to admit it but he was just plain scared, yet part of him was drawn to her as if she had him on an invisible piece of string which she could pluck at pleasure. The worst of it was that he did not think she realized the effect she had on him: he did not figure large in her life, so wrapped up was she in her snake-haired companion, and she probably did not believe she counted for much in his.

A shout from behind: 'Ah, Col! There you are. I've been looking for you. Your gran wants you home for six.'

Col spun round in horror, realizing he had only seconds to avert a catastrophe. His father was swaggering out of the trees, smoothing his black hair out of his eyes and stretching lazily.

'Thanks. See you then,' Col shouted back, waving at his father and making as if he was about to go.

'Wait!' Mack was jogging over to catch up with him. 'I'll give you a lift on the bike. I'm going out for the evening.'

With Evelyn, no doubt, thought Col, now changing direction and running towards his father to head him off. He did not want this bit of information shouted across the clearing with his mother in earshot. 'Fine . . .' His voice tailed off. It was far from fine. His mother had reappeared in the doorway of the van, holding a package.

She stood frozen on the top step, her look as stony as a gorgon's but, fortunately for Mack, without the killing power.

'Hello, Cassie,' Mack said heavily on seeing her there.

'Cassandra,' she said curtly.

'So you've decided to join us protesters, I see,' Mack continued in a doomed attempt at polite conversation. 'I s'pose I should've guessed you'd come.'

'Not join you!' she snapped. 'I'll never make that mistake again.'

Mack bristled at the insult. 'Ha! You never really did even when we were married! Too busy grubbing around looking for snakes, if I remember—funny way to behave on our honeymoon.'

'It was no honeymoon for me, believe me! You—off in the slimy embrace of your tentacled friend! "Let's go to the Bahamas," you said! Oh, I was so gullible then. I should have known it was the Kraken rather than the beaches that interested you.'

'So you were jealous!' Mack cried in triumph.

Col looked furtively around: the row was attracting the attention of other campers; a small crowd was beginning to gather. Col saw Rat and his family coming out of their bus and wondered if he could slip away before they noticed him.

'Jealous—jealous of you? Ha! You second-rate creep who only feels big when roaring about on that ridiculous bit of tin!'

'You—you scheming viper!'

Col flinched as if ducking blows as the slanging match continued over his head. Mack's last insult brought a burly man with a shaven head out of the crowd.

'Is he bothering you, love?' the man asked Cassandra.

As if she needed help, Col thought.

'He's always bothered me,' Cassandra replied smartly, 'but I can handle him, thanks.' She flashed the man a brilliant smile; he moved to stand at the bottom of the step, a self-appointed bodyguard.

Hoping the escalating confrontation was sufficient distraction from him, Col tried to slide away but his father grabbed his collar.

'Don't you go, Col! Don't let shame of your mother drive you away!' Mack said loudly.

Col could now feel the eyes of the onlookers turned to him. He could have shrivelled up with embarrassment.

'Shame of me!' Cassandra shrieked, darting down the step to seize Col's arm. 'Thankfully he's inherited his mother's courage—none of that Clamworthy weakness.'

'You're deluding yourself as usual, Cassie: he takes after me. Ask him!'

They both turned their fierce eyes on Col, breathing hard after all the shouting. Col wished at that moment that he were anywhere else on the planet but here.

'If you want the truth, I don't want to be like either of you!' he burst out, pulling himself free of their grasp. He turned on his heels and ran away as fast as he could, heading back to Hescombe—to anywhere where they weren't.

When his breathing had become so painful that he could run no more, he bent over by the side of the road, panting. He wished he could keep on running for ever—leave them both behind and never have to see either of them again. His eyes were burning but he was too old now to waste tears on his parents, he told himself. Furious at his weakness, he brushed them away and walked slowly down the hill.

The roar of a bike gave him ample warning of his father's approach but he was hemmed in by high banks on both sides of the road so had no choice but to stomp on, pretending he could neither see nor hear anything. The bike screeched to a halt right in front of him, forcing him to check his pace.

Mack lifted his visor. 'Here!' he said and held out a brown paper package. 'Your mother wants you to have this.'

Despite himself, Col took the parcel, amazed that his father had deigned to run an errand for Cassandra. He could only imagine that for once he had managed to put out the blazing row by his abrupt departure.

'Get on,' Mack said, gesturing to the back seat of his bike. 'It's a long walk home.' He held out the spare helmet.

Col hesitated. Putting up a fight now would be pointless. Besides, though he would never tell his father, he rather liked zooming along on the bike—it beat walking. He took the helmet.

'So, what are we going to do about Connie?' Dr Brock asked the Hescombe members of the Society who had gathered in Mrs Clamworthy's kitchen. The wooden table was bathed in soft light from the lamp overhead. Around it sat twelve anxious people.

'Jane and Anneena got in to see her,' said Col. 'They say it's like a prison over there. The old bat won't let Connie out.'

'Then we'll have to get in too,' said Mr Masterson, a local farmer and owner of land where many Society activities took place in secret.

'We've been trying,' said Col's grandmother. She got up, went to the sink and ran her fingers under the tap. Feeling the atmosphere in the room change subtly, the others fell silent. The water curled round her hands taking the shape of one of her water sprites until the creature was standing in the basin, his form rippling like transparent silk. Mrs Clamworthy closed her eyes and hummed softly. All the other members waited reverently for the encounter to finish.

'I've never seen her do that before,' Evelyn whispered to Col.

'Neither have I,' Col admitted.

Mrs Clamworthy broke off her bond with the water sprite, letting the creature flow down the plughole. She smiled at Col and Evelyn.

'Who's to say you can't teach the old dog a new trick? It was Issoon's idea actually. He doesn't like doing it much, but now I'm getting on a bit, he thinks he should make the effort to come and see me at home more often.'

'What did he have to say, Lavinia?' asked Dr Brock.

'That there's no way in to see Connie. The garden's hopeless—not a pond or a fountain in sight. No access to the water system.' She glanced out of the window at her own garden which was full of running water and pools. 'They're keeping watch as the Trustees asked, but it has to be from a distance.'

'But we all know it's not enough just to guard her,' said Dr Brock. 'There's Connie's training to think about. The Trustees are most insistent that this is not neglected. They, like us, have heard rumours that Kullervo has regrouped and creatures are once again flocking to his side. An entire coven of banshees has recently disappeared—we think to join him. We've got to get to Connie before Kullervo or his followers do.'

'That's all very well, Francis,' said Evelyn, nettled by his mention of the defection of some of her companion creatures, 'but are the Trustees volunteering to go and tackle my aunt themselves? She sent me away with a flea in my ear when I tried so I don't fancy their chances.'

Dr Brock frowned. 'We know that Godiva is something of a special case. She'll deny that she can even see them, if I know her.'

'You've met her before?' asked Col. He could've sworn that Dr Brock blushed.

'Yes, we used to be friends once upon a time. A very fine looking girl she was in her youth.'

'Then perhaps you should talk to her?'

'No!' he said sharply. 'That would do more harm than good. No, I think we should try something else. Is Hugh still living with her?'

Evelyn nodded. 'But I fear that she rules the roost.'

'I'd expect nothing less of her. But I have an idea how we might winkle Connie out of the house. All we need is the right bait.'

Aunt Godiva leafed through the pamphlet on the national curriculum she had picked up from the local education authority. 'What have we come to?' she muttered. 'Citizenship lessons—what on earth is that?'

Connie sat silently at the desk that had been allotted to her in the former nursery, her fingers playing with an old-fashioned ink pen. Godiva would not allow pencils in her class.

'Well, we can forget about all that, can't we?' Godiva announced coming to a decision and throwing the leaflet aside. 'This is about curing you of the Society. What a young mind like yours needs is a diet of grammar and arithmetic, leavened with a modicum of scientific fact. We'll start with an hour of sums, an hour of composition, and an hour of Latin.'

'Latin!'

'Of course, a very good subject for teaching intellectual rigour. In the afternoon, we'll study science and domestic accomplishments.'

'You are joking?' asked Connie hopefully, but her great-aunt's face told another story.

'I've never been more serious in my life. You are suffering from delusions, Connie, no doubt hearing voices and seeing things, all encouraged by those mad people in the Society. Hard application to these subjects will bring you back to yourself.'

The pen spurted ink over Connie's fingers. 'I'm not deluded, Aunt.'

'I beg to differ. If I took you to any medical expert, they would say the same. What you think you feel during those Society meetings of yours is not real—it's a form of group hysteria. I didn't realize it myself at first, but I now see that the Society is a particularly virulent cult that brainwashes its members—dragons and flying horses, I ask you! I've no doubt they use banned substances too these days to induce even wilder hallucinations.'

'You were a member too once, weren't you?' Connie asked quietly. The mystery of her great-aunt's behaviour was beginning to fall into place.

Godiva stalked to the window and looked out. Her silence seemed to confirm Connie's guess.

'What is your companion species?'

Godiva swooped round in a fury. 'I do not have a companion species—neither do you. The sooner you realize how you've been duped, Connie, the better. And my task is to make you see the truth—I'll do it even if it kills me!' She was breathing heavily, her hair starting to escape from the tight bun she had pinned it into. Putting her hands to her head to repair the damage, she continued. 'Open your book at page one—start solving the long division sums you find there until I say you can stop. I want you to think of numbers—nothing but numbers.'

The morning was already wearing on when the gate bell rang.

'I'll go!' Connie said, abandoning her post at the desk, desperate for some fresh air.

'No, you will not, young lady. I'll go. You never know who it might be round here,' Godiva said.

When she had gone, Connie went to the window. It was raining hard. She could see Hugh had beaten her aunt to the gate and was bringing two people into the house under the shelter of a big green umbrella: an elderly West Indian man with white grizzled hair and a young girl with tightly braided plaits. Connie tiptoed onto the landing to listen.

'What do they want?' Godiva asked Hugh as he shook out the umbrella on the top step.

'Hello there, Miss Lionheart,' came the rolling tones of a familiar voice. 'I'm a friend of Connie's. I understand she's here for the summer and I wondered if she'd like to meet my grand-daughter, Antonia?'

Godiva opened the door wider, revealing Horace Little standing dripping with rain in the porch, a girl with bright brown eyes at his side. The companion to selkies and his granddaughter had come to visit her.

Godiva sniffed suspiciously. 'How do you know my great-niece, sir? Are you one of those Hescombe Society people?'

Horace smiled, delighted that the question could be answered quite truthfully. 'No, no, I'm from London. I come sailing down here from time to time.'

'Like sailing, do you?' asked Hugh brightly.

'It is a great passion of mine. I was in the navy.'

'So was I! Which ship?' Hugh was clearly set-tling down for a long discussion of all things naval.

Godiva gave her brother an indulgent smile.

So she does have a weak spot, thought Connie. It's Hugh.

'Well, you'd better ask him in then. You can take him through to the kitchen,' Godiva said primly, watching the pools of water gather on her spotless stone floor.

Not believing her luck, Connie ran down the stairs.

'Mr Little, it's great to see you!'

Horace patted her on the shoulder, looking searchingly into her face, checking all was well. She gave him a small smile.

'So, Connie, how are you?' he asked aloud.

'Fine,' she replied briefly, wondering when Godiva would realize that one of the members of the forbidden Society had slipped under her guard.

'Well, Mr Little, would you like to dry off in the kitchen?' asked Hugh. 'You're soaked to the skin.'

'Oh, what's a bit of wet? I'm used to it.'

'Well, a cup of tea then?'

'Don't mind if I do. Connie, why don't you show Antonia around? This looks a very interesting house.' He nodded at the windows in the front door.

'You can take her up to your room,' countered Godiva crossly. 'We'll resume our lesson later.'

Connie led Antonia upstairs to her bedroom.

'Hey, this is really cool!' the girl exclaimed, admiring the many posters of animals ranging from unicorns to dolphins and seagulls that Connie had pinned on the walls to relieve the austerity of the room. Antonia sat on the edge of the bed and looked straight up at Connie, her face eager and alert like an otter, twitching in expectation of fun. 'What's it like being the universal then?'

Connie felt a great wave of relief: at last here was someone she could talk to after days of having to pretend that she was normal.

'It's amazing. I s'pose it's a bit like what you feel on your first encounter, but repeated again and again.' Connie sat on the edge of the metal table and smiled back as she remembered the creatures she had met over the past year.

'Grandpa's been really worried about you— they all have. Dr Brock asked us to try and call because your great-aunt doesn't know us. He thought Grandpa might be able to charm them into letting you out a bit.'

'I hope he can. My aunt thinks the Society's some kind of evil cult—she's trying to cure me of it. If she suspected he was a member, he wouldn't be sitting in the kitchen now.'

Antonia flicked through a photo album lying on the bed, looking at the pictures of Hescombe, of Col, Anneena, and Jane. She paused over a snapshot of Scark the Seagull, perched on top of his favourite lifebuoy. Connie felt a pang of grief: it was her only photo of the bird. She had taken it before Kullervo crushed the seagull to death for trying to save her.

'Not much chance of being cured, is there? I can't imagine my relatives wanting to keep me out of it,' Antonia added. 'They were thrilled when I turned out to be a companion to wood sprites as none of my brothers had inherited the gift.'

Connie was interested by this, not having come across a family, apart from her own, where some members did not share the gift. 'Hasn't that caused a problem in your family?'

'Oh no,' Antonia grinned. 'You don't know my brothers. They couldn't care less what I do. They have their own life—football, music, y'know—they just think my going off to the Society is, well, just my thing.'

'Are there many wood sprites in a city? It must be hard being a companion to them in London.'

'Not as hard as you might think. Every tree is like a world in itself. Even in Brixton you can find sprites in the back gardens and parks.'

'I'd like to meet one. What are they like?'

'They're . . .' Antonia stopped, looked at Connie and laughed. 'No, I'm not going to tell you. You're the universal companion: you can meet them. Why get your information second hand?' She glanced out of the window. 'Not here though. Not a tree in sight, is there?'

Connie went to the window and looked out at the sterile garden. That was what was wrong with it: there was nothing wild for any creature to live in. No wonder she'd been feeling so weakened over the last few days—her link to the natural world had been severed.

'Connie,' Antonia interrupted her thoughts hesitantly, 'Grandpa told me all about what happened last year—about you and Kullervo. Do you mind me asking what he's like?'

Connie's knuckles went white on the windowsill.

'Only I've heard so much about him all my life—Mum and Dad have always talked about him—but he's never really seemed real to me. I couldn't believe it when I heard you'd encountered him. I can't even begin to imagine what that's like.'

Connie turned to look at Antonia. The wood sprite companion's face was eager, hungry for information. She wouldn't look like that if she had met him herself, thought Connie.

Antonia's bright expression dimmed. 'I'm sorry. That was stupid of me. Of course, you don't want to talk about it.'

'No, it's OK,' said Connie with a sigh. 'I don't

blame you for wanting to know.' She dropped her gaze to the carpet. 'He's not like any other creature I've encountered. He's dark—like a sea. When you're with him, you feel like a ship being battered to pieces on the rocks. All you know is that he hates you for what you are—but yet needs you.'

Antonia shuddered. 'You're very brave, Connie. I mean, living in the knowledge that he could grab you again at any moment. I'd be terrified.'

'I am. But what choice do I have? I can't change the fact that I'm a universal just because I'm scared.'

'I s'pose not. But I still think you're brave.'

By an unspoken agreement, the girls chatted about lighter matters for a few more minutes before going to the kitchen. Uncle Hugh and Grandpa Little were talking amicably, reliving their youth spent on the high seas.

Horace reached inside his jacket pocket. 'I've got something here that might interest you and Connie, Hugh. I was given some free tickets to the boat show at Olympia by my old commander. Would you like to come with us?'

Hugh's face lit up, then dimmed as he remembered his sister.

'I don't know, Horace . . .'

'We're going back to London tomorrow. You

could come with us on the train. It is Connie's summer holiday after all.'

Hugh glanced at Connie. 'Would you like to go, my dear?'

'Yes, please.'

He sucked his teeth for a moment, his eyes gazing hungrily at the tickets. 'I'll see what I can do. A trip to London won't do any harm, surely? I'll explain to my sister that you'll be safe from corrupting influences from Hescombe.'

'But, Uncle, I'm not sure . . .' began Connie. She didn't like lying to him. He should at least know the truth if he was to brave Godiva.

'After all,' Hugh continued with a wink at Horace, 'she only said to me that she didn't want you to have anything to do with the Society people from Hescombe. Horace here is from Brixton— that's quite another story.'

Connie, Uncle Hugh, Horace, and Antonia were standing in front of the underground map at Paddington Station.

'I'd better just check the tickets again,' said Horace. He clapped his hand to his forehead. Antonia grinned and squeezed Connie's arm. 'Would you look at that! I must be losing my marbles: I should've read the small print. The special offer is for navy veterans only—an exclusive preview.'

Hugh shuffled his feet miserably. 'Well, I suppose we should see when the next train back is then.'

'Don't be silly, Uncle, you must go now we're here,' said Connie, sensing this moment had been planned all along.

'Yes, yes, it's all my fault, my dear chap. Why don't you go on ahead to Olympia, and I'll drop the girls off at Antonia's library. They'll be quite safe there—we can collect them later this afternoon.'

'A library, you say?' asked Uncle Hugh shrewdly. 'What sort of library?'

'One with books,' said Horace smiling. He knew what Hugh suspected.

'And nothing will happen to her there?'

'What do you think could happen in a library, Hugh?'

Hugh scratched his chin, torn between his desire to feast his eyes on boats all day and his duty to shield Connie from Society influences. 'You promise you'll stay there, Connie, not go on any foolish expeditions?'

'Of course, Uncle Hugh.'

'What'll you do all day?'

'Read, I guess.'

'Hmm. All right. I'm trusting you to keep your

word. And don't tell my sister I let you out of my sight.'

'I won't.'

Relieved of his responsibility, Hugh stabbed his finger on the underground map. 'Olympia it is, then. I'll see you there, Horace.'

'Where're we going?' Connie asked happily as she made her escape with Horace and Antonia to the Bakerloo line.

'Charing Cross,' Horace replied.

'Charing Cross? That's right in the centre of town, isn't it? Why are we going there?'

'Well,' began Horace, casting a look over his shoulder to check they could not be overheard, 'when the Trustees heard that you were not allowed to continue with your practical training, they decided that we should try to start you on the theory. That's why we're taking you to the Society's headquarters—there's something rather exceptional there that you should see.'

Leaving the train at Charing Cross, Horace led the girls up the escalators and through the crowds pouring onto Trafalgar Square. Sensing her arrival, a flock of pigeons flew in from the park. They spiralled into the sky, forming a column to rival Nelson's over Connie's head.

She nodded up to them, acknowledging their welcome, then waved her hand to scatter them before too many people noticed. Horace and Antonia said nothing but smiled at each other. Horace picked up his pace and guided the girls down the side of a large church with an impressive portico and onto the fume-filled bustle of the Strand before any more of London's wildlife decided to mark Connie's arrival with flamboyant displays. After walking down the street for five minutes, he took a right hand lane between two shops. They entered a different world from the traffic-clogged Strand, a backwater where old London had clung on. The buildings were so close together that the pavement at their feet was in deep shade, cold and unwelcoming.

Horace turned sharply to the left and pushed open an ornate double gate that Connie would have missed if he hadn't directed her towards it.

'Down here,' he said, beckoning Connie through an archway and into a cobbled court-yard, leading her out of shadow into the sunlight.

There in front of them stood an elegant build-ing, its walls mellowed by age to the colour of ripe barley. Light glanced off the high mullioned windows which were set symmetrically on three storeys around the pillared entrance. To Connie's eyes the building looked like a cross between a church and a small palace. It was crowned by a lantern dome with a weathervane in the shape of a compass.

'Here we are,' announced Horace, 'the head-quarters of the Society for the Protection of Mythical Creatures.'

5
Snake

C onnie had never been anywhere like this before. It felt very private and very old. She hesitated, doubtful that she would be allowed to go in. It did not look the kind of place to welcome children. Horace, however, was already striding determinedly across the cobbles. Antonia gave Connie a nudge.

'Go on. It'll be fine,' she said. 'I felt like that too, the first time.'

With this encouragement, Connie abandoned her doubts and followed Horace. She lifted her eyes to the roof. Water sprite gargoyles supported the guttering, ready to spout through rounded mouths as if they were singing rain. As she crossed the courtyard, she saw over every window a frieze of creatures: centaurs jousting with pegasi; dragons flying just out of reach of a writhing mass of Kraken tentacles; sirens singing on their rocks while griffins wheeled in the sky; rock dwarfs hammering on an anvil with a weather giant working the bellows. Each was like a carved advertisement for the Society's secret purpose laid out for all to see, but in a way that only members would understand.

She paused before a magnificent pair of stone dragons crouched before the front doors, teeth bared at intruders, half the size of the real thing and carved in polished dark green granite. She would have liked to linger but Horace ushered her straight on. As she entered, she caught a glimpse of a compass motif in the circular window over the entrance and felt a tingle of excitement: that was her symbol. She belonged here.

They came into a marble-floored foyer. A vaulted ceiling rose two floors up, creating a pillared space with the same echo and respectful hush of a cathedral. Antonia smiled at Connie's wide-eyed expression of wonder.

'It's amazing!' Connie exclaimed in a whisper.

'I know,' agreed Antonia.

'Do non-Society people ever find it?'

'Course,' Antonia snorted, 'you can't hide a great big building like this in London! But if they come, they're told it's a "members only" club and are turned away. Grandpa says there are private clubs everywhere so no one's surprised.'

Horace had been signing them in with the porter on duty in the lodge while the girls had been talking.

'Come along—we've been given the green light,' he said cheerfully. As they passed the porter's hatch, Connie noticed that the man had put down his newspaper and was staring after them—after her to be more precise. She hurried up the red-carpeted stairway.

Reaching the first floor, they were faced by a set of ebony doors with the gold lettering 'Library' over them. So they really were going to the library after all. Horace pushed the right hand one quietly open and stood back to let the girls pass.

They were in a large circular room with every inch of the walls covered in books. In the middle, a round desk for the librarians was flooded in pale sunlight streaming in from the windowed lantern set in the centre of the dome overhead. The light spilled out to the rows of tables that radiated like wheel-spokes from the hub. The room was divided by a low wooden partition into four sections—two rows of desks to each segment. The curved roof above each quarter left no doubt as to which company each belonged: to the north, a mural of creatures of the four elements intermingled in a riotous dance—the Company of the Four Elements; to the east, creatures flew in a great burst from the central symbol of a pair of wings—the Company of Winged Creatures; to the south, sea creatures played amongst the waves while dragons spouted flames in the sky—the Company of Reptiles and Sea Creatures; to the west, two- and four-legged beasts and beings processed through a garden studded with flowers—the Company of Two- and Four-Legged Creatures. The air was heavy with the scent of beeswax and book-dust.

Horace led the way over the gleaming wooden floor to the librarian's station. A thin man with sparse white hair and spectacles perched on the end of his nose looked down at the girls curiously.

'Mr Little, what can I do for you today?' the librarian asked in a reedy voice, his watery eyes turning to Horace. 'I'm afraid I still haven't tracked down *Selkies of the Hebrides* for you.'

'No, it's not that today, Mr Dove. I want to sign in a new reader.'

'Oh yes? And which of the young ladies is that?' Mr Dove smiled pleasantly at Antonia and Connie, opening a great ledger on the desk in front of him with pages coded in four colours: green, brown, orange, and blue.

'Antonia—my granddaughter here—already has her pass for the Elementals,' Horace replied, resting his hand proudly on Antonia's shoulder. 'The new reader is Connie Lionheart. I think the Trustees have sent the Senior Librarian a letter on her behalf.'

Mr Dove did the smallest of double-takes before closing the ledger with a thump and putting it to one side. He took a minute silver key out of his waistcoat pocket, retrieved a battered wooden box from a drawer in the cabinet behind him and used the key to unlock it. He drew out a slim black book.

'The Universals' Register,' he explained. 'We'd forgotten where it was—the letter from the Trustees sent us into quite a panic, as you might imagine.' He pushed it across the counter to Connie and handed her a heavy gold-nibbed ink pen. In front of her lay a nearly blank page ruled into columns. It had only a few entries: Suzanna Caldicott, 1703; Gilbert Hollingsworth, 1742; William Blake, 1793; Martha and Millicent Applethrop, 1850; James Proud, 1899; and Reginald Cony, 1921. She felt ashamed of her clumsy round handwriting in comparison to her predecessors' fine copperplate flourishes.

Mr Dove took the book back, blew on the page to dry it, before locking it in the box.

'Well, Miss Lionheart, arrangements for you are a little unusual. You are welcome to refer to works in any of the sections on this floor, but you also have access to a special reading room up there.' He pointed to the dome above with his spindly index finger. Connie saw that there was a gallery running around the lantern, bordered by a white railing.

'How do I get up there?' she asked.

'With this.' He handed her a second key, this one with a fob in the shape of a four-pointed star, attached to a length of turquoise satin ribbon. 'The door is over there. I think it leads to the stairs.'

'You think?' interjected Horace, surprised at the vagueness of this direction.

'Indeed so.' Mr Dove smiled apologetically. 'As Miss Lionheart will find out, only universals are allowed up there. No one has been in for years. The doorward will not let us pass.'

Horace raised his eyebrows. 'It sounds as if it might be a bit dusty then. Well, you'd better make a start, Connie. You have only a few hours before I have to come back to fetch you.'

'But why the doorward?' asked Connie. 'What's up there that needs guarding?'

Mr Dove smiled. 'You are better placed to tell us the answer to that question than anyone still alive, Miss Lionheart.' He leant forward. 'Though from the catalogue of books we have, I should say there's some pretty dangerous information up there—stuff that only universals can do. When the Trustees said that you were to be given access to your room, some of our members . . .' (he gave a derisive sniff) '. . . argued strongly that you should not be allowed up there unsupervised. They only gave in when we pointed out that they would be eaten if they tried to accompany you.'

'Eaten?' Connie asked in bewilderment.

'But you've no need to worry—you're a universal. No one's going to have you for supper.'

This wasn't very comforting. Connie fingered the key nervously as she set off through the rows of desks to the door in the far wall. She always hated being singled out and the short walk to the universals' entrance suddenly seemed a very long way. As she passed, a few readers looked up from their books, nudged their neighbours and, like a ripple spreading across a pool, soon the whole room was buzzing with excited whispers. Connie hurried forward, tripping in her haste to get out of sight.

When she reached the small door, she paused, surprised to find that it had no keyhole, only a brass handle in the shape of a compass. She turned it and the door swung open smoothly.

That was odd, she thought, if it was open all along, why the key?

She stepped across the threshold into the dark stairwell beyond. Steep stone steps bordered by a handrail carved like a twisted snake led upwards into the gloom. She groped around the wall for a light switch, but there wasn't one.

Probably no one had been up here since the invention of electric light, she thought grimly.

With no light to help her, she resolved to use the rail as a guide up the stairs. She stretched out her hand to touch it.

'Aargh!' She jumped back several paces with a smothered scream.

The handrail was alive.

Her touch had roused the doorward: the twisted end unfurled to reveal the head of a python with jaws that looked as if they would have no problem swallowing Connie in one gulp. The head slithered to her feet, its forked tongue testing the air a hand's breadth from her trainers. Now Connie understood why the librarians had not dared to venture up the stairs. With the unblinking eyes of the snake boring into her, she doubted she would be able to summon the courage to pass it.

'May I go up?' she asked, her voice a whisper.

The snake continued to stare at her.

She took a step forward. It reared up, jaws wide, tongue flickering, fangs exposed, hissing like water dropped on hot coals.

'OK, obviously not then,' she said, retreating until her back was pressed against the entrance.

Perhaps she should show it the key? Maybe that was some kind of pass?

She held the key out but the snake's head now danced above her ever closer; she could feel its dry breath on her cheek. Connie struggled to contain a sense of rising panic; it felt as if a knot of snakes had just untwisted in her stomach.

She was a universal, she was allowed up here. She willed herself not to make a bolt for safety, but her hand was already groping for the doorknob.

Then another voice spoke inside her head: 'So what would a universal do that others could not?' Connie only had to think for a moment: she had to do the last thing she wanted and risk an encounter with the snake. Stretching out her hand still holding the key, she touched the top of the snake's diamond-patterned head.

'Key. Mouth.'

Like a snake bite, the two words struck her hard and fast in the pit of her stomach: she knew now exactly what she had to do. Gingerly, she ventured her hand into the open jaws of the snake, expecting at any moment to feel them close upon her. She dropped the key into its mouth.

In an instant, the snake turned and slithered swiftly up the steps. There was nothing for it but to follow. Connie kept close on its tail, guided by the pale golden glow that shone from its scales. The light grew stronger, turning from bronze to white, as she climbed up. Moments later, she stepped out of the stairwell and onto the sunlit floor of the lantern gallery. It was like entering a bath of sunbeams after the darkness of the winding stair. Light poured in through the high windows over the tops of the bookcases; blue sky could be glimpsed outside breaking through ragged grey clouds. The snake was now curled in a tight spiral by the door, its eyes closed, a long blue ribbon hanging from its mouth like a bizarre tongue.

Connie heaved a sigh of relief. She had made it.

Peering hesitantly over the rail (she did not like heights), Connie saw Horace and Antonia down below looking out for her. She gave them a wave to show that she had survived the encounter with the doorward and they turned to go—Antonia heading to the northern quarter, Horace to the exit to rejoin Hugh at the boat show.

Connie stood back and surveyed her surroundings. So, what had the great snake been set to guard? What secrets were there for her to discover?

The outer circle of the wall was lined with tall bookcases. Connie scanned them quickly and pulled out particularly attractive volumes at random, in the process disturbing clouds of dust as Horace had predicted. She found that they corresponded more or less with the sections downstairs. The eastern shelves were stocked with manuals on flying: one particularly beguiling volume showed the recommended stance to be adopted by a human companion on the backs of a bewildering number of winged creatures, accompanied by a long discussion of balance and maximum load. To the west, she paused over a giant bestiary of 1603, full of vibrant woodcuts of animals from all over the world. She recognized the unicorn and the dragon quite easily, but spent some minutes puzzling over an illustration of one very improbable creature until she deciphered its name as 'elephant'. Smiling to herself, she thrust it back and turned to consult the inner ring of low bookshelves that ran round the railing.

With a rush of excitement, she realized at once that these books contained the dangerous knowledge of which Mr Dove had spoken for they were devoted to the *Art and Science of the Universal*, as one title put it. She pulled out this work eagerly and studied the contents. She recognized the name on the spine: Suzanna Caldicott, one of her predecessors who had also passed the doorward.

Some of the techniques described she already knew—the shield and the sword, for example, though from the pages given over to both these subjects, she saw that she did not yet know the half of it. There were many other tools listed in the index, all given names drawn from armour and weaponry: the helm, hauberk, lance, to name but a few.

She stood for a moment with the book weighing heavily on her palm. There was far more to being a universal than she had known, a vast and as yet untapped potential in her gift—a world of weapons and tools, both deadly and defensive. Here she was surrounded by the knowledge of her kind: it was the nearest she would get to talking to a universal as they were all long since gone. This room was the key to becoming who she really was.

Her heart fluttering with eagerness, she sat down at a small round table and began to read.

Introduction to the universal's tools

Welcome, my fellow universal, to a new world of knowledge—a place like the Americas to us dwellers in the old, full of wonders as well as dangers. Take heed of what is written in these pages so that you may avoid the errors of the past.

I have devoted my life to the study of our craft, sorely feeling the lack of any guidance when I first assumed my mantle as leader of the Trustees. I pray you will benefit from my labour.

The most important thing that you must know when setting out on your voyage of discovery is that universals are weak. Without our companion creatures, we are nothing. We can defend ourselves, but nothing more. Even the humble snail with its shell can claim as much. Think upon this when the privilege and power of your status makes you boastful.

Connie looked out of the high window and watched the clouds sail by. This felt so true: she had always seen herself as feeble compared to others. Suzanna Caldicott now confirmed it.

87

I. Of tools

The implements of our company were first identified by our forefathers and mothers not long after the birth of the Society. Their names take the colouring of that chivalric age. Mental tools can take any shape: it is their use, and not their title, that matters.

There are two kinds of tools belonging to a universal. First, and most important to the wellbeing of the universal, are the defensive implements, shield, helm, and their like. These lie in the universal's mind. They are the key to controlling contact with your companions. Without these, the descent to madness is swift and unstoppable. History is littered with examples of members of our company who have failed to learn these skills and fallen into insanity. Study hard so that you may not be the next.

Connie thought involuntarily of Godiva's warning against voices in her head and delusions. Her great-aunt was partly right then—her gift could lead to madness.

A few defensive tools, such as the hauberk, are the result of harmonious co-operation between universal and creature. In them, you become one with your companion and take on the properties that make them what they are.

Connie picked up her pen and began to take notes, underlining each tool in heavy black ink.

Many universals have devoted their time to the learning of the weapons of battle, such as sword, arrow, and spear. Be warned: it is these tools that enable us to reach beyond our puny selves and manipulate those around us, but in them lies great danger. We only act as channels for the power of others—we are not the power itself. If we take where we are not welcome, we will pay. Many fear us now; if we abuse our gift, they will reject us, turning us from the king among them to the leper beyond their gates.

Some hours later a distant bell rang down on the main floor of the library, warning her that her time was almost up. She was deep into a chapter about mental exercises for controlling shared thoughts—the helm—and was reluctant to stop. She was trying to imagine what it would be like to use this tool, thinking through the process described of using the helm to defend a mind against invasion by another, a useful alternative to the shield. Could she take books out? she wondered.

Picking up the volume, she moved to the stair. On her approach, the snake sprang into life once more and hissed a warning, blocking her exit with a furious weaving dance.

'I think I've got my answer,' Connie said to herself, beating a hasty retreat to put the book back on the shelf.

Once she was bookless, the snake had no objection to guiding Connie down the stairs with its eerie copper glow. At the bottom, it dropped the key at her feet and returned to its vigil, curling itself around the handrail and becoming as still as if it had really been forged from metal. Relieved to be getting out of there in one piece, Connie picked up the ribbon, closed the door behind her, and returned to Antonia by the desk.

'Well?' asked Mr Dove curiously, holding his wrinkled palm out for the key.

'A bit fierce, isn't he?' she said, handing it over still damp from the snake's mouth. Antonia looked mystified but Mr Dove gave a grim smile and locked the key back in the box with the universals' register.

'We call him Argonaut.' Seeing Connie's expression, he continued, 'It's our little joke, you know. Long ago, Jason and his Argonauts got past one of its kind to steal the Golden Fleece. The great snakes have made up for it since by never sleeping on watch. But we librarians like to remind the doorward of Jason, just to keep him in his normal good humour, which doubtless you enjoyed today.'

'Yeah,' Connie muttered to Antonia, 'I'll never complain about paying a library fine again.'

Horace joined them in the entrance hall. Over his shoulder, Connie could see her great-uncle outside, sunning himself against the old stone dragons, looking up at the building in wonder.

'I hope you've learned something today,' said Horace as they signed themselves out.

'Yes, loads of things, thanks,' said Connie, showing him her fat notebook. 'I only wish I could try them out. I know I won't really understand them until I do.'

'Oh, I didn't mean that,' Horace replied, his broad smile beaming on her. 'I was thinking that you might have learned that where there's a will, there's a way.' She looked at him blankly. 'What I mean is, that where you have a will to do something, a way will be found. A universal cannot be kept from her destiny.'

'Ah, Miss Lionheart, I heard that you were in the building.' Mr Coddrington, the assessor who had originally refused Connie membership of the Society, glided stealthily from behind a pillar to intercept them on their way across the foyer. A tall, thin man with limp brown hair, he had the etiolated look of a plant kept in a dark room, straining to grow towards the light. Connie's party stopped.

'Oh, it's you, Coddrington,' Horace said, his

normally genial voice laced with disdain. 'How's the New Members Department treating you?'

'Same as usual,' Mr Coddrington replied evasively, his eyes still fixed on Connie. 'I wondered if I might have a brief word with Miss Lionheart. Alone.' He attempted a pleasant smile that was truly painful to behold.

Horace glanced at his watch. 'Well, if Connie doesn't mind, I suppose we have a few moments.' Connie wished he had not said this, wished he had given her a decent reason to excuse herself for now her head was full of the last time Mr Coddrington had spoken to her 'alone': the rush of wings, the terror of being swept away by a black dragon and taken to Kullervo.

'Good. If Miss Lionheart would not mind stepping this way into my office, I have something I would like to ask her in private.'

Connie was too shy to be overtly rude to him. She followed Mr Coddrington down a tiled corridor leading off the entrance hall. There were many doors opening on either side, some ajar, giving her a glimpse into the administrative heart of the Society, but she was too preoccupied by what Mr Coddrington might want with her to take much in. The assessor paused by a closed door marked 'New Members Department', unlocked it and ushered her inside.

There were three desks in the room but no occupants. Two desks were piled high with files, adorned with children's pictures and pot plants. One desk was meticulously tidy—not a stray paperclip in sight—with a pale grey blotter set square in its gleaming centre and an in-tray in one corner. Behind the desk on the wall, it was another matter: a huge map of the British Isles was covered with tiny pins, each colour-coded for one of the companies and bearing a number.

'It is fortunate that my colleagues are out assessing,' Mr Coddrington said, nodding at the two untidy desks. 'Please have a seat.'

Connie sat down nervously in a low chair across the desk from him. Avoiding meeting his eye, her gaze drifted to the map. She realized with a jolt that on the spot marking Chartmouth there was single silver pin—the only one on the whole map.

'Oh yes, I like to keep tabs on everyone,' he said with a wintry smile when he noticed her staring at the map. 'Literally, that is. Each pin is cross-referenced to my filing system with a note of date assessed and eventual allocation of companion species. They are all filed in one of my cabinets.' He nodded at four metal filing cabinets standing along one wall. 'I did not know what to

93

do with you: your entry is still here, waiting to find a home.' He picked up a thin piece of paper from his in-tray, the only thing in it, holding it between his finger and thumb, before dropping it back down. 'I suppose I will just have to get a new cabinet, won't I?'

Connie was not sure what she was expected to say to this so said nothing, her eyes now straying to the despised piece of paper that recorded her membership details.

'Actually, it is about this that I wanted to talk to you, Miss Lionheart.'

Filing cabinets? Connie had lost track of what he was saying.

'I was wondering if you could give me any idea just how many of you there might be out there—to help us adjust our systems to cope with the burden you will place on them.'

'Me?' Connie stared at him in surprise. 'How should I know?'

Mr Coddrington leaned forward intently, elbows on his blotter, fingertips touching lightly. 'We thought you might be in a position to find out. At the very least you might have your suspicions about other universals.'

Connie recalled the 'suspicions' she and her aunt had had about her brother Simon some time ago but not had an opportunity so far to follow up. Mr Coddrington would be the last person with whom she would share these thoughts.

'I really have no idea, Mr Coddrington,' she said as sweetly as possible. He frowned slightly and sat back.

'Well, if you change your mind, you'll let us know immediately, of course,' he said, rising to his feet. 'Here, take my business card in case you want to ring me. Call any time. It is very important that we understand whether you are an aberration or the beginning of a revival of a whole new company. If the latter is the case, then there will be many adjustments to make.' He sighed, the frown lines on his brow deepening.

'Sure, I'll bear that in mind,' Connie said quickly, also getting up. 'Can I go now?' He nodded curtly and Connie bolted for the door without a backward glance. Half running down the corridor, she could not get the image of that map out of her head. There was something about Mr Coddrington that was just not right. It could be the creepy way he always looked at her as if he were plotting something against her; or perhaps it was his opposition to her very existence in the Society. She had believed for many months that Mr Coddrington was in league with Kullervo, despite Col and Dr Brock's scepticism on the subject. Information as to the whereabouts of every companion would be very valuable to Kullervo—make it absurdly easy for him to anticipate and neutralize the counter-attack the Society was preparing. And the person best placed to betray this information was sitting in the heart of the Society headquarters, allowed to continue unchecked.

And as for her membership details, Connie had been in the Society for almost a year now: when was he going to accept that he was over-ruled and she was a full member? Or perhaps he did not expect her to survive long enough for it to be worth his while to move her from his pending tray? With these dark thoughts she rejoined Horace and Antonia.

6
Gorgon

Col sat cross-legged on his bed with his mother's parcel on his lap. His bedroom, every inch decorated with pictures of horses, even the duvet cover and curtains, was flooded with golden evening sunlight. He liked to be surrounded by them, even though they weren't a patch on Skylark, the real thing. He should have felt safe in these surroundings but the package loomed before him like an unexploded bomb. He was right to be nervous: his experience of his mother's gifts was not encouraging. He was not sure that he had ever got over being given a rattlesnake's rattle—with original owner still attached—for his third birthday. Only the rapid intervention of his grandmother had prevented disaster. His mother had been testing whether or not he had inherited her particular gift and had seemed surprised by the family outcry at her choice of birthday present. Well, at least this present did not appear to be alive—he had already prodded it with a stick before taking it up into his room.

What had his mother said? He had grown up. Seen danger and mastered his fear.

OK then.

He ripped off the paper and laughed with relief as onto his lap fell a polished circular mirror, the unreflective side decorated with a bronze head of a snake-haired gorgon. A note fluttered out. He saw his mother had written it in looping green ink:

Use this when you visit me. Remember, the first rider of the pegasus braved the gorgon: do likewise and you have nothing to fear.

Col, of course, knew exactly what she meant: in Ancient Greece Perseus had foiled the gorgon's killing gaze by looking at her in the reflective surface of his shield. According to the legend, the blood spilt at that encounter had given birth to the first pegasus which Perseus had then ridden. However, more important to Col was the fact that his mother was actually inviting him back: it was the first time she had recognized him as a companion to pegasi, as an equal. Her talent for choosing presents was improving. He rubbed off the mist left by his breath on the mirror and stowed the gift carefully away in his backpack, determined that he would one day soon show her that he was as courageous as Perseus.

He didn't have to wait long for the invitation. Col was camping out with Rat. They had begun the evening tending the animals in Rat's impromptu hospital that he had made in the space under the bus. First, Rat showed Col how to put a splint on the wing of a blackbird they had rescued from the roadside. He then went on to introduce Col to his other charges—a fox with a bandaged tail, two orphaned rabbits, and a pheasant with a broken leg. Col marvelled that the family dog, Wolf, an impressive black and tan Alsatian, allowed these residents to live undisturbed only a few metres from his nose.

'He's an old softie when you get to know him,' Rat said as Wolf bared his teeth at Col and growled.

'Oh yes?' said Col, unconvinced.

'He does what I tell him,' Rat said with a shrug, 'even looks after them for me. I have more problems persuading the fox not to go for the others.'

Yes, the fox did look a bit resentful, thought Col as Rat shut the rabbits and the pheasant back in their temporary hutch. The blackbird he placed on the bus dashboard, ignoring his mother's protests that he should 'get that filthy animal out of here'.

'She's not serious,' he said airily to Col. 'Her voice sounds different when she means it. She doesn't mind really.'

Now they were lying in the open, wrapped warmly in sleeping bags, contemplating the constellations overhead. Rat turned out to be very knowledgeable about the star systems—a training he put down to one summer spent at Cromer with a cousin who told fortunes for a living.

'A load of rubbish,' he admitted cheerfully, 'but she was really into stargazing, science and all that stuff. The telling was just to make money to buy a half decent telescope.'

Col turned onto his elbow and lay for a moment watching the sharp profile of his friend as Rat pointed out two more constellations—the Great and Little Bears—for Col's benefit.

'Don't look much like bears to me,' Rat was saying. 'I s'pose if you kind of think of them as skeletons it works . . .'

'Rat?' Col asked abruptly.

'Yeah, what?'

'Are you gonna come to school with me after the holidays?'

Rat looked a bit shifty and turned his head away. 'Sure, I'll go to school. It's the law, ain't it?'

'Well, if you do,' Col said, lying back down, 'you might find you can do more stuff about planets and stars in science lessons. You're really good at it already.'

'Yeah?' Rat sounded pleased.

'Yeah.'

There was a silence and then Rat spoke again: 'I can't read. Not that I'm thick or nothing,' he added defensively. 'Just not got round to it.'

Col was surprised: Rat had managed to get by very well without showing he could not read.

'Come to school with me then. About time you got round to it.'

They lay in silence listening to the sounds of the wood at night. The leaves whispered to each other in the gentle breeze; distant bursts of laughter came from the main encampment; an owl hooted mournfully in a nearby tree. A police siren wailed into the night. Col wondered who was causing trouble now: had Rat's dad and his mates broken into the builders' compound again? They'd been threatening to decorate the JCBs with luminous green paint. Or perhaps one of the tunnellers had been discovered in his hideout beneath the field scheduled for clearance the next day?

Rat's breathing was now coming deep and even: he had fallen asleep. Col put his arms under his head, thoughts of Connie stealing into his mind as they so often did when he stopped for a moment. He was missing her: he wanted to talk to her about his mother—introduce her to Rat—he felt sure they'd get on together. And she'd be so interested to hear about the gorgon. He knew she would be feeling terrible without her companion creatures. Was there really no way of getting in to see her?

He gazed up at the stars that formed the Pegasus, wondering where Skylark was now. He longed to be flying with him in the skies above; if he spent too long apart from the pegasus, he started to feel weak, as if a key part of him was missing. Skylark was probably chasing the wind in some remote part of the moor. They'd be seeing each other soon. Col turned over and drifted off to sleep.

'Colin?'

He was woken some hours later by a firm shake of his shoulder. He sat up abruptly to come face to face with his mother. Her fair hair glimmered frostily in the moonlight; her eyes were in shadow.

'What's matter?' Col yawned.

'Nothing. It's time to come with me.' She looked across at Rat. 'But do not bring your friend—this is for you alone.'

Col, still disorientated by sleep, rubbed his knuckles into his eyes to drive his drowsiness away. It appeared that now would be a very good time to have his wits about him. Shuffling out of his sleeping bag like a moth emerging from a chrysalis, Col scooped up his things and shoved them into his backpack. As he did so, his hand touched a cool, smooth object; he seized it and stuffed it into his jacket pocket. His mother watched his preparations in silence. She moved off the instant he was ready. They were heading deeper into the wood. Col gripped the mirror, finding its cold hardness against his skin a comfort.

'Where are we going?' Col asked. He instinctively kept his voice low.

'To meet her, of course. She wants to see my hatchling.'

'Your what?'

'You.'

Col swallowed. There could only be one 'her' as far as his mother was concerned: the gorgon.

Forcing himself to follow, he stumbled after her into the trees. The wood was full of shadows of half seen creatures flitting through the patches of moonlight. A light flutter caught his ear and he saw what he thought was a bat whisk past him. His mother was leading him into a part of the wood he had never seen before—the deepest, densest thicket of oak trees and holly bushes. Brambles grabbed at his clothes and scored his fingers as he shook himself free. It seemed as if they were almost reluctant to let him through.

'Is it far now?' he asked.

Cassandra had not been hindered by the thorns. She seemed to glide past all obstructions.

'No, not far. It is a special place, Colin. I'm trusting you with my biggest secret by bringing you here.'

Col felt a flush of pride. 'Does it have a name, this place we're going to?'

'Snake Hollow. It's where the gorgon always returns—the nest where she hatches her hair-serpents. She must come here every year.'

'And if she can't?'

'Her serpents will not be reborn and she will die.'

They reached a bank that plunged steeply down from a rocky lip. Cassandra stood at the very edge and pointed.

'The nesting cave's not far from here—that's where she's waiting for you.'

'For me? Why—aren't you coming with me?' Col's voice shook. He did not want to be left alone now with the gorgon so close.

Cassandra then did something she had not done for many years. She put her arm around her son's shoulders and drew him into an embrace. Col felt a rush of fierce love for her. He had been so starved of any sign of her affection that this small gesture was like an earthquake inside him.

'No, she wants to meet you alone—without another human present. She wants to explain. Please listen to what she has to say. I want you on our side when it all happens.'

'When what happens? Mum, what are you talking about?'

Cassandra ignored his questions. 'I'll drop you down onto the ledge and I'll wait here until you return. Don't forget—use your mirror and you have nothing to fear.' She hesitated again and cleared her throat. 'And, Colin—don't anger them.'

'Them?'

She shook her caped head, refusing explanation. 'Give me your hands: I'll lower you as far as I can, then you drop the last few feet onto the ledge. Do you understand?'

Col swallowed, wondering if he could turn back even now. But how could he repay her belief in him by refusing to go ahead? His relationship with his mother was so fragile: he would surely shatter her good opinion of him if he did so. She was so fanatical about her companion that she never saw the danger for anyone else in her drive to do her best by the gorgon. Like now: she seemed to think nothing of dropping her only child over a cliff. Before he could decide what to do, his mother had seized both his forearms and was guiding him to the edge.

He had to do it: falling was better than failing.

Col surrendered himself to the inevitable. They both knelt—Col with his back to the edge, his feet already hanging in the air.

'Off you go,' Cassandra said. 'I'm sure you'll make it.'

As Col inched his way backwards on his stomach, his mother stretched out at full length, taking his weight. He soon found out why there was no climbing down—the edge was in fact the lip of an overhang; only an insect could crawl down this incline. He was now dangling over the void, his wrists complaining in his mother's grip.

'I'm going to release you on the count of three. Be careful!'

'A bit late for that, isn't it?' he muttered.

'Lean forwards—not back,' he urged himself, desperate not to lose his balance on the shelf. One mistake and he'd end up at the foot of the slope.

'One, two, three!' Her grip opened and Col dropped onto the ledge. He threw himself forward to hug the rock face, bruising his temple as he collided with stone. He was down. Cassandra's head appeared above him.

'I told you you'd be all right. Now follow the ledge round to your left. It'll lead you down to the cave. I'll be waiting here to help you back up.'

And she was gone. No word of praise for getting down safely, nothing. Col shuffled along the narrow sill, fear running like an electric charge through him. Stepping on a crumbling piece of the ledge, his left foot gave way. Stones clattered down the sheer drop as he scrabbled to keep a hold. Nails scraped on bare rock. Gripping on to a tree root, he just managed to save himself. He pulled himself back up and collapsed, panting, against the cliff.

Clinging like a fly to a wall, Col saw the full absurdity of his situation. A mad laugh bubbled up uncontrollably inside him. He was risking falling to his death to meet one of the most deadly creatures alive. He must be mad.

There was nothing for it now but to go on. He shuffled along until he turned the corner. The path descended in steps into the black heart of the forest. It began to spit with rain, making the muddy rock slippery underfoot. To his relief he found that he now had tree branches to hold and made faster progress. In the murk ahead he thought he could see a dark hole—the mouth of the cave perhaps?

It was time to 'be careful'.

He groped inside his jacket for the mirror, pulled it out and held it in front of him so he could look closely at the cave entrance. As far as he could tell in the weak moonlight, it seemed empty. An orange light flickered within. She had a fire then.

'Hello! I'm here.' His voice echoed off the hillside in a mocking imitation of his own words: 'Lo! Ear!' There was no other reply. Col continued to edge forwards only stopping when he was within an arm's length of the entrance. What should he do now? Risk entering or wait until he was invited in?

He tried again: 'It's me—it's Col.'

Above the gentle patter of the rain on the leaves around him, Col heard a rustling and hissing noise within like the dry scrape of a besom broom on a pathway. It stopped, only to be followed by a soft voice speaking in a sibilant hiss:

'Ss-step inside. Ss-stand with your back to me. Hold out the mirror ss-so you can ss-see me.'

Not at all sure he wanted to see the speaker, Col sidestepped into the entrance of the cave and spun himself round so that he was facing outwards. He lifted the mirror with a shaking hand, struggling for a moment to find the right angle that would show him the creature. She flashed into sight briefly—a blur of bronze—then came back in sharp focus at the centre of the mirror when he steadied his hand. A pair of hard jet-black eyes stared back at him. They were set in a heart-shaped face with skin that glowed tawny gold in the firelight. Long folds of hair fell back over the creature's shoulders, looking strangely solid as if each lock was carved from sandstone. At first glance the gorgon seemed draped in swathes of silky material but Col then saw she was wrapped in her own golden wings. He was astonished: he had imagined something monstrous and fearsome, not this beauty.

'You had something you wanted to tell me?' he asked, his voice cracked with fear.

She nodded, displacing one of her tresses as she did so. It slid over her slim shoulder, blinked a pair of small black eyes coolly at him and slithered back to join its siblings. Col gave a start that he tried to disguise as a cough.

109

'Well, I'm listening,' he said, uncomfortably aware of how exposed his back would be should any of these benign snake-locks change their mind and choose to strike. Rain was now dripping down his forehead and into his eyes, spotting the surface of the mirror and distorting the gorgon's face, making her look as if she was melting with tears. He wiped the glass quickly with the sleeve of his jacket, losing the reflection of her face as he did so.

'Come into the cave,' the gorgon said softly, rustling a little closer. 'Ss-sit here while we talk.'

Col could not see where she was pointing and did not much like her invitation but he remembered what his mother had said about not angering 'them'—perhaps she had meant the snakes? He shuffled backwards until his heels struck an obstacle. Reaching out behind him, he touched the flat top of a boulder. He sat down and, a moment later, felt something gently brush his collar. Instinctively, he jumped away, thinking it was one of the snakes paying him a visit, but he was wrong. The gorgon's hand, cool and dry to the skin, now caressed his cheek; he could just see the tips of her almond-shaped fingernails at the edge of his vision.

'Yes-ss, Cass-ssandra ss-said you were a ss-strong boy—I can ss-see it in your face-ss and in your shoulders-ss. You will be a fine man ss-soon.'

Col shifted uneasily under the creature's touch, both embarrassed and pleased by her words. He was flattered to see himself through her eyes for a brief moment. Squaring his shoulders, he resolved not to flinch again from her hand.

'Mum—Cassandra—said something's going to happen. Is that what you want to talk to me about?' He flashed the mirror around the ceiling, the rock wall, until, there, he found her again.

'Ha!' The gorgon gave a shout of laughter, making him start. To Col's dismay, the laugh opened her mouth wide, wider than any human mouth, revealing great teeth, like the tusks of a boar, curling up from her lower jaw to meet dagger-like fangs descending from above in a fearsome bite. 'Ss-something might be happening—but we need ss-someone to make it work.' Her tongue flickered black in the red maw of her throat.

Col, mesmerized by the contrast between her smooth beauty when her face was at rest and the monstrous teeth revealed when she spoke, only half took in her words. It was like watching a sleeping python with the feeble line of its closed mouth suddenly roused to face danger, hissing, jaws open, fangs dripping venom.

'W . . . who do you need to help you? Me?' he stammered.

She smiled enigmatically. 'Why not you, my bold one? We creatures-ss need to fight to pres-sserve our exiss-stence before humans-ss stamp us-ss out. Look what is happening to me—to my la-sst refuge. But even that is to be torn away from me. And why?' She gave another of her bitter laughs, shaking her head back and this time stirring all her snake companions as they sensed her rising anger. 'Cass-ssandra told me the wood is doomed because it creates-ss a bend in a human-road, making it slower for those machines of yours-ss.' The snake-locks wove in and out of each other in an angry dance, creating a writhing halo about her head, all eyes glaring at Col in his mirror. 'Is this-ss all the excuse humans need to make others homeless-ss—to drive some of us into extinction? Will you let this happen? Or will you help save us-ss? Ss-ave me?' Her voice dropped to a soft plea, the snakes no longer lashed the air angrily but swayed sinuously on her shoulders, all eyes still fixed on him. Their gaze was like a cold breeze chilling his back; under this scrutiny, he had no difficulty understanding the power of her deadly eyes.

'Of course I don't want this to happen. What can I do?'

'Fight with us-ss. Do not wait until the machine crushes us-ss, but act now.'

If Col had been thinking straight he would have been suspicious of her arguments, but he was under the spell of the image the gorgon was reflecting back to him. Her words painted an alluring picture of a young warrior ready for combat.

'Show me what I must do—how I can help,' he offered eagerly.

The gorgon smiled and nodded. 'Good. It is-ss as we hoped: you are ripe for the tass-sk we have for you.'

'Task?'

'Your mother will tell you more when we are ready.' Her finger caressed his cheek again. 'I must tend to my hatchlings. You ss-should go.'

As Col got up, he almost turned to take a last good look at her before he left but caught himself just in time.

'Idiot,' he hissed at himself. If he was going to help the gorgon, he couldn't start by getting turned to stone.

7
Argand

Connie bent over her Latin grammar book and tried to make sense of the introductory lesson. So far, all she had noticed was the dog-eared state of the pages and the cramped writing; the words were sliding in and out of her mind making no impression. Idly, she flipped to the front and looked at the title page again: Sybil, crossed out, Robin, crossed out, Hugh, crossed out, Godiva still plain to see. Her great-aunt obviously thought what was good enough for her and her brothers and sisters was good enough for Connie. Picking up her pen, Connie struck through her aunt's name and added her own underneath. The latest in a long line of Lionheart Latin martyrs, she thought grimly.

'How are you doing, Connie?' asked Godiva. She was sitting at a table embroidering a cushion with the Lionheart compass.

'Fine,' lied Connie. She turned back to the first chapter. Someone had underlined certain words in pale blue ink. She traced them through, skipping from page to page—horse, bear, tree. Whoever it was had picked out all the words to do with nature. Wolf, serpent, dragon.

Tap-tap.

Connie looked up, feeling a strange burning sensation in her stomach. Godiva raised her eyebrows, warning her to re-apply herself to her work.

Tap-tap.

This time, Connie sneaked a glance at the window—and almost dropped her book in surprise. There, dancing in the morning sunlight, was a small golden creature, wings glistening with all the colours of the rainbow like a dragonfly—but it wasn't a fly. Seeing Connie watching, the dragonet Argand looped the loop with excitement.

A cold sweat broke out on Connie's brow. Her companion was bobbing about only a few metres from Godiva's head. What could she do?

She waved her hand at the window. 'Go away!' she mouthed.

Argand waved her tail back with a friendly gesture.

Connie shook her head and repeated the hand signal.

'What are you doing, Connie?' barked Godiva, laying her sewing to one side.

'A wasp's bothering me.'

'Well, really, don't you know better than to wave your hands in that stupid fashion—you'll only annoy it. Sit still and it'll go away.'

But this particular 'wasp' didn't. Thwarted by the glass, Argand began to dive-bomb the barrier, trying to smash her way in. Connie gulped. Godiva appeared to be ignoring the thumping sound behind her. She had to do something—and quick!

'May I open the window, please?'

Godiva turned and took a long look outside. Surely she must see the little dragon now? She gazed back at Connie, her expression set.

'No, you may not. You will do five extra pages of exercises as punishment.'

'Punishment for what?'

'For inattention.'

This was so unfair! Godiva must have seen Argand too—why was she pretending she hadn't?

'You can see the dragon, can't you?'

'Eight pages!'

'Her name's Argand. She hatched last month.'

'Ten pages!'

'She's my companion.'

Godiva leapt from her seat and thrust her face right up to Connie's.

'Listen, there is *no* dragon—*no* companion. You are ill, Connie, very, very ill. If you carry on talking such drivel, I will have to take drastic measures.'

At that moment, the glass shattered and Argand zoomed merrily into the room, heading straight for Connie. Godiva screamed.

'That damned parakeet!' She started throwing anything to hand at the dragonet. 'The organist really must keep it under better . . .' Crash! '. . . control!' Thump. The last missile, Connie's Latin book, struck Argand on the snout and burst into flames.

'Quick, quick! Put it out!' shrieked Godiva.

Connie stripped off her hooded top and smothered the book and the irate dragon underneath. Scooping them up, she ran out of the room, calling, 'I'll take it out into the garden,' over her shoulder.

Godiva was leaning against her desk, panting hard.

'Be back here in two minutes—or else!'

Connie ran down the path to the stone seat at the far end of the garden. Argand struggled in her arms, protesting at this rough treatment. Placing the bundle on the bench, Connie unwrapped the contents. Immediately the way was clear, a very angry dragon darted into the air, spitting sparks at Connie.

'Hey, hey!' said Connie soothingly. 'It wasn't me!'

Argand circled once and then flew into her chest with a thud, knocking her back. The dragon dug in her claws and clung to Connie's T-shirt, shivering. Gently, Connie tried to extricate the most painful talons which were pinching her skin.

'Calm down,' she crooned. 'It's all right now. The nasty lady has gone.'

Argand gave a low fluting sound of distress. Connie dipped into her mind, seeking the bond with her companion. She swiftly found her—Argand was still in a nightmare of loud noises and missiles. Stroking the creature along her scaly spine, Connie led Argand back to the daylight and to peace. Opening her eyes, she found the little dragon gazing adoringly at her, her tiny fire-bright eyes full of trust.

'There now, that's better, isn't it? What are you doing here? Does your mother know where you are?'

If dragons could look sheepish, Argand now did.

'No? Well, you'd better hurry home. Can you remember the way?'

Argand nodded.

'You can't come here like this, you know. I'll have to think of another way for us to see each other. Will you wait till I send word?'

The dragon shook her head.

'Please?'

A pause, then Argand nodded.

'Right, off you go!' Throwing Argand up into the air like a ball, Connie watched the dragon flit away over the wall, her wings flashing with rapid strokes.

Knowing her two minutes had been up long ago, Connie picked up her scorched top and the smouldering remains of the Latin book.

It seems she was the last in a long line of Lionhearts to use it, Connie thought as the pages drifted away in black flakes. A noble end for a family heirloom.

Col was waiting in his grandmother's boat for his father to arrive. Mack was late—of course. Seagulls mewed overhead, etching figures of eight like ice-skaters in the sky. Bored with watching tourists mill around the gift shops, Col busied himself coiling ropes, involuntarily thinking of them as snakes and wondering what his mother and the gorgon were up to.

'Hi, Col!' He looked up, shading his eyes against the slanting rays of the sun. Anneena, dressed in fuchsia pink, was standing on the gangplank; Jane hovered shyly behind her.

'Oh, hi,' Col said brightly. 'Come on board. I haven't seen you all week: what've you been doing?'

'Busy working on these,' said Anneena, gesturing to a bundle of posters Jane was carrying. The girls leapt lightly down into the boat.

'What are the posters for?' He took them from Jane and put them on a dry spot on the engine hatch.

'We're appealing for teams to take part in the carnival procession,' Jane said, patting the scrolls proudly.

'Oh yeah?' Col had seen the pageant in previous years: it was not his kind of thing—a bunch of enthusiasts dressing up in daft costumes for 'Michaelmas', one of the old quarter days that fell in late September and the traditional start of the festival. He was always more interested in the music that followed.

Anneena took over. 'This year we want to make it really good because my sister—you know Rupa's landed a job with *The Times* in London?—well, she's going to do an article about it for the weekend magazine—they're running a story about the festival. It's all part of the publicity about the new road.'

'Really?' Col replied with a distinct lack of enthusiasm.

'Yes,' Anneena continued, unperturbed by his reaction. 'You ride, don't you, Col? You'd be great—all you need is a costume.'

'Oh no, you don't,' Col said firmly. 'You are absolutely not going to rope me into it.'

'Think about it—please!'

'I don't need to think about it.'

Anneena's face was a picture of disappointment. Col felt a bit bad letting her down but the last thing in the world he wanted to do was to team up with the ageing amateur dramatic society who ran the pageant and make a fool of himself in some stupid costume. He couldn't think of any circumstances under which he would willingly take part.

Jane nudged Anneena to stop her arguing it any further today. 'Go on, tell him,' Jane muttered. Evidently, they had not called in at the boat by accident.

Anneena said: 'It's about Connie.'

'What about her?'

'We saw her again yesterday. She really wants to see you.'

'And I want to see her. But how can I? Her aunt won't let her near anyone from our Society.'

Jane smiled sadly. 'Yeah, she thinks you're all a bunch of tree-hugging nutters.'

'And what's wrong with that?' laughed Col.

'I dunno,' said Jane, shrugging. 'Poor old Connie: she's really hating it in Chartmouth.'

'Did she say if she can get out of there?'

Anneena nodded. 'She's had an idea. She wants you to meet her in the abbey tomorrow at midday—she's got a favour to ask.'

'What kind of favour?'

'No idea—she was very mysterious about it.'

It must be about the Society then, thought Col. 'Sure, I'll go to the abbey.'

'She said to hide in case she's with her aunt.'

'Fine—I can do that.'

'So, Col, I see you've got company!' Mack had arrived and was looking down at the threesome with an unnecessarily broad grin. 'Shall I come back later?'

The girls both glanced at Col, not knowing what to make of the arrival of one of Hescombe's famous characters. Col wished that the earth would swallow him up but he had to say something.

'Anneena—Jane—this is my dad,' he said heavily.

Mack jumped into the boat. He then reached up to the quayside to lift down his diving gear, knocking Jane's posters into a puddle of water. He swore and shook them out.

'Sorry, love. What's all this then—a pageant?' he asked, catching sight of what was written on them. 'You're looking for volunteers? You should come up to the woods and ask the protestors—they've plenty of time on their hands. Getting dressed up in weird costumes would be right up their street. I expect you'd think that some of them wouldn't even need to change.' He gave Jane a conspiratorial wink. Col felt a pang of pity for her and wished he could spirit his father away. Then it got worse: Mack peeled off his jacket and shirt to put on his wetsuit, revealing a tattoo of a great tentacled creature on his back. Jane did not know where to look. 'Fancy an expedition, girls?'

'Er . . . no thanks, Mr Clamworthy,' Anneena excused them hastily.

'Mack, love, call me Mack.'

Col noted dismally that everything he hated about his father seemed magnified in the presence of girls.

Anneena looked flustered. 'Thanks, Mr . . . er . . . Mack, but we've really got to get these posters up.' Jane was already abandoning ship with the scrolls stuffed haphazardly under her arm. 'Some other time, perhaps.' The girls hurried off, shouting their goodbyes before the invitation could be pressed any further.

'So,' said Mack, leaning on the wheelhouse and assessing his son, 'you've not yet started to make headway with the girls then? Give it a few more years.'

Col was bored waiting for his father to surface from his dive, having tired of staring out across the same patch of ocean for several hours. He wished Connie was with him—at least with her there would have been a chance of catching sight of a siren, or a selkie, or any mythical creature in the vicinity, come of think of it.

He thought back to the most recent Society meeting only last night. Dr Brock had stressed that they were far from ready for Kullervo's next attack with Connie unable to continue her training. The adult members were working hard in secret for the expected confrontation with the shape-shifter and his supporters—even junior members like Col were being taught ancillary tasks, like treatment of weather injuries for the unicorn companions, search and rescue for the selkie companions, and evasion techniques for pegasus and dragon riders. They all expected Kullervo to unleash a devastating revenge, an assault that would require everyone to play their part—especially the universal. Col hated the feeling of powerless panic that hit him every time he thought about the shape-shifter. He wanted to be braver—stronger. He had wanted to learn how to fight, to know how to protect Connie from Kullervo. He'd be good at it, he was sure of that, and he'd enjoy learning the skills. But Dr Brock had firmly put him in his place when Col had expressed this wish.

'The Trustees are strongly of the opinion that children must not be used in battle. When you are eighteen, you can apply to join one of our active units, but until then you must be content with learning these other, equally useful skills,' the doctor had told him.

Watching the sea lap against the fenders, Col yawned. Adults were all the same really: there was Dr Brock spoiling his plans, just as Connie's great-aunt was determined to spoil hers.

There was an explosion of bubbles in the sea and a masked head bobbed to the surface. Col helped pull his father's gear over the side, before Mack slithered back on board, dripping liberally, shaking himself like a dog emerging from a bath.

'How was it?' Col forced himself to act interested.

'Amazing,' Mack replied, his eyes still bearing a far-off look as if part of him had not yet returned.

'Yeah, right,' said Col, starting the engine. 'Connie said the Kraken was one of the weirdest creatures she'd encountered.'

Mack looked up abruptly, anger sparkling in his dark eyes. 'Weird? She knows nothing then.'

Col, already irritated by his father's crass behaviour earlier, scaring off his friends, sprang to the absent Connie's defence.

'Nothing, huh? A universal and she knows nothing? Well, Dad, for one thing she knows a lot more than you'll ever know about mythical creatures and if she says the Kraken's weird, then it's weird.'

Mack peeled off his wetsuit jacket and threw it to the floor.

'That's right, son,' he said with a bitter edge to his voice. 'Live in her shadow. Play lapdog to the universal if you must. You're just like your mother—a slave to someone else. Some of us prefer to stand on our own two feet.'

As Mack was wearing bright yellow flippers when he said this, the remark would have been funny if it had not nettled Col so badly.

'You're so blind, Dad. Mum's not a slave. The gorgon's amazing.'

'The expert now, are you? What has your mum been telling you?'

Col said nothing; he didn't want to share his secret visit to Snake Hollow with Mack of all people. He started the engine and pushed it into top gear so that the engine whined with an angry hum, jerking the boat into motion. The two Clamworthys returned to Hescombe Harbour sitting at opposite ends of the boat.

8
Inheritance

Connie decided that breakfast was the best moment to broach the subject of a visit to the abbey as Hugh would be there. She waited until her aunt had satisfied her hunger with several rounds of toast before taking the plunge.

'I've been wondering, Aunt,' she began.

'Yes?' Godiva was instantly suspicious.

'You mentioned something about the Lionhearts being an old family—merchants, I think you said.'

Godiva smiled. This was a safe topic.

'Indeed. I'm glad you're taking an interest in them.'

'Uncle Hugh said they were sailors too.'

Hugh rustled his paper. 'That's right, my dear—it

goes with the territory, you might say—oldest son in the warehouse, younger in the shipping business. Shocking number of them lost at sea, of course—those sailing ships may be beautiful, but they were treacherous.'

Connie wondered fleetingly how many of her ancestors had fallen foul of the Kraken on their voyages, but knew better than to speak this thought aloud.

'I'd like to see their memorials in the abbey. Would it be OK if I went this morning?'

Godiva sniffed, trying to scent the hitch.

'Perhaps Uncle Hugh could come with me and show me about a bit?'

'Delighted, my dear. I have a favourite tomb I'd like to take you to—remember, Godiva, Charles Lionheart's one under the south window?'

Godiva smiled at her brother. 'Of course, I remember, Hugh. We could hardly tear you away from it when you were a boy. Yes, you go and show Connie that.'

Hugh, with old fashioned gallantry, offered his great-niece his arm as they crossed the Abbey Close a few minutes before midday.

'Are you managing all right, Connie?' he asked once they were out of sight of Godiva. 'I mean, I know my sister can be a bit fierce but she means well.'

Connie said nothing.

'It's just that you're looking a bit peaky. I was beginning to worry. She said you had to go through this to be cured. I hope you understand.'

'I'm not ill, Uncle.'

He glanced at her sideways. 'You probably don't see it like that. I understand. Who understands better? I came from a whole family of people who had only a vague connection with sanity—my sister Sybil was completely . . .' He checked himself. 'I loved her all the same. It was terrible what happened to that nice young man of hers.'

There weren't many visitors in the abbey that morning. Sunlight streamed in through the round south window, staining the floor with rich splashes of colour. Connie walked forward and stood in the centre of the ring. She looked up. The vast circular window was in the shape of a compass—it was breathtakingly blatant—here for everyone to see.

'Lovely, isn't it,' said Hugh, rubbing his hands. 'They say it stands for the ring of eternity—the snake with its tail in its mouth. The compass is a parable of how the heart leads us to our Maker.'

But it's also about me, thought Connie. Someone in the family knew what the symbol meant—they must've done. 'Who paid for it to be put here?' she asked lightly.

'The couple in this tomb—this is what I really wanted to show you.'

Hugh beckoned her over to a marble sarcophagus. The sides were decorated with images of the sea—ships in full sail, mermaids, dolphins, and fish. The lid was covered by a carving of the compass. Connie bent over to read the inscription.

Here lies Charles Henry Benjamin Lionheart,
beloved husband and father. Born 1670.
Departed this life 1742. 'The Sea calleth him home.'
And also his relict, Suzanna Caldicott Lionheart,
a universal mother to us all. Born 1682.
Died 1743. She encompassed every virtue.

'Very nice, isn't it?' said Hugh, touching the lid affectionately, taking her stunned silence for admiration of the stone-cutter's craft. 'Never have been able to track down the quotation—probably from the Bible.'

Or from his Company. Charles was a companion to the mermaids, Connie was sure of it.

'Bit over the top about his widow, though. Every virtue? Sounds pretty awful to me,' he continued.

Suzanna Caldicott—her great-great—Connie didn't know how many 'greats'—grandmother.

She had already begun to learn from Suzanna thanks to that book in the library, not realizing she had also inherited her gift from her. No wonder Suzanna's old house was full of the universal's symbol!

'If you don't mind, Uncle, I think I'll just stay here for a moment. I want to think.'

Hugh smiled and patted her on the shoulder. 'You do that. I'll toddle off and see if I can buy you a postcard of the tomb.'

Connie sat cross-legged in the middle of the compass reflection. She hadn't forgotten that she was here to meet Col, but she hadn't realized that the trip would prove such an eye-opener. Well, if hearing other creatures in your head was madness, as Godiva claimed, at least now she knew that the insane streak ran deep in the family. But she wasn't mad: Godiva was, to shut herself off from the family inheritance.

This was how Col found Connie: sitting in the middle of her symbol, lost in thought. Multi-coloured lights danced magically in her hair. He was almost afraid to break the spell.

'Connie?' He knelt beside her.

'Col!' She reached out and held his hand fast in hers. 'Look, my sign. It's in my blood!'

He looked up and whistled. 'That's pretty cool. I've never noticed before.'

'I don't think anyone but us knows what it really means—they all think it's here because the Lionhearts were sailors. But she was a universal.' Connie nodded at the tomb.

'Who?'

'Suzanna Caldicott Lionheart—she's in the library register.'

'Wow.'

'I'll bet you anything she probably had weird eyes and funny hair like me too.'

'Probably.' Col smiled and ruffled Connie's black mop of hair. 'How's things?'

She grimaced. 'Terrible.'

Yeah, she did look bad, thought Col. She had dark shadows under her eyes and she was very pale.

'I'm missing everyone—particularly you and Argand.' Connie glanced over to the bookstall where her great-uncle was just paying for his purchases. 'I haven't got long, but Col, can you do me a favour?'

He spread his hands wide. 'Anything.'

'Can you bring Argand up to Mallins Wood at the weekend—Saturday night around nine?'

'Why?'

'I'm going to try and slip out. I don't think either Argand or I can bear being apart much longer.'

'But why the wood?'

'I think it's the last place on earth my aunt will want to go to look for me.'

'You're not making sense.'

'Maybe not, but I have my suspicions about her.'

'Dr Brock said he knew her.'

Connie nodded: that followed. 'I bet she knows a lot of them—Mr Masterson, your grandmother. Ask them about her for me, won't you? I think it'll help if I knew.'

'Knew what?'

'What it is she's running away from.'

A packet of postcards fell into Connie's lap.

'And who's this young man?' asked Hugh.

'A friend from school,' Connie supplied quickly. 'He's got a boat.'

'Really? What kind?'

As Col began a detailed discussion of *Water Sprite*'s specifications with Hugh, Connie rose to her feet. Col winked at her—sealing his promise to meet her as she asked.

'We'd better get back,' broke off Hugh, checking his watch. 'I promised I'd not keep you more than an hour. Nice to meet you, Col.'

'And you, Mr Lionheart.'

'See you around,' called Connie over her shoulder.

'Yeah, see you,' answered Col, watching her until she disappeared back into the lodge.

Col called by Dr Brock's house the next day to ask permission to take Argand up to Mallins Wood. He found Dr Brock stoking a big bonfire at the end of his long, narrow cottage garden. The borders were full of bright red and orange flowers as if they too were burning.

'Hello, Col!' called Dr Brock, pitchforking dead branches onto the blaze. 'How's your holiday been? Looking forward to starting at Chartmouth next week?'

'Not much. I'd prefer to hang out with Skylark.'

Dr Brock chuckled. 'Of course.'

'And Connie won't be there.'

The doctor leaned on his fork, his face serious. 'No, it seems that she won't. How is she, by the way? Your grandmother told me you'd seen her.'

'I dunno—miserable, I think. But she's got plans to escape at the weekend and see Argand.'

'Good. It doesn't do for companions to be separated for too long.'

'I know—I feel rough when I've not seen Skylark for a few days.'

'It's more than that. Your bond makes you reliant on each other—you both need each other

135

to be truly yourself—at least, that's how it seems to me after all these years with Argot.'

'So can I borrow Argand?'

'Ask her yourself.'

Dr Brock pointed to the heart of the fire where Col now saw a little dragon was basking.

'Won't she get hurt?' He had half a mind to fish her out with Dr Brock's pitchfork.

'Oh no, that's the amazing thing about pure golden dragons—their hide protects them from even the hottest flames—they're practically indestructible.'

Col watched with fascinated delight as Argand fanned the flames with her wings to make it blaze a little hotter around her rump. She wriggled with pleasure as the fire tickled her.

'Argand!' called Dr Brock.

She ignored him.

'Argand, pay attention: it's about Connie.'

Instantly, the dragon whirled up from the fire, circled, and landed on Dr Brock's shoulder, cheeping and whistling in his ear.

'Will you go with this boy to see her in a few days?'

Argand's eyes turned to Col. A flourish of raspberry coloured flames burst from her mouth.

'Now stop that: what would your mother say? I

know he's not a dragon companion but he is Connie's friend. She chose him.'

Argand let out a sceptical whistle, then nodded.

'Well, that seems to be agreed. Come and fetch her from here on Saturday. I'll have words with her to make sure she behaves.'

'Thanks.' Col turned to go but then remembered what else Connie had asked him to do. 'Dr Brock, what do you know about Godiva Lionheart?'

Dr Brock frowned and wiped his hand across his face, leaving a soot mark. 'Why do you want to know?'

'It's not me—it's Connie. She's worked out that her great-aunt knows a lot about the Society.'

'Yes, she does.'

'How come?'

Dr Brock stroked Argand thoughtfully. 'I'm not supposed to talk about it—about her. That was what we agreed.'

'Agreed? When?'

Dr Brock shot Col an astute look. 'Well, it seems Connie's guessed quite a lot already. I'll tell you something about it—but not all, mind. I took an oath and I intend to keep it.

'Two Lionhearts in that generation had a gift—Sybil and Godiva. Fine girls, the pair of them—broke many hearts in the youth section of the Society just before the war.'

'You mean the Second World War?'

'I suppose I do—but I was thinking of the last war with Kullervo. Sybil was the elder—she married a very powerful companion from the Two-Fours. As for Godiva, well, I suppose you could say she and I were walking out together.'

'You were dating Godiva Lionheart?' Col found it hard to imagine anyone fancying that old battleaxe.

'I was.' Dr Brock sighed. 'She'd only just joined as a full member—"sweet sixteen" and I . . . er . . . made sure the rest of the song didn't apply.'

Col looked puzzled.

' "And never been kissed"? Surely you've heard your grandmother singing it?'

Col shook his head.

'Heavens, you make me feel old, Col. Anyway, the violent deaths of Sybil's husband and many others came as a great shock to us all. Godiva reacted more severely than any of us—I think she went almost out of her mind. I couldn't reach her—she pushed me and everyone else away. It was particularly sad as her sister needed her more then than at any other time. Iva started . . .'

'Iva?'

He smiled sadly. 'Her pet name. Iva started saying that the mythical creatures were all made up—a hysterical delusion. She even rejected her own companion. It died and something in Iva died too that night.'

'Her companion died?'

'Yes. It was terrible. Of course, it happened during wartime: we were surrounded by death and destruction. But that one death—the suffering as her companion pined away with Iva refusing even to say goodbye—that was the worst.'

'That's . . . that's awful.'

'Maybe, but grief and love make us do strange things.'

'What was her companion species?'

Dr Brock shook his head. 'I'm sorry, I can't say. We agreed never to reveal that once she handed back her membership badge—or threw it at me, I should say. It's the protocol for when members leave: they are no longer mentioned and their companion species struck from the record. Fortunately, she didn't know many of our secrets—only the basics of her own company. I suppose you could say that leavers become as mythical to the Society as the creatures are to most people.'

'But that's daft. You can't deny she's got a gift.'

'It's not us denying it—it's her—it's her choice.'

'And she's trying to force Connie to do the same. We've got to stop her.'

'I know, but the law of this country is on her side. We can't go marching in and take Connie away. I've no doubt she'd soon get the authorities to have the lot of us arrested as a dangerous cult kidnapping children. No, what you are doing is the best way—keep Connie in touch with her companion, support her as a friend.'

Dr Brock unwound Argand's tail from his neck and placed her gently in Col's hands. 'If I were a betting man, Col, I'd put my money on Godiva cracking before Connie does. After all, she doesn't know it, but she's up against a universal— that's way out of her league.'

9
The Chest

Though Connie had committed herself to escaping from the lodge on Saturday night, she had still to work out the details of her plot. She knew she needed the gate key and some way of getting up to Mallins Wood. During her lunch hour on Friday, she decided to explore the coal-shed and was rewarded with the discovery of an old bike. Dragging it out onto the lawn, she examined it to see if it was still roadworthy.

'Goodness, where did you find that?' asked Hugh, coming in from his daily trip to the newsagents, gate key clinking at his side. 'I've not seen that old boneshaker for years. Now let me see . . . ah, yes, it was Godiva's—I thought as much. Sybil must have taken hers with her when she decamped to Hescombe.'

'Do you think I could do it up?'

'Frankly, my dear, no I don't.'

Connie's face fell.

'But I could. Right up my street something like this—stop the old seadog feeling completely useless.'

'Thank you. Do you think it'll take long?'

'Why? In a hurry to leave us?' he asked shrewdly.

'I was just hoping I'd be allowed out this weekend. It's been weeks since I've seen the other side of these walls—apart from the abbey, of course.'

'Well then, I'll take it along to the bike shop this afternoon and see what I can do. No promises, mind!'

'Thank you, Uncle Hugh.' Impulsively, Connie kissed him on the cheek. He flushed pink with pleasure.

'Now, now, don't mention it,' he said. 'You may be a funny little thing, Connie, but I can't bear to see you upset. I'm pleased I can cheer you up with this. I wish I could do the same for my sister—it's sixty years since she was last really happy.'

'That's a very long time.' She too had sensed that something had sucked all the happiness out of her great-aunt, like a lemon squeezed of its juice. The atmosphere changed when Godiva entered a room, becoming heavy as if presaging a storm. Connie found it hard to spend so much time in her company.

'Yes, isn't it? I sometimes wonder whether . . . well, never mind. Let me get going on this. Come and find me in my room after lessons and I'll tell you how I got on.'

Hugh's cabin, as he liked to call it, was at the far end of the house up in the roof. Connie had not yet been allowed in and so was curious to see what it was like. She knocked on the door.

'Come in!' called Hugh.

'Wow!' Connie stood transfixed in the doorway. In contrast to the deadness afflicting the rest of the house, this room was vibrantly alive. It was crammed with wonderfully carved furniture—wardrobes, chairs, tables, screens—so much that there was barely room to move.

'Sorry, it's a bit cluttered,' said Hugh.

'No, I love it.'

He looked pleased and stroked the top of a wooden chest under the window. 'I couldn't let Godiva get rid of them, you see. They've been in this house for centuries. So here they are—in my sanctuary.'

'Why would anyone want to get rid of them?' Connie was admiring a filigree screen chiselled into the shape of a fruiting apple tree. The wood seemed to hum contentedly under her touch.

'I think she . . . they make her uncomfortable. She says it's a kind of allergy.'

'She's allergic to furniture?'

'No, just to wood. She only feels safe from it at sea.'

The last piece fell in place. Connie now knew what Godiva's companion species had been.

'Can I take a look around?'

'Of course, my dear, they're yours too—all family bits and bobs.' He watched his great-niece examine each article, tracing each carving with her fingertips. There were mythical creatures from all companies in here—dragons, griffins, snakes, water sprites, minotaurs. Hugh lived surrounded by them but did not know that they had been carved from life. Connie finally settled down before the chest and placed her hands on the compass symbol that decorated the lid.

'Ah, I see you too like my favourite piece. It reminds me a bit of that tomb. I've always reckoned this was the family safe. It's full of old papers and ledgers.'

Connie's heart began to beat a little faster. 'May I take a look?'

'Certainly. I've leafed through it myself several times—a lot of it is mumbo jumbo.' He opened it and with the knowledge of long acquaintance rifled until he reached a bundle of papers. 'Like this lot—I guess someone was translating from Arabic—see these squiggles here—that's what it looks like to me.'

Connie took the crackling pile of yellowed parchment from him and read the title. It had been written in English on the left-hand side of the page, leaving a column for some kind of script on the other. Though the English was flawless, the script had many crossings out and inkblots as if the pen had hovered over the page too often as the writer searched for the right word.

She looked back at the title: *Fighting Within the Gate: A Universal's Guide to Repelling Hostile Encounters.*

'What do you think, Connie?' Hugh asked her, perplexed by her sudden stillness. 'I thought it might be a translation of some Arabian Nights tale or some such—or a crusader's handbook.'

'I think it's a translation all right, but from English into this other language,' said Connie. She didn't add that she had a shrewd suspicion that the language was not one spoken by men.

The author, she guessed, was Suzanna Caldicott, but why she should then go on to translate it was a mystery. Connie's fingers burned to turn more pages but she tried to hide her excitement.

'Can I take this with me and see if I can make anything of it?'

Hugh sucked his bottom lip. 'I suppose so,' he said reluctantly. 'But wouldn't you prefer to choose something else?' He pulled out a big family Bible. 'How about this? Or this? The accounts are fascinating—all that ballast, rum, and cordage—it keeps me amused for hours just looking at the sums involved in keeping a three-masted ship afloat.'

Connie shook her head, smiling. 'I think it'd send me to sleep.'

He laughed. 'In that case, you can take those. It's far too old to be of any consequence now, isn't it? Godiva won't think I've broken her rule.'

So he was suspicious that it had something to do with the Society, thought Connie. She leafed through to the end. 'Look, Uncle Hugh, the family compass is here again. Perhaps it's something to do with why we chose that as our coat of arms. It seems to mention all those mythical beasts right out of heraldry, doesn't it?'

This common sense explanation pleased him.

'Yes, it does. I hadn't thought of that. Take it

away with you then.' She got up, eager to make her escape. 'But, Connie?'

'Yes?'

'Don't you want to know about the bike?'

In her excitement, she'd forgotten all about the main purpose of her visit.

'Of course—sorry. Did you manage to fix it?'

'It's as fixed as it'll ever be. It'll take you around town but not on the Tour de France.'

'That suits me fine. Thanks, Uncle Hugh.'

Connie sat on the floor between her bed and the window, hidden so that her aunt would not see what she was doing if she put her head around the door. It was getting dark. Connie put her bedside lamp beside her and sat in the pool of light with the papers spread out on the rug. Hugh's chest had yielded a totally unexpected treasure: she had thought that she would have to arrange another trip to the Reading Room to consult her predecessors again, but here in Suzanna's handwriting was a draft of another chapter—and Connie hadn't even had to brave the snake to find them.

She began to read.

It was nearly midnight when she finished. Her legs were numb from sitting on the floor so long, but far more uncomfortable was the knowledge that she had just absorbed. She had learnt that universals were by no means immune to attack if a creature so willed it—and as Suzanna's rough illustrations rather too vividly showed with their images of men being stabbed, trampled, burnt, frozen, and torn apart by an assortment of ravening mythical creatures. Universals could be electrocuted by a storm-bird's lightning, turned to stone by the gaze of the gorgon, paralysed by the cold grip of stone sprites, gored by a great boar, even driven to madness by the siren's song. Their only hope was either to raise their shield in time or make a safe bond with the creature. But a bond had to be entered into by mutual agreement—no help if you were under hostile attack—and the shield was only as strong as the universal that wielded it—that defence could be breached if strength failed.

She'd had a close escape last year, Connie realized. The sirens had wanted to encounter her and so had forged a complete connection that had done her no harm. Had they wanted to attack, she would have drowned. Knowing nothing on her first encounter about closing her mind with the universal's shield, she was lucky to be alive.

* * *

Col arrived in the wood in good time on Saturday night because he had first arranged to have supper with his mother. He'd spent more time with her over the summer holidays than he had during all the last six years. He couldn't honestly say he felt any more relaxed in her presence, but he did at least have a sense that she approved of him—unlike his father who these days did nothing but moan about how he was turning out.

'He's jealous,' said Cassandra, threading some mushrooms on a stick and placing them over the fire. 'Don't think I don't know that he doesn't want me anywhere near you.'

This was probably true, but Col didn't feel he should even enter that debate as he still did not want to take sides between his warring parents.

'What's Evelyn Lionheart like?' Cassandra asked suddenly.

She'd heard the rumours then, thought Col.

'Dunno really.'

'Is it serious?'

He wished she wouldn't grill him like this. He felt like the mushrooms slowly roasting over the fire.

'Dunno. Dad hasn't said.'

She smiled and shook back her long hair. 'No, he wouldn't. I pity her.'

Argand peeped out from Col's jacket, lured by the scent of the food. Cassandra threaded a mushroom off the spit and threw it to her. Deftly, Argand caught it in her jaws and swallowed it still piping hot.

'Magnificent creature,' said Cassandra appreciatively.

'I s'pose being in Sea Snakes you've had quite a lot to do with dragon riders?'

'Never had much time for them, but as for the dragons . . . that's different.'

She leant over and gently caught Argand's front paws and pulled her out into her arms. She stroked the smooth golden scales, hissing between her teeth.

'If it weren't for the wings, she'd almost be like one of the young of a golden-haired gorgon.'

'I didn't know there was such a thing.'

Cassandra nodded. 'She lives in the Pacific and Indian oceans, spawns with the yellow-bellied sea snake, highly poisonous.'

'Spawns? I don't understand.'

Cassandra smiled mysteriously. 'Few people do. The gorgons live symbiotically with their snake species.'

'Symbiotically?' Col knew he'd heard the word but was not clear what it meant.

'It means when two creatures join to live to

their mutual advantage—the gorgon hosts the young, the snakes become part of the gorgon.'

'And your gorgon?'

'She hosts the adder.' Cassandra drew her diamond-pattern cloak closer around her and Argand. A cool light rain had begun to fall. 'She incubates the eggs and they hatch into new hair.'

Col tried not to shudder but the thought was putting him off his supper. He checked his watch.

'So you're still meeting Connie at nine then?' his mother asked carelessly.

'Yeah, at least I hope so.'

'I told them you were. They want to meet her.'

'Who does?'

'The gorgon.'

And her snakes, Col added silently.

'Well, I s'pose I could ask her if she's interested. I mean, she's here to meet Argand really.'

'But this is no weather for a young dragon to be out in. Why don't I take her to the cave? You can bring Connie there. Send her in on her own so you don't meet the gorgon's eye by mistake.'

'Well, I dunno . . .'

Argand crooned happily in Cassandra's arms.

'Look, she's a lazy little thing,' laughed Cassandra. Her laugh was brittle—he would've said nervous if his mother ever felt anything as weak as that. 'You can tell she'd prefer it. You can't have been intending to let them meet out in the open—there are far too many people about.'

Col cast about for an excuse. He'd been looking forward to having Connie all to himself—and Argand, of course. This unforeseen expedition sounded very complicated. 'But what about the climb?'

'I'll leave the rope I use for you both.'

'Well, OK, I suppose I could . . .'

'Good, that's settled.' She handed him a mushroom kebab. 'Now tell me about Skylark.'

Connie had chosen Saturday evening to make her bid for freedom because Godiva often listened to the concert on Radio Three, sending Connie up to bed early so she would not be distracted. At seven, Connie knocked on Uncle Hugh's door.

'Hello, my dear.' Hugh was whittling a piece of flotsam into a dolphin.

'That's beautiful.'

'Thank you. It's for you, you know. Birthday coming up at the end of the month, haven't you?'

'Yes, I have.' She'd almost forgotten that September was already here—her school holidays had disappeared down a tunnel of lessons and lonely spells in her room. 'Uncle, would it be OK if I took the bike out for a little before it gets dark?' She crossed her fingers behind her back as, whatever the consequences, she knew she had no intention of returning before the light completely went.

'I suppose so.' Hugh fished around in his waistcoat pocket. 'Here's the key to the gate— the bike's not locked. Promise you'll not go far?'

Connie's hand was outstretched, the key dangling over it.

'Of course, I . . .'

'Hugh!' The door banged open and Godiva stood on the landing. Even now, she dared not cross the threshold. 'What are you doing?'

Sensing trouble, Connie grabbed the key and tried to duck round her great-aunt but sharp fingers caught hold of her hair.

'Ouch!' yelled Godiva as the hair spat sparks at her like an angry cat. She let go but seized Connie's arm instead. 'How dare you!' she bellowed.

'Now, now, Godiva, don't frighten the child. She's not done anything wrong. I just said she could go out on her bike for a little while.'

'Not done anything wrong!' exclaimed Godiva, shaking Connie in her fury. 'Then how do you explain this? I went to check on her and found them in her room.' She held out a fistful of crumpled pages.

'Now, I say, don't do that!' said Hugh indignantly, trying to take the papers from her before she did any more damage. 'I said she could have those to look at.'

'You don't know what you gave her, do you?' breathed Godiva heavily. 'But I bet you she knew the moment she laid eyes on them.'

'Know what? Connie thought it might be something to do with heraldry—mythical beasts and all that.' Hugh looked puzzled.

Godiva seemed on the point of saying something but held back. 'I'm afraid it's much worse than that, Hugh. It's exactly the kind of stuff with which they have been polluting her mind in Hescombe. I didn't know we still had it in the house—I thought I'd destroyed it all.' She turned on Connie. 'You must break this, my girl, or it'll break you. It's like . . . like an addiction. You must not indulge in even the least daydream or you'll tumble all the way back into your pernicious habits.'

She addressed herself to her brother again. 'She is certainly not going anywhere tonight.' She prised the key out of Connie's fist and handed it back to Hugh. 'I see now that I have been too lenient with her. It's time I attacked this problem root and branch. Connie, follow me.'

With sinking heart, Connie traipsed after her

great-aunt to her bedroom. Her aunt marched in and turned to face her.

'It starts here: tear these things down now!' She pointed with a trembling finger at the posters.

Connie gaped. 'But why?'

'They are nourishing your delusions—they must go.'

'But I can't.'

'Then I will.' Godiva reached up and ripped the unicorn poster from the wall, sending drawing pins ricocheting around the room.

'No, please, don't!'

But Godiva was merciless. She tore all the pictures down and crumpled them into a ball.

'Turn out your things.'

Connie sat down on the chest, determined to defend her photo album from Godiva's assault. 'No.'

'Get up!'

Connie shook her head. She was furious. At that moment, she wished she had some power—a gorgon's gaze or a siren's song—to strike down her great-aunt. 'Just because you don't want to be a companion to the wood sprites, doesn't mean I have to be like you!'

Something snapped inside Godiva. Her eyes were lit with a mad fury.

'There are no such things as wood sprites,' she

hissed, her spittle flying into Connie's face. 'Now move!'

When Connie remained sitting, Godiva seized her by the arm and pushed her to the floor. Her claw-like hand dived into the chest and pulled out the album. She held it high out of Connie's reach, ripping the pages out one by one.

'Poison . . . filth . . . lies!' she shrieked, stamping on the picture of Scark, the seagull killed by Kullervo. Connie tried to snatch it back but Godiva crushed her fingers under her shoe. 'You are not to touch—not to think—not to mention anything about the damned Society ever again, you understand?' She bent down and swept up the crumpled paper from the floor. 'This lot goes on the bonfire. You stay in your room until I say you can come out.'

As a parting shot, she took the shell from its place on the windowsill and stormed out of the room.

Connie stood in front of the bare walls, nursing her bruised fingers, and burst into tears.

Col grew restless waiting by Rat's bus for Connie to arrive. She'd said she'd be here at nine. He'd allowed her an extra hour but still no sign. Something must've gone wrong.

156

'All right there, Col?' Rat stuck his head out of the door. He had the blackbird perched on one shoulder and the rabbit on a piece of string.

'Yeah. What're you doing?'

'Just taking them for a walk. Me ma doesn't like them pooing in the bus.' He jumped down the steps, closely followed by the rabbit. Wolf whined inside.

'What's wrong with him?' asked Col jerking his head in the direction of the dog. If he was going to wait here any longer, he'd prefer to know what kind of mood the beast was in.

'Dunno. He's been acting up all evening. Took one sniff of the air and bolted inside. He's crazy.'

Col now noticed that the rabbit had stopped leaping after Rat and was quivering with terror on the bottom step. The blackbird peeped and flew back into the bus.

'Looks like whatever's worrying him has got to them too,' said Col.

Rat scanned the skies. 'D'you reckon there's a storm on the way? I can't sense anything.'

'No, neither can I. I'd better get going. I don't want to get caught in it.'

'But what about your friend?'

'I think she must've run into trouble getting away. She's got this mental great-aunt who keeps her locked in the house.'

157

'Sounds as if she needs rescuing.'

'Yeah, you're right. Perhaps I should try.'

'Count me in—I'll bring Wolf—he'll sort out the great-aunt. Eats great-aunts for breakfast, he does.'

Col laughed. 'Yeah, right. I'll just tell my mum I'm off. See you soon.'

'At school—on Monday—don't forget.'

'You're really coming?'

'Yeah.' Rat looked proud but a little sheepish.

'Great. See you then.'

Col jogged off into the wood, eager to fetch Argand and get home before the storm arrived. The thought of going to Chartmouth with Rat prompted Col to laugh. He couldn't wait to see what Rat made of his other friends and what they would make of him. It was such a shame Connie wasn't going to be there. He thought Rat would feel comfortable with her.

He needed his torch to help him find his way along the ledge. Arriving outside the cave mouth, he called out a warning of his approach.

'Hi, I've come to fetch Argand.'

The echo was interrupted by the gorgon's voice.

'Ss-send the child ins-sside, hatchling. S-sshe can fetch the dragonet.'

'I'm sorry but I can't.' Col could now hear a distressed whistle from inside the cave. 'Is that Argand? Is she OK?' He crept nearer, patting his pockets for the mirror until he realized he'd left it at home.

'Why can't the universal come in?' hissed the gorgon threateningly.

Col didn't fancy explaining himself to her and he was worried for Argand—she sounded really upset. 'Mum, are you there?'

'Don't cry for your mother, boy.' The gorgon was getting closer. 'S-sshe had faith in you, but it s-sseems you have failed.'

Instinctively, Col half turned away. Part of him wanted to run for it, but he knew he couldn't leave Argand behind.

'I'm sorry. Something must have stopped Connie coming.'

'It was you, wasn't it? You made her suspicious of us-ss.'

'What? No—I haven't seen her. She doesn't know anything about you. I'm sure she wanted to come, but she couldn't.' Col now had his back pressed against the rock wall, his eyes screwed tight closed. 'Look, just give me Argand and I'll go. I'll try and bring Connie here another night.'

A cold fingertip touched his cheek—no, it wasn't a finger: it was the flicker of a snake's tongue. He swallowed his cry of alarm. Another snake glided over his shoulder, wrapping itself around his neck. He could feel the dry breath of the gorgon on his face.

'S-sshall I kill him?' the gorgon asked.

The question was answered by the noise of hoofs inside the cave.

'I think not,' said a voice that Col had never heard before. The sound chimed through his body, making his bones quiver. 'Leave him to me. He can still be useful to us. Turn your eyes away so he can see me.'

Col felt the snakes retreat.

'Boy, come and greet me,' ordered the voice.

Cautiously, Col opened his eyes a crack. The gorgon had her back to him and was staring at the entrance of the cave. Out of the shadows stepped a pegasus, larger than a Shire horse with vast iron-grey wings, powerful shoulders, blue-black mane, and strong muscled legs. It snorted once and trotted towards Col, graceful despite its size, coming near enough for him to see into the horse's eyes, an odd pair, golden and acid yellow, all wrong for the creature.

Col hesitated. He felt dazed and confused, unable to think straight staring into these eyes. Something was not right: he could not sense the pegasus from afar as he could Skylark.

'Greet me!' the voice threatened again, this time inside Col's head. It felt as though the door to the bond he shared with Skylark was being prised open with a crowbar. He put his hands to his temples.

'Coward, greet me!'

This time, Col had no choice. He reached out and touched the pegasus.

Crack! A charge flashed through him. He screamed but could not remove his hand: it was as if an iron fist had gripped his wrist. This was no encounter: it was an invasion. Col was driven down, trampled in the stampede of the dark presence. It thundered over him until he no longer knew who or where he was, kicked and buffeted aside by uncaring hoofs, stunned into submission. He fell against the pegasus, his face half-buried in the creature's suffocating mane, and then slid to the floor.

Pleased to have conquered so easily, the pegasus nuzzled Col possessively. The boy stirred.

'Come,' the pegasus said.

Obedient now to another's will, the boy rose to his feet and stroked the creature's neck, drinking in its presence like poison.

Somewhere inside him, the dying embers of Col watched this stranger he had become clamber astride the pegasus. He was powerless to stop what was happening, his screams unheard as if he were shouting and thumping the walls of a thick glass cage. Then another pulse of energy from the false pegasus stamped out even this resistance.

Argand chewed her way through her tether in time to see Col flying away on Kullervo's back, heading into the night. The gorgon was slithering up the path and into the trees. Argand peeped in distress. Why had everyone left her?

10
Colin

Connie thought she would go mad. The walls of her room had closed in on her; the faded tendrils of rose-patterned paper wove into her dreams, choking her with their thorns. She'd been shut away for a week, not allowed out except to use the bathroom. Godiva had banned Hugh from going anywhere near her, making it sound as if she was contagious, and visiting only to hand out and collect school work and meals.

Perhaps she really believes what I've got is catching, Connie thought, staring at the ceiling. Perhaps she thinks she'll fall ill again, wake up and hear the trees talking to her as they should.

As much as Connie hated her great-aunt for this treatment, she could not help but be fascinated by her. How could Godiva have taken the step of denying the evidence of her own eyes—of her own heart even? She had viciously pruned off the shoots of her true self to produce not even a bonsai, but a dry stick. But she couldn't escape her gift—the hiding from anything wood proved that. It still hummed under her fingers like it did for Connie—that's why she hated it—and why she loathed Connie. But did she know that the much praised family coat of arms was based on the Universal's symbol? Connie thought not—or she'd have eradicated that from the house too.

Spending hours in solitary confinement, Connie had plenty of time to wonder what Col, Anneena, and Jane were doing at school. She measured out her hours by theirs, thinking of them chatting at the bus stop, kicking a ball in the playground at break, doing their homework together in the Nuruddins' kitchen. She hoped Col understood why she hadn't shown up at the weekend, but she still was surprised that he'd not even tried to call or get a message to her through Anneena.

Saturday came round again. Connie wondered whether her aunt would expect her to work like during the week—she thought on balance that she would. Connie had got through the last few days by not speaking to her, except for 'yes', 'no', and 'thank you'—the barest minimum she could get away with. Her heart burned with the injustice of her imprisonment but there seemed no one to turn to.

She was allowed that breakfast time to eat with Hugh and Godiva in the kitchen. Let out on parole for good behaviour, she thought.

'Feeling better now, Connie?' asked Hugh anxiously.

'I've not been ill, Uncle Hugh.'

'Well, well.' He patted her wrist, clearly preferring to avoid an argument.

There was a ring at the gate bell. Godiva got up and peered through the window.

'It's those two friends of yours,' she said over her shoulder to Connie. 'Did you invite them?'

'No . . . who?'

'The girls.'

'Oh, you mean the nice ones—the safe ones,' supplied Hugh. 'Shall I go and see what they want?'

'They'll want to see her, of course.' Godiva looked at her great-niece's bowed head. Connie dared no longer show any enthusiasm or pleasure in anything in case it was whipped away from her.

165

'And can they?' asked Hugh. 'See her, I mean?'

'I think she's learned her lesson. Haven't you, Connie?'

'Yes, Aunt.' Adding under her breath, 'No, Aunt, three bags full, Aunt.' She'd got to the stage where she would say anything to see someone other than Godiva. She'd even welcome an interview with Mr Coddrington if it came to it. I must be feeling desperate, she thought ruefully.

'Righty ho. I'll go and fetch them,' said Hugh, brightening. He too had been suffering in sympathy with his great-niece.

A few minutes later, Anneena and Jane were standing in the kitchen, trying to persuade Godiva to let them take Connie out for the morning. Their pleas were seconded by Hugh.

'I've done up your old bike for her,' he said. 'You can't keep a young thing like her indoors the whole time—she needs a run from time to time. It'll stop her dwelling on *other things*.'

This argument proved the most persuasive.

'In that case, you can go. But you're not to go to Hescombe, Connie, nor anywhere near Evelyn and her friends, do you understand?' said Godiva.

Connie could've hugged Anneena and Jane—they were her knights in shining armour come to rescue her.

'Yes, Aunt,' she replied, keeping her face under strict control. She felt like dancing for joy.

'And be back by one o'clock.'

'Yes, Aunt.'

'Well, then, what are you waiting for?'

For any more orders, Connie could've said, but she didn't want to push her luck.

It felt wonderful to escape into the air. The three friends didn't say anything at first, by mutual agreement wanting to put some distance between them and Lionheart Lodge in case Godiva changed her mind. Connie just let herself enjoy the sensation of pedalling hard after Jane's bent back, feeling the wind in her hair. After ten minutes they had reached the outskirts of Chartmouth, not far from the refinery. It wasn't a picturesque spot. Connie wondered why Anneena had brought them here.

'Shall we have a rest?' Anneena suggested, her face glowing with the exercise.

'OK. But where are we going? I can't go to Hescombe—not when I promised.' Connie looked up the steep hill that separated Hescombe from Chartmouth. It was much changed since she'd last seen it—one side was a raw scar of turned earth and concrete as the construction work on the new road got under way; on the other, the land was as yet untouched. At the top of the hill, the first of the trees of Mallins Wood waved on the horizon. Police cars were parked in the layby near the summit with a couple of officers flagging down vehicles—usually old, battered ones.

'What are they doing?' she asked.

'Looking for protesters—there's already been some trouble,' explained Jane. 'The police tried to move the camp last week but they wouldn't budge, so now they're trying to stop more joining. It's all getting a bit heated—and the festival's only a week away. There'll be so many people then that they're saying the police won't be able to handle it.'

'Mr Quick from the refinery said they should call in the army to clear the camp. I saw him on TV myself,' snorted Anneena. 'Actually, Connie, that's where we're going.'

'Where?'

'Up there to the wood. You see, there's a problem.'

'What problem?'

Connie had a foreboding that something serious was coming. Anneena sat down on a concrete block lying by the roadside.

'It's Col. He's not turned up at school this week.'

'What!'

'Yeah, I know. It's not like him. He's disappeared somewhere with his mother. We don't know where she's taken him, but I thought he'd at least ring to let us know what he's doing. Even his grandmother doesn't know what he's up to. She's really upset—and as for Col's dad, he's—well, you can imagine.'

'But where does Col's mum live? Have they checked if he's there?'

'She doesn't live anywhere much, except in a campervan she drives about in. It's not around here at the moment—Jane and I cycled up to the wood to check yesterday. No one's seen her.'

Connie was quickly thinking through all the people who might be able to help. Presumably Mrs Clamworthy had tried all the obvious sources of information: Dr Brock, Col's mentor Captain Graves, Skylark. Who did that leave?

'Look, Anneena, I've had an idea. I think I can find out where Col's mum might be from some-one in London. Can I borrow your phone, Jane?'

'Sure.' Jane held it out. 'Where's yours?'

'Confiscated by my great-aunt.'

'Is she . . . quite all there?' Jane asked delicately.

'No, I really don't think she is.'

'You should tell your parents.'

'Don't think I haven't. It's just that they take the view that she's the sane one and I'm the one who's barmy.' Connie tried to make light of it but she couldn't rid herself of the sense of betrayal

169

that her parents sided with Godiva rather than with her.

'What about your uncle? He seems OK.'

'Except he sees things her way too—he doesn't like what's going on but he agrees that you've got to be cruel to be kind.'

'It's inhuman what they're doing to you—it's like you're in prison or something. Isn't there something we can do?'

'For me at the moment? No. But at least I might be able to help Col. Just give me a minute.'

Connie dug in her jacket pocket, pulled out Mr Coddrington's business card and rang the switchboard at the Society for the Protection of Mythical Creatures.

'We're sorry but our offices are closed at the moment. If you'd like to . . .'

She ended the call. Of course, it wasn't open. It was Saturday. No one would be there. But she wouldn't have another chance once she handed the phone back since Godiva had hers; she decided to give the direct line a try, banking on Mr Coddrington being such a workaholic that he might well be in at the weekend.

The phone was picked up before it had even rung twice. 'Hello, Coddrington here.'

'Oh, Mr Coddrington, I wasn't really expecting you to be in the office.'

'Who is this?' His voice had a snap like a mantrap.

'It's Connie Lionheart, Mr Coddrington.'

'Ah, Miss Lionheart, Connie.' She could almost see him fawning over the phone as he spoke. 'How good of you to call. I assume that you've given further thought to our conversation last month and you have something to tell me?'

'What?' Connie realized that he had jumped to conclusions as to why she should choose to contact him.

'I assume you want to tell me about how many universals you think there are,' he said patiently. She heard rustling in the background as if he was poised to take notes.

'Er, no.' She glanced nervously at Jane and Anneena who were listening in to every word. 'I'm with some people at the moment. I can't say too much.'

'I understand. Perhaps we can make another time when you are at liberty to speak more freely to me.'

'Er . . . yes, of course. Actually, Mr Coddrington, that wasn't why I called.'

'Oh? So why did you then?' He now seemed genuinely curious.

'It's about a friend of mine—Col Clamworthy. He's gone missing with his mother. I just

wondered if you knew where she might be, seeing how good your filing system is?'

'Oh, is that it?' She could tell that her flattery
was hitting the desired mark. 'Well, I might be
able to tell you—as a favour between friends.
You understand that all the information has been
gathered strictly in confidence. If I tell you this,
I'll be bending the rules to help you.'

Connie understood that what he meant was
that he expected a favour from her in return, but
this did not matter as long as she could help Col.

'Thank you. I'd be really grateful.'

'What is the mother's name?' She heard the
clanking of cabinet drawers being pulled out.

'Cassandra Clamworthy—at least I think so.'

'Let me see—Cassandra Clamworthy. What is
her companion species?'

Connie searched her memory, not even sure
whether Col had ever told her this. He had not
talked much about his mother. 'Sorry, I don't
know,' she admitted.

'Never mind,' Mr Coddrington said, as if this
was good news. 'All my files are cross-referenced.
I should still be able to find her for you. Your
friend is a companion to pegasi?'

Connie wondered how he knew this about
Col. Perhaps he remembered him from last year?
Col had said that he had trained once with

Mr Coddrington and Shirley Masterson. 'Yes, that's right.'

'Ah, here he is. Hmm, from quite a family by the looks of it: a Kraken and a gorgon companion—a most unusual combination—but resulting in a child with a fairly common gift. Well, there is no Cassandra Clamworthy here: you are looking for Cassandra Lang, a companion to gorgons. She reverted to her maiden name after her divorce from the Kraken companion.'

'And do you know where she is?' Connie wished he would stop showing off and tell her what she needed to know.

'Oh yes, this one has given us a lot of trouble from the evidence of her record. Dear, oh dear: quite disgraceful. It seems that she can most often be found as an irregular tenant of a cottage in Wales, in the Brecon Beacons to be precise. Bwlch is the uncouth name of the place—' he spelt it out for her, '—at least, that is where I have elected to put her pin, just to the left of it. If you are looking for your friend, I suggest you start there.'

'Thank you for your help.'

'And you won't forget our little discussion, I hope? Ring any time if you have anything you would like to tell me.'

'Er, thanks,' said Connie, ending the call. Jane and Anneena were still watching her. 'I've got a lead—Col might've gone to Wales to his mother's cottage.'

'Great.' Connie could tell that Anneena itched to ask to whom she had been speaking. It was a measure of their friendship that she held back, knowing Connie well enough to understand that she hated being interrogated about the Society. 'That's really helpful. His grandmother will be pleased to have something to go on. She's been having a terrible week—we found her in tears. Apparently that friend of yours, Dr Brock, is really angry with Col for not returning something, and that hasn't helped.'

'When was this?'

'Last Saturday night apparently.'

Col hadn't returned Argand—now she was convinced something terrible had happened.

'Come on, I want to see what's going on in these woods,' said Connie.

'Let's go and find Rat then,' said Anneena, mounting her bike as a tanker rumbled by filling the air with fumes.

'Who?'

'Col's friend from the camp. He's a bit odd but actually . . .' she looked at Connie from under her lashes . . . 'I think you might have a lot in common.'

Colin Clamworthy was woken early by his mother. He floated up from his dreams of darkness like a diver rising from the depths, but he did not break the surface, staying submerged just below the point of true consciousness.

'Colin, it's time for your combat training,' Cassandra said gently, helping him to his feet. Colin automatically reached for his new padded flying jacket and helmet—both were black and were worn with matching leather arm protectors and shin pads.

'How are you feeling today? Better now?' Cassandra asked as he tied on his gear. He nodded and admired his reflection in the cracked mirror on the wall of his cell-like bedroom. He looked cool.

'I know it's hard for you, Colin,' she said, biting her lip, 'but he's promised he won't hurt you. He says that as the plan failed—as you and I didn't bring the universal to him—that he needs you now to make it right.' She frowned slightly when the boy made no sign. 'Are you listening, Colin?'

'Yes, Mother,' he replied in an expressionless voice.

This was to be expected, Cassandra told herself. The distant mood would pass once the shock of meeting Kullervo had settled down. The shape-shifter had said that he had taken her son under his wing—told her to think of it as an honour. She'd get Colin back soon. She had to be brave for them both. He would thank her one day.

'Come,' she said, watching him anxiously. Though she told herself he would be all right, her instinct was saying something different. She was torn between her loyalty to Kullervo, who had promised to save the gorgon, and her feelings for her boy. 'Your teacher is waiting.'

They stepped out of the cottage into the chill air of the dawn to where a pegasus was standing, snorting plumes of steaming breath, shaking his magnificent black mane so that it sparkled in the gathering light. He trotted over to the boy.

'Boy,' the horse greeted him.

'Kay,' Colin replied mechanically.

'Mount.'

Obeying the order instantly, Colin vaulted nimbly onto the bare back of the pegasus and laced his cold hands in the mane. The pegasus cantered to take off, rising until they were up in the clouds. The water vapour stung Colin's eyes. He reached for his visor, but checked his hand with a moment's indecision. He had remembered something—a girl clinging to his waist, another pegasus, but not this one.

176

'Colin, you are not paying attention. I shall have to punish you,' whinnied Kullervo angrily. A throb of pain swept through Colin and the memory was extinguished like a candle snuffed out. Kullervo snorted, relishing the vindictive pleasure of bending a human to his will—a human moreover who was dear to the universal. That added spice to the victory.

Colin did not heed, or even remember, the pain for long. He was now looking down at the mountain slopes below him, admiring the ranks of creatures practising their combat exercises. Kullervo's supporters were growing in number, believing him to be the only hope now for their own survival. Every day, fresh outrages by humanity—the felling of forests, the pollution of inland waterways and seas, acid rain: the assaults were too numerous to mention—brought more over to Kullervo's side. He promised them that he would rid the world of humanity—in one blow giving them a secure future and revenge on those who had pushed them to the brink of extinction. The creatures were training in earnest and their leader had promised that their moment would soon arrive. They only needed one more thing to perfect their attack. A universal. As Colin watched, two black boars gored and hacked at each other with their bloodstained tusks, surrounded by a ring of yelling banshees, their screeches drowning out the grunts and squeals of the fight. Weather giants hurled hailstones and thunderbolts at the hillside, causing the valley to echo with explosions as each one hit. Ahead, a black dragon wrestled with a white one in mid-air, their bodies intertwined in a vicious knot of teeth, claws, and hooked wings.

Kullervo landed by a small grove of hawthorn trees, close to a stack of sharpened poles.

'Take a javelin, boy. You are to aim for that kestrel there.'

Colin looked to the treetops and saw a bird of prey glaring down at them, its yellow eyes confident and cool.

'He does not think you will hit him,' mocked Kullervo. 'How does that make you feel?'

A wave of anger, propelled by Kullervo, ripped through the blank mind of Colin. He reached for a javelin and threw it clumsily at the bird. It clattered harmlessly to the ground, well short of its target.

'Pitiful,' sneered Kullervo. 'You threw with your feelings and not your judgement. Try again.'

Colin grabbed another weapon and this time aimed carefully, assessing distance and height before he let go. The javelin sailed cleanly from his hand and hit the leaves at the kestrel's feet, forcing the creature into the sky with a startled cry.

'Much better. No longer so proud, is he?' laughed Kullervo. Colin laughed too but the sound was mirthless and grated on his throat. 'Take three more javelins: we will see if we can catch him on the wing.'

Colin seized two poles in his left hand, holding another ready in his right. Kullervo took off and set out in pursuit of the kestrel, flying swiftly to outpace it. The bird dipped to the left but Colin had anticipated this move and let fly his javelin. It struck the bird on the wing and the kestrel fell spiralling to the earth, its limb broken.

'An excellent shot,' Kullervo gloated. 'You shall have a reward.'

Colin then felt a surge of triumph course through his veins, vitalizing every inch of his deadened being. He punched the air with his free hand, threw back his head, and crowed with delight.

'You are a warrior now, boy, a true warrior,' Kullervo exulted.

'I want to do that again,' Colin said and held up another javelin, ready to strike.

11
Beacons

The three cyclists had now reached the edge of Mallins Wood. Connie barely recognized the picnic spot: it was draped with rainbow-coloured bunting and decked with signs bearing slogans, such as 'Trees not tarmac', 'Save the planet—get on your bike'. As her feet touched earth dismounting from the bicycle, Connie felt sick and angry at the thought of all the creatures that would soon be homeless and all the trees that would be lost. Standing here, she could feel the throbbing life in the grass, rising up to the tree tops, but soon that would cease, leaving a dead scar on the landscape—and inside her. That loss would never heal. Each tree was irreplaceable. She wondered what the

Society was doing to save what they could. Organize an evacuation for the creatures, take cuttings to new homes? But there were few areas of woodland left in this part of the world. She wished she was still on hand to help as there would be so much work involved, so much that only she could do.

First things first: she had to find the missing dragonet.

Anneena pointed at a banner strung between a white bus and a tree. 'Arthurian Pageant—volunteers wanted'.

'Look, we've chosen our theme for the carnival procession.'

Connie was eager to start searching for Argand and wasn't paying full attention.

'That's great.'

'Yeah, but it's better than you think—and all thanks to Jane.'

'What do you mean?'

'We're bringing local legend in on our side to fight the council. Jane, you explain.'

'Well,' said Jane, 'the wood has a fascinating history. Did you know that it used to be called Merlin's Wood? The name got corrupted over time to Mallins. I did some digging around in the library and found a story that claimed it was the place where Merlin was imprisoned by a sorceress named Nimue. He was supposed to be trapped in a cave at the roots of an old oak tree.'

'Really? That happened here?'

'Well, probably not really—there are hundreds of other places that make the same claim. But that doesn't matter—as long as we can convince enough people to care about the wood and its history, it might just stop the council in its tracks.'

'Yeah,' added Anneena, 'stories like this make the wood more important to everyone—to people beyond Hescombe. We think we can get a really good campaign going—use the procession to launch it nationally.'

Connie began to understand the possibilities. 'Then you need some new banners: how about, "Don't mow down Merlin!"'

Jane laughed. 'You're right. We must get painting. I'm sure your aunt will help—she did the first set.'

'Have you seen her? Is she OK?'

Jane and Anneena exchanged looks. 'Yes, we've seen her around,' Anneena said awkwardly, avoiding Connie's eye.

'On the back of Mr Clamworthy's bike, I suppose?' guessed Connie.

'So you know about that?' Anneena looked relieved. 'Yes, she's fine, but missing you, of course. She's always asking after you in case we've heard anything.'

They left their bikes chained to a picnic table under the trees. Connie followed Anneena and Jane as they made their way over to a white bus from which fiddle music was blaring out of every open window.

'Brace yourself,' Jane whispered to Connie as Anneena knocked on the door. It opened with a bang as a flame-haired woman erupted onto the doorstep. An Alsatian dog charged from behind her legs, nearly knocking her over. The dog began to bark and snarl at Anneena who rapidly retreated down the steps. Unperturbed, Connie reached out a hand. At first, the Alsatian sniffed it with suspicion, then he licked her fingertips. He sat at her feet, eyes closed, leaning against her, allowing her to scratch his ears.

'You again, is it?' Siobhan said loudly to Anneena, but casting a curious glance at Connie as her guard dog now rolled over onto his back and begged for his tummy to be tickled. 'You'll be wanting Rat, I suppose?'

'Yes, if he's here,' said Anneena more timidly than was usual for her.

Siobhan shrugged. 'He's around the place somewhere. Try over by the builders' compound. Here, Wolf, you soppy old beast!' The Alsatian ignored her, now whining with ecstatic pleasure as Connie stroked him.

'Off you go, Wolf,' Connie whispered to him, patting him on his head. He leapt to his feet and trotted obediently back into the bus. Siobhan took a good look at Connie but said nothing.

The girls eventually found Rat at the edge of the perimeter fence that guarded the road builders' machinery. He was well hidden, lying on his belly with a pair of wire-cutters, and it was not until Connie spotted a flock of sparrows flying out of a tree in alarm that they discovered he had been the source of the disturbance as he had just snipped through a piece of the mesh.

'Who's this?' he asked, giving Connie a distrustful look.

'A friend of ours,' Anneena explained, glancing uneasily at the fence. 'Should you be doing that?' Rat grinned and cut another strand. Anneena sighed. 'She's found out that Col's mum has a place in Wales. Do you know anything about it?'

'No,' Rat said, snipping another piece of wire. 'That mad cow could be anywhere. Real creepy she is—scary eyes when you see her up close. I'll ask around.'

'I think she lives near a place called . . . well, it's spelt BWLCH. Don't know how you say it,' said Connie.

Rat looked awkward. 'You'll have to write it down for me.'

Connie found a scrap of paper in her pocket and, borrowing a pen from Jane, wrote the place name out clearly. Handing the paper over, she touched Rat's fingers for a moment and was filled with an odd sensation—she had only ever felt it when she had touched a wild creature: Rat was alive to the world, really alive, as few people were. He must have felt something too because he gave her a sharp look.

'You've got the same eyes as Col,' he said.

'I know.'

'Col's my best friend—I don't want nothing bad to happen to him.'

'I know.'

Satisfied with that, Rat turned back to the wire fence.

'Oi! You lot! What do you think you're doing?' A policeman came pounding along the perimeter towards them, his belt jingling heavily with handcuffs and truncheon.

'Split!' hissed Rat. He slithered out of sight, emerging the other side of the bush to pick himself up and run into the trees. Jane gave a panicked scream and darted back the way they had come, closely followed by Anneena. Connie hesitated, then set off in the opposite direction, heading towards the coastal path, hoping to lose any pursuit in the dense oak trees that grew in this part of the wood. The last thing she needed after persuading a reluctant Godiva to let her out was to end up in trouble with the police.

She ran into the trees and paused. Was she still being chased? There came a crashing noise behind her and the sound of a man swearing as he tripped up over a tree root—she was the unlucky one, he was on her tail! She started to run again.

'Stop! Police!' he shouted.

She was making too much noise in the thick undergrowth: it was easy to track her each time she moved. Her heart was thumping, her legs had turned to jelly. She felt like a fox being pursued by a hound, but at least she didn't have to stay on the ground. Thinking quickly, she looked for a place to climb. She broke from cover to run into the space under a decrepit old tree, jumped to swing up on a low branch and climbed into the yellowing canopy of oak leaves. A moment later, her hunter fought his way through the undergrowth, and passed right beneath, still cursing her for giving him the run-around, but fortunately he did not think to look up. Connie waited until all sounds of his passage through the wood had died away.

The normal noises resumed: the song of the birds, the rustle of leaves, and the whisper of the breeze, carrying the tang of the sea inland. It appeared that it would be safe now for her to find a way down and look for Argand. But it did not prove so simple: her fear had driven her high up the tree; it no longer looked such an easy climb from here.

Then Connie gave a muffled cry of surprise. A pair of brown eyes was staring at her from a split in the tree bark: a wood sprite, the spirit of the tree, was watching her. She had never yet been close enough to encounter one. Intrigued, she reached out a finger and touched the crack. A twiggy claw emerged and its tip stroked her hand experimentally. The creature's presence unfurled in Connie like a bud opening. She felt as if she was merging with the tree, becoming an extension of its life, a new branch or cluster of leaves, waving up here in the wind, yet connected to the deep places of the earth where the roots delved. Down there it was dark and moist, while up in the leaves above, all was light; birds sketched patterns across the sky, carrying the acorns away to drop in new seedbeds far from the parent tree. The oak was ancient. A thousand years of memories ringed its trunk.

Old enough to remember Merlin? Connie wondered.

The creature shuffled out of its hole, whiskers twitching, and came to sit on the branch beside Connie. The sprite perched on its back legs like a squirrel, sniffing the air. Its rough pelt was dark green, shot through with brown and yellow, but Connie noticed that it shed leafy bristles with every puff of wind. These floated gently to the ground, leaving patches of silver-grey skin bare to the elements. The wood sprite's blunt, rounded snout was smooth olive green, dimpled with little brown pits around the nostrils. It whispered a soft greeting, like the flutter of leaves.

Connie thanked it for its welcome and for allowing her to take refuge here.

'Is Merlin buried under you?' she asked it.

'Merlin? What's that?' rustled the sprite with interest.

Connie smiled. 'Not what—who. A magician from long ago.'

'Know nothing about such things. No magician under my roots. Have own magic—not man's magic.'

The universal could feel it—the pulse of life in the sap, the strength in the roots. But she couldn't stay to learn more: she had to find her companion.

'Have you seen a little golden creature in your wood? A dragonet?'

The sprite scratched at the bark, thinking, feeling in the earth. 'She in dark place over there. Sadness. Scared.'

'I must go to her.' Connie began to scramble down. 'But how shall I get to the ground?'

'Like the acorn—you drop,' came the response.

Not thinking this very helpful advice, Connie reluctantly turned round. But the wood sprite was right: she had no choice in the end but to drop to earth from the lowest branch. Falling heavily, Connie rubbed her hands together where she had grazed them, licking the cuts like a cat, tasting the salty tang of mingled bark and blood. She looked back up into the tree to see the sprite was still watching her. It pointed into the trees. She waved farewell and it darted out of sight.

Pushing her way through the thickets, she reached out for Argand through their bond, calling her. A golden glimmer lit up one corner of her mind—faint and fearful. She hurried on, homing in on that presence. Finally she came to the edge of a sheer slope that dropped away to the hollow below. She couldn't get down this alone.

'Argand! It's me,' she called, feeling she was close enough now to use her voice.

A streak like a golden firework burst from the darkness and flew at her. She opened her arms wide and caught Argand, hugging her close. The dragonet was shivering. She was cold, tired, and—Connie reached into her mind—terrified of something.

'What happened? Where's Col?'

A series of images flashed through Argand's head—horseboy, dark creatures, snakes. Col screaming.

'Has something happened to him? Something bad?'

'Yes, yes!' peeped Argand.

Connie stroked the dragonet into calmness. 'Look, companion, you need to go back to your nest. I'll show you the way.' Drawing Argand closer, she showed her a mental image of the way back to the moor. 'Did you get that?'

Argand nodded.

'Tell your father what happened here. Now go.'

Argand fluttered into the sky, bobbing off over the trees. Connie hobbled back towards the camp, hoping no one would think her extended absence strange.

Her two friends and Rat were waiting for her by the bus.

'Thank goodness, Connie!' exclaimed Anneena, seeing her emerge from the trees. 'We were just getting ready to come back in after you. I thought you'd been caught.'

'Almost, but not quite,' Connie admitted. 'But I think I've found a good contender for Merlin's tree—over there, in that grove of oak trees by the fence.'

Rat nodded. 'I know the one you mean—the old one.'

'That's it.'

'It's in a part of the wood that they're going to cut down.'

'No—they can't!' Connie cried, thinking of the wood sprite and the community of creatures that were housed in the canopy.

'But that's good,' said Anneena, half to herself.

'What!' Rat and Connie rounded on her indignantly.

'It can be our symbol—something for the story to focus on. We can call it Merlin's Oak. We need some photographs, someone to front the story—yes, yes, it's perfect.'

'What's she on about?' Rat asked Connie in a puzzled tone.

'She's got an idea . . .' Connie began.

'And when Anneena has an idea, we all hear about it sooner or later,' finished Jane. 'Usually sooner.'

Rat looked at Anneena doubtfully.

'Do you think your mum would help?' Anneena asked him.

'Help with what?' He did not seem too sure about a suggestion involving his mother and had begun to edge away from them.

'Tell the reporters about Merlin's oak, of course!' Anneena seemed genuinely surprised that he was not following her train of thought.

'Dunno. You ask her yourself. Look, I've gotta go.' Rat slipped off and started running towards the wood. 'Gotta finish that fence.'

Anneena continued to spin her plans as the girls returned to Chartmouth on their bikes, shouting snatches of them to Jane and Connie as they all enjoyed the smooth ride downhill, a reward for the hard climb earlier.

'But what about Col?' Connie asked her when they got back to Lionheart Lodge.

Anneena's face fell. 'Sorry, I was getting carried away. I'd almost forgotten. But what can we do?'

'Someone needs to go and look for him,' Connie said firmly.

'But we can't do that! How would we even get to Wales?' Anneena protested.

'I want to do something too,' Jane said as she leaned her bike against Connie's, 'but I really don't know what we can do other than tell his grandmother everything, as we've been doing.'

'Perhaps you're right,' Connie replied, 'but I know I can't sit back, just hoping that he'll turn up. What if something really bad has happened?'

'But it can't have done,' Jane said, shocked, 'he's with his mother.'

Connie had difficulty sleeping that night, worried by the images Argand had shown her. She wanted more than anything to speak to someone in the Society, someone in whom she could confide her fears, but her great-aunt had cut off all channels of communication. What exactly it was that Connie was afraid of she couldn't say. As Jane had said, Col was with his mother: he should be fine. But even though Argand's mind was still unformed and could not hold complex thoughts, she had given Connie a sense of something snakelike—Cassandra's gorgon perhaps?—and also a dark creature with hoofs. Then there had been a flash of a picture of Col distressed, ensnared, screaming.

Connie couldn't bear it. It wasn't enough to send Argand with a message to Argot in the hopes that the dragon and Dr Brock would understand how serious this was. She had to do something. But what? She had no way of getting to Wales to see for herself.

Tossing on her bed, it took Connie a moment to realize that the hair on the back of her neck was tingling as she felt the presence of another creature.

She threw the covers back, and stumbled over to the window. There on the lawn was a white stallion with folded wings: Skylark. She threw the sash window open. Here it was: her way out! Why hadn't she thought of it before? She put her fingers to her lips to silence Skylark's joyful greeting.

'I'll be there in a minute,' she called softly.

Laughing inside, Connie scribbled a note for Godiva and left it on her pillow. Then, pulling her flying suit out from the bottom of the chest, Connie prepared herself with layers of warm clothing for the long flight she hoped to be undertaking if she could persuade Skylark. They could go and look for Col together!

There was no sound from her great-aunt's room as Connie ran past. Then she was out of the front door and had her head buried in Skylark's mane. A flood of communication passed between them as her touch made the familiar connection. She could read everything the pegasus was thinking and feeling. Skylark was desperately worried about Col and eager to do something. He had heard from Mrs Clamworthy that Connie had found out where Col's mother lived. Frustrated that no one had set out to look for Col immediately, Skylark had resolved to come to fetch her. It took no time for them to agree to be off.

'I'm going to be in so much trouble,' she muttered as she climbed on his back. But just then she didn't care.

Early on Sunday morning, while it was still dark, Skylark and Connie reached the Brecon Beacons. Frail strings of lights marked the small villages and isolated farms that fringed the mountain mass, but its interior yawned black to the sky, like a great hole ready to suck in the stars that twinkled overhead.

'What do you think, Skylark?' Connie asked her mount, who had far more experience of aerial reconnaissance than her. They had been circling about for some time and knew they were near their goal. 'That might be Bwlch. Mr Coddrington said he's put the pin to the left of it on his map.'

Skylark dived lower.

'See over there,' he said, 'that's a bonfire. It's very odd to have a fire now. Let's go a little nearer.'

Like a barn owl swooping down on its prey, Skylark silently glided towards the flickering light. Connie strained her eyes to see what was going on but could only make out indistinct figures in a farmyard passing to and fro in front of the flames.

'The van!' Skylark exclaimed. His keener eyes had made out the dusky shape of the van parked by the barn. 'This is it.' He began to descend for landing.

'Pull up!' Connie ordered, stung by a sudden intuition like a slap in the face. Skylark responded immediately and propelled them higher, out of sight of the farm.

'What is wrong, Universal?' he asked her.

'I'm not sure, but I felt something. There's a mythical creature down there—or maybe many— I can't be sure. I think it might be safer to arrive in daylight.'

They hid in a copse not far from the farm, waiting for dawn. Connie huddled on a pile of leaves, wishing she had thought to bring a blanket, and tried to catch a few winks of sleep. Skylark moved restlessly, keeping watch. The sun crept slowly above the horizon, illuminating everything in a cold, cruel light. Connie got to her feet and stretched her cramped limbs.

'You'd better stay here,' she said to Skylark, 'in case there are any people other than Col and his mother around. I'll come and get you when I can give you the all clear.'

Skylark snorted with frustration but accepted this advice: he could not go trotting into a farm and risk meeting the farmer.

The light grew stronger as Connie walked down the track, pushed the gate open, and entered the yard. All was quiet. In front of her sat the light green van parked by a wooden barn, to her right was a ramshackle stone cottage, and to her left a number of outhouses. The yard seemed empty: the embers of the bonfire still glowed hot in its centre but all traces of the people she had seen dancing round it were gone. Her skin still tingled: there were creatures close by, but she could feel nothing for certain, no distinct natures. It was as if they were purposely trying to disguise their presence from her. She rubbed her arms thoughtfully, wondering if she should risk proceeding without knowing what she was facing. But what about Col? Decision made, she approached the cottage door and knocked. After a few moments, a woman with straggling locks of blonde hair opened it.

'So you did come after all,' the woman said, looking disdainfully at her visitor.

'Mrs Lang?' Connie asked.

'*Miss* Lang,' Cassandra corrected her.

'Can I see Col?'

'I suppose so,' she said coldly. 'Wait here a moment.' She went back into the house, leaving Connie on the doorstep. Connie wiped a hand across her tired eyes, feeling confused: it seemed too easy, but also odd. Cassandra Lang was clearly not surprised to see her—how could that be? No one knew she was here. She did not have time to solve this puzzle as she could now hear footsteps approaching. Cassandra Lang returned, followed by a boy dressed in black leather riding clothes.

'Col!' Connie exclaimed, rushing to hug him. 'We've been so worried about you.'

The boy received her hug unresponsively. He looked over to his mother.

'Col, what's the matter with you?' Connie asked, stepping back. Inspecting him close to, she saw that his eyes were dead; there was none of Col's usual animation about his face: no grin, no laugh. 'What have you done to him?' she asked his mother.

Cassandra frowned. 'I've done nothing. Kullervo has taken him for training.'

'Kullervo?' Connie's mind whirled as she tried to understand what was happening. 'How could you let this happen? Don't you know what being taken by Kullervo means? He's destroying him!'

198

'That's not true,' Cassandra sneered. She was angry; she didn't want to hear her own doubts voiced by this child.

'But look at him! Kullervo's done something terrible to him. This isn't Col!' Connie made a grab for Col's arm, intending to shake him, to wake him out of his stupor, but the boy pulled away.

'Kullervo's told me that he'll be all right once he is used to it.'

'You've betrayed Col!' Connie said desperately.

'And you betrayed all mythical creatures when you refused to join us!' Cassandra spat back.

Connie turned away from Col's mother in disgust. If Kullervo was around, she had to get Col out quickly. 'I'm not staying here. Come on, Col, we're going.' She made another grab for his arm and began to pull him towards the gate, thinking that if she could get him to Skylark then maybe he would snap out of this strange daze.

'Stop her!' Cassandra shrieked.

Out of the building closest to the gate glided a bronze figure, wings unfurling like a cobra's hood around her hissing, spitting head as she reared up before the two friends. Connie felt Col being wrenched from her grasp.

'Fool: don't let him see her eyes!' Cassandra hissed, ripping her son away from Connie so that

199

he was no longer in direct sight of the creature. 'She's all yours!' she shouted to her companion, giving a triumphant laugh.

Standing alone in the middle of the yard, Connie turned to face the gorgon.

12
Helm

The dark eyes of the gorgon blazed at Connie, beating down upon her with awesome power. Connie felt it as a burning coldness scorching her skin, entering her flesh, and freezing her to the spot. Connected to the creature through its gaze, her hair began to rise from her scalp, writhing with the angry, tormented dance of the snake-locks. The gorgon snarled, baring her teeth in a vicious grimace, confident that she had caught her victim. She could now begin the slow process of the kill as her power to turn to stone worked inwards to still Connie's pounding heart.

The universal's shield, thought Connie frantically.

The constricting grip of stone had reached her chest. Her breath became laboured and her throat choked. The attack had penetrated too far. She couldn't conjure the shield—but she had to! Slowly, inch by inch, trying to forget her pain and fear, she raised in her mind the silver shield, a barrier between her and death. She could feel the power of the gorgon's gaze now beating against it, trying to turn it into stone so it would be too heavy to hold.

The balance of the fight wavered: who would prove the stronger?

Then the creeping paralysis stopped and began to recede. The gorgon redoubled her attack, hissing with anger as she felt her power leach away into the ground at Connie's feet, petrifying the weeds that grew through the cracks in the concrete.

Now for it, thought Connie.

With an immense effort she thrust her mind-shield forward to throw back the gorgon's gaze. The creature screamed as the cold fire singed her skin, freezing her hair in mid-air so that the snakes stood out from her head like curling icicles. With a sob and a strangled cry she fell back to the floor, her sight temporarily blinded. Wounded, she slithered away to take refuge in an outhouse.

'What have you done to her?' shrieked Cassandra, pouncing on Connie and grabbing a fistful of hair to pull her head back. Connie's eyes watered with the pain.

'Let go! I've just done what she was trying to do to me,' Connie said, attempting to free herself.

Cassandra gave a whimper, released her hold on Connie and ran after her companion.

Connie turned to Col. 'Right, let's go while we've a chance.'

But he was not looking at her, nor at the building into which his mother had disappeared: he was staring past Connie's shoulder with a nasty greedy expression shining in his eyes. Hearing the steady beat of hoofs behind her, Connie spun round, hoping that perhaps Skylark had ignored her advice and come to her aid. It was a pegasus she saw, but not Skylark: a great blue-black creature with mismatched fiery eyes and furled wings like those of a huge eagle. Connie was not fooled by outward appearances. She knew the beast for what he was the moment she felt his dark presence this close: it was Kullervo.

'Quick, Col, run!' she yelled, sprinting to the gate, but Colin remained stock still, smiling in a strange lop-sided manner. 'Come on!' she called frantically.

'He will not run,' whinnied Kullervo softly. 'He does not want to. Come here, boy.' Colin turned and walked with the jerky steps of a marionette to stand beside the pegasus. 'Do you want to go with this girl?' Kullervo asked him.

'No,' said Colin.

'Do you want to stay with me and fight as a warrior by my side?'

'Yes.'

'Do you want to taste blood again, to kill to save the creatures of this world from humanity?'

'Yes.'

Kullervo relished taking Colin through this vile litany in front of Connie, knowing that every word would be a torment to the universal that had so injured him on their last encounter.

'That's not Col speaking,' Connie said fiercely as she hesitated by the gate, unwilling to leave without her friend. But what else could she do?

'Oh, it is the new Colin speaking,' Kullervo said, shaking his mane carelessly. 'Don't you think I improved him?' His eyes sparkled with malevolence. She could feel their mesmerizing power pulling her in. She closed her own against them.

'No, I want the old one back,' she said. She couldn't run for it and leave Col to Kullervo— she just couldn't. But neither could she make Col come with her unless this bond with Kullervo was broken.

And then she realized how to do it. Her reading over the summer had taught her this, though she had not had an opportunity to try the exercises out for real. Well, now seemed like a good moment to make the attempt. Keeping her eyes closed to concentrate, she looked inside for the tool in the universal's armoury that she needed. She found it, shining with a dull golden gleam just within reach. Buckling on the helm, Connie reached out to Col's occupied mind. Given entry by Kullervo's counterfeit pegasus bond, she found the way open and slid in using the wave of dark energy connecting creature and Col to mask her intrusion. She then cast off disguise and called her friend's name as she wandered through the echoing chambers of his being. His mind stretched in a bewildering labyrinth in all directions; she felt lost in a nightmarish crypt where all presence of Col had nearly been extinguished.

It did not take long for Kullervo to sense her trespassing on his shared thoughts with his prey. He immediately tried to evict her. She resisted. His malice beat harmlessly against her helm like water off a windowpane.

'Col—I'm coming for you!' she called.

Kullervo attempted to drown out her voice, howling like a tempest in the empty places he had made for himself in Col's mind. Driven by her love and concern for her friend, Connie faced into the storm and staggered on. Darkness whipped around her. She gritted her teeth, determined to find him, but Kullervo's power was so strong, she began to fear she would not survive it. Finally, with the last of her strength, she stumbled upon a small child lying curled up in a corner, shaking and sobbing, an image of a younger Col.

'Col, it's me,' she said, stooping over him.

'Connie?' The boy turned his head, his eyes igniting with his old self again.

She knelt beside him and raised him up. 'Yes, it's me. Let me put this on you.'

He submitted as she buckled her helm on his head. His connection with Kullervo was instantly severed, but Connie, her mind no longer protected, was now caught in the link. She could hold Kullervo off with the shield, but she could no longer break the bond. All her force had been spent in saving Col. The storm consumed her.

Col came to himself and found that he was standing in a strange farmyard with a black pegasus by his side and Connie, crumpled to her knees in the mud, holding her hands over her head as if warding off blows. He staggered back in disgust from the creature: this was no pegasus, this was a counterfeit. He could feel its evil nature oozing from every pore as it concentrated its hatred on his friend.

'Stop it! Stop it!' Col yelled. He dashed to Connie, trying to protect her with his body from the presence of the creature. But it was futile. She was twisting in agony, shaking her head this way and that. The attack on Connie was happening in a realm far from the physical world and he could do nothing to help.

His cry disturbed Kullervo from his assault. The shape-shifter relented a little, taking a moment to despatch the boy he no longer needed.

'You can go. I have got what I wanted,' he said. Col watched with horrified fascination as a change swept over the pegasus and he melted into a dark pool of matter. But before Col had time to pull Connie away, the blue-black substance began to coil and writhe into a new shape. A great hydra with nine serpent-heads rose out of the pool, nine black tongues hissing at Col, forcing him to back away from Connie with their foul breath. The hydra coiled itself around the girl, binding her in its loops.

'I'm not leaving without her!' Col shouted.

'It is what she would want,' Kullervo laughed, each of his nine snakes' jaws split wide open, displaying white fangs and cavernous mouth. The horrid bubbling noise of his laugh burst like poisoned gas from his gut. 'She would beg you to take your chance. You will find a pegasus—a real one—' (one head darted forward and smiled at Col, tongue flickering lazily in the slack line of its closed mouth) 'waiting for you in the trees up the track. You had better go—that is, unless you want to join us: you made a very good warrior, Colin.'

Col shuddered. The events of the recent days came back to him as if he was watching flashes of film involving an actor playing his role: the kestrel, the training, the gorgon.

A door banged behind him.

'You!' Col spat at his mother who had just emerged from the nearest building. 'You let him do this to me! You've betrayed both Connie and me!' He advanced on her, his fists balled by his side, longing to hurt someone for all the pain he had been through. Cassandra fell back, feeling the heat of his anger bearing down on her.

'She has not betrayed Connie: you did that,' Kullervo hissed wickedly, enjoying the scene of pain and treachery that he had concocted.

'No!' Col turned back to the serpent in disbelief.

'Oh yes. It's her love for you that brought her here. What with that, and a few pieces of choice information that I allowed to be passed to the Society, I have been expecting her for days.'

'You used me as bait,' Col said in a hollow voice.

'Exactly. Though there was always the chance that you might really join us. Your mother certainly hoped so. You could not truly be my companion, of course, only the universal can be that,' (the hydra's coils tightened around Connie's chest causing her to gasp for breath) 'but the simulation I devised for your training worked almost as well as the reality. A good soldier doesn't need a soul.'

Cassandra strode to her son's side and took a tight grip of his forearm. 'Join with us, Colin. Don't disappoint me. The gorgon will die if we don't stop humans bulldozing her nest. The Society is being useless as usual and those ecowarriors won't stop the road with their protest. We need to fight for what we want. If you really care about mythical creatures, about their fate, then you'll stay with us willingly. If you don't, then go—we have no further use for you.'

Shaking her off, he said savagely, 'I'm called Col now. It's about time you learnt to call me by my proper name.' Mother and son glared at each other.

A weak voice interrupted them, barely rising above a whisper:

'Go, Col. There's nothing you can do for me.'

'Connie!' Regardless of the hydra's fangs, Col scrambled to her side. Her eyes were closed, her face pale and skin clammy. She seemed to gleam with a silver light, but it was fading fast.

'I'm caught in darkness,' she moaned, wandering off into incoherence. Her mind was bending like a tree before the onslaught of a hurricane—any moment it might crack and leave her helpless, roots splayed in the air.

'Connie!' Col tried to pull her from her living prison, his touch returning her to the present.

She opened her eyes briefly. 'Please, go!' she begged. She had little energy for speech. She only knew that from this mess Col at least should escape.

Col had never been good at knowing when to give up, rarely recognizing that a battle was lost, but for once in his life, he realized that he could do no good here. He needed help if he was to save Connie. He jumped to his feet and began to sprint up the track, every step that took him away from his friend like a stab in his stomach, but he did not look back.

Col stumbled up to Skylark who had been waiting anxiously in the trees. The pegasus whinnied with pleasure but broke off when he saw the state of his companion.

'Where's Connie?' Skylark asked as Col fell against him. He looked down the track but could see no sign of her. 'Where's the universal?'

'It was a trap,' gasped Col. 'We must get help!'

He pulled himself clumsily onto Skylark's broad back and slumped over his mane, allowing his mount to read all that had happened, glimpse all the pain he felt, in the sparking connection that ran between them. The horse neighed with anger and began to canter back to the farm, set on revenge and rescue.

'No, no,' Col shouted. 'We can't save her that way! We can't take on Kullervo alone!'

Brought to his senses, Skylark wheeled round and galloped to take off.

'It's broad daylight, Col,' Skylark said as they strode into the air. 'What if we are seen?'

Col swore. 'Who cares?' he said. 'We'll fly in the cloud as much as possible, but so what if every person between here and Hescombe sees us? We've got to get help. Connie's in pain.'

Skylark whinnied his agreement and kicked hard against the wind, determined to fly the fastest he had ever done in his life.

Four hours later, Col left Skylark imperfectly hidden with Mags at the allotments and ran, half-staggering, back to his home. He burst into the kitchen to find his grandmother sitting at the kitchen table, her eyes wet with tears. Dr Brock and his father stood either side of her. They looked up in astonishment when he erupted in upon them.

'Col!' shrieked Mrs Clamworthy, jumping up to hug him.

'Is Connie with you?' Dr Brock asked, relieved to see him. 'We thought she must have gone to look for you when we heard she'd run away.'

'Where's your mother? I want a word with her,' growled Mack, thumping Col on the back.

'Shut up! Shut up, all of you!' Col gasped, struggling to free himself from the tangle of his grandmother's scarves. 'It's Kullervo—he's got her. At least, he had me and he's now got her. It was all a trap.'

Dr Brock's face drained of colour and Mrs Clamworthy collapsed into a chair. Mack was the first to move.

'Where's he got her?' he asked, guiding Col to a seat. 'Tell us everything.'

'Kullervo was trying to get her in Mallins Wood but caught me instead. He . . . he took me over. Connie must've known something was wrong—she came to rescue me from Mum's cottage in Wales. She seemed to be able to break the link he had bound me with, but ended up caught herself. It was ...' He choked on his words, '... terrible. It was like she was being drowned or something and I could do nothing to pull her out.'

Dr Brock pulled on his motorbike gloves. 'We need a search party. We must find out if he still has her there. Are you coming, Mack?'

Mack squeezed his son's arm. 'Yeah. Let's go. I'll go by road. I suppose you'll fly?'

Dr Brock nodded. 'We'll bring Argot's youngster, Argand: as Connie's companion, she should be able to sense her if we get near enough. Lavinia, you raise the alarm—send the others.'

'I'm coming too!' Col leapt to his feet.

Mack pushed him back down. 'Not this time. You've done what you can—leave it to us now.'

After the noise of their departure had died down and the alarm call been made, Mrs Clamworthy turned to her grandson. 'I'm sure she'll be all right,' she said in an unconvinced tone of voice. 'They'll find her.' She patted Col on the back and bustled about to make him some tea. 'You look all in.'

Col stared down at the plate she put before him, not feeling the slightest bit hungry, though he did have an unquenchable thirst. He drained his first mug of tea and accepted a refill, drinking it greedily. He was tormented with regrets. Images of the past few days were still swirling about in his head: the Colin who had been inside him for that period had been proud to be chosen as Kullervo's boy; the Col who sat at the table now was ashamed to find he had been only a pawn and the means to lure his friend to possible destruction. What was worse, he knew that Kullervo had fed Colin these illusions because they were already part of Col. Kullervo had known his weak spots and exploited them mercilessly, driving Colin to become the fighter that Col had idly dreamed of being. But as a warrior he had caused death and was now sickened by the memory. He hoped he would never have to fight again, and knew that if he did, it would only be as a desperate last resort.

'And what about Cassandra?' Mrs Clamworthy asked him gently. 'Is your mother all right?'

Col shook his head. He realized he had forgotten to make plain to Mack and Dr Brock the role his mother had played in all this, how she had handed him over to be Kullervo's instrument. The thought of this was like the twist of a knife in his guts. 'No, she's been taken by Kullervo too. But she went willingly.'

'Then there's no saving her. She's lost to us.'

'Good. I never want to see her again,' Col replied angrily. But even now his heart whispered another story.

13
Battering Ram

The rescue party returned late on Sunday evening empty-handed. They had found the farm deserted, only tyre tracks by the barn to show that the campervan had ever stood there and not a sign of Kullervo's army. Col, sitting wrapped in his duvet in an armchair by the Aga, felt his last flicker of hope go out.

'There's nothing for it: we'll have to send out the general call-up and gather everyone at the Mastersons,' Dr Brock said heavily, taking Argand from his jacket pocket and placing her on the stove to warm up. She flickered her tongue at Col, sniffing his scent curiously. 'If Kullervo is planning to use Connie for some purpose of his own, then we must be ready for him.

215

There may be more than her life at stake if he is able to wield his power through her.'

Mack grunted. 'I don't understand. What is all this about her being used against us? She's a tiny thing—not much power in her, I'd've thought, even though she is a universal.'

Col said nothing, but was once again struck by how stupid his father could be.

'It's not about size, Mack,' Dr Brock said, wearily unlacing his jacket sleeves to remove his gauntlets. 'And in any case, I have a suspicion that Connie is far more powerful than any universal we have ever known before. Her first encounters were remarkable. The Trustees haven't told her, but they said they'd never met a mind like hers—and some of them, like Gard and Morjik, have known many universals in the past. Her potential is huge—but perilously untrained. If Kullervo can turn that potential to his own purposes, we don't stand a chance. That would certainly explain Kullervo's persistence in pursuing her—he must sense this too. But it makes her dangerous to us, more dangerous than you can imagine.'

Argand let out a sorrowful croon. Dr Brock scratched her gently on her neck.

'So far Connie has been strong enough to resist Kullervo, but I am worried by this most recent attack. He clearly took her at her weakest and who knows how long she can hold out? If she co-operates with him, even if it is against her will, she can channel his power into our world. She has told us that she feels his presence in her as a tide of darkness, sweeping over everything to drown her in his malice. If she lets him use her, then this tide becomes a very real deluge that will crash down on the rest of us. Noah's flood is nothing compared to what Kullervo has in store for humanity. There will be no ark to carry any of us through, I fear, except perhaps for a few chosen companions, but even they would not survive long—that is not Kullervo's way.'

There was a knock at the door. Dr Brock and Mack looked uneasily at Mrs Clamworthy.

'Are you expecting anyone?' Dr Brock asked. She shook her head.

Mack moved to the door and flung it open, ready to challenge any stranger. There, on the doorstep, hand raised to knock again, was Anneena, behind her a worried-looking Jane. Anneena was about to say something to Mack but she caught sight of Col.

'You're back! Thank goodness!' She pushed past Mack, quite forgetting that she was intimidated by him, and dashed over to Col. Mrs Clamworthy quickly threw the tea-cosy over Argand.

'Yeah, I got back today,' Col said, forcing a smile. Jane darted to Anneena's side, and stood staring down at him, hardly daring to believe her eyes.

'But have you heard about Connie?' Jane asked.

'What?' Col said eagerly, for one fleeting moment thinking that by some miracle she had turned up.

'She's gone missing,' Anneena said. 'Her great-aunt stormed over to my place this morning with the police. They'll probably be round soon as they're asking all her friends if they've heard from her. She thinks your Society people are hiding her. She's trying to get them to arrest Evelyn. She says Evelyn's been trying to get in to see Connie ever since she took her away to Lionheart Lodge. She's even saying that Evelyn must've snatched Connie.'

'What!' exploded Mack, halfway to the door.

'But they won't arrest her—not without proof anyway,' Anneena added.

'I did think,' said Jane nervously, 'that Connie might've gone looking for you. She was really worried. You don't think she has, do you?'

Col avoided their eyes. 'She might've, I suppose.'

'She found out about your mother's place in Wales, but she wouldn't have gone there, would she?' Anneena pressed him. 'How could she get there anyway? It's in the middle of nowhere from what she said.' Anneena was talking in a continual stream as much to work off her worry for her friend as to wait for an answer from Col.

'We've checked the farm,' Dr Brock interrupted her. 'Evelyn thought that too and some of us went to have a look. She's not there.'

'Oh,' Anneena said in a flat tone, disappointed of her one hope.

'She'll be all right,' Col said firmly, though he did not quite believe it himself. 'She'll turn up.'

'Yes,' said Dr Brock, 'she's more resourceful than many give her credit for.'

The kitchen door burst open again. This time it was Evelyn Lionheart who entered, not waiting to knock.

'I've just got your message that Col's back,' she panted, having run all the way from her house. 'He's seen Connie?'

Dr Brock shot a quick look at Mack from under his brows. Mack took the hint.

'Col's fine, Evie. Come with me and I'll tell you all about it.' He put his arm round Evelyn and steered her out of the room before she could say anything further in front of Jane and Anneena.

'Would you like a cup of tea, girls?' Mrs Clamworthy asked hospitably to cover this abrupt exit. She made to pick up the tea-cosy but thought twice. 'Or perhaps you'd like coffee?' She gave a worried glance over her shoulder in the direction of the sitting room from where they could hear the murmur of Mack's voice.

'Er . . . no thanks, got to get back,' said Anneena. There was a muffled scream from the front room—Mack must have just mentioned Kullervo. Anneena and Jane looked suspiciously at each other but Mrs Clamworthy pretended not to hear the interruption.

'If you're sure. Come back and see Col when he's rested, won't you?'

'Will you be at school tomorrow, Col?' Anneena asked on her way out.

Col was astounded that she could be thinking of such things at this time—then again, she did not know the truth. 'Um . . . perhaps not. I've not been feeling myself lately.'

'Right,' she said, hovering by the door. 'Well, get better soon. Don't forget, the festival kicks off on Friday. School's given us the day off to help with the procession. I hope you'll be well enough to come and see that. And perhaps Connie'll be here too by then. She really wanted to do something for the wood.' She gave him a shaky smile, trying to remain optimistic. 'After all, what with the local television and press reporting Connie's disappearance, it can't be long before someone finds her.'

Connie was lying on the top bunk of the camper-van gazing up at the plastic ceiling that glimmered grey in the darkness. The engine was quiet now: they must have parked for the night, but still she did not move. She felt exhausted, as if all the reserves of her energy had been drawn from her and she was now like a dried-up well. She was too tired to be as terrified as she knew she should be. Even if her hands had not been tied, she did not think she could muster the strength to make an attempt at escape. All she could manage was to keep hold of the frail fragment of shield that remained to her, knowing that Kullervo's presence was still out there, beating down upon her, waiting for her surrender.

As she lay there, she listened to the sounds around her. Cassandra's breath rose and fell evenly somewhere in the darkness below. Outside, she could hear the distant whine of passing cars, but sensed that the road was some way away. She guessed that the van was in a wooded spot because the rustle of leaves and hooting of an owl also travelled to her ears through the stillness of the night. But there were not only trees out there; she knew that many other creatures besides Kullervo were close by. She could feel their wild energy pulsing on the air in a feverish throb. They were excited, celebrating something—celebrating her capture. That was the worst—she had never felt so rejected and alone.

'You feel it, do you not, Universal?' A voice insinuated itself into her thoughts like a maggot eating its way into the core of an apple. Kullervo had begun to inhabit her mind.

'Feel what?' she asked wearily.

'You feel how your stubbornness has taken you out of your true path. It cannot be right that the universal should be so closed to others. Listen to them.'

'I don't want to listen to them,' she said. But it was hopeless: the weight of the shield was too much for her tired mind and she let it fall. She had no choice but to hear. Creatures crowded in upon her.

'They have destroyed my home; crushed my children!' howled a great bear, rending apart the remaining fragments of shield.

'I choke. The air is thick with their vomit,' cried a weather giant, searing her mind with a bolt of his anger.

'Help us!' wailed a banshee, tearing her hair in despair. 'We are hunted, driven out.' Connie felt anguish as if the banshee had plucked out a handful of her hair.

The universal reeled. She fumbled for her armoury of defences—sword, shield, and helm—but they had all crumbled away. She was standing unprotected in the dark surrounded by their misery; she could no longer shut it out. Voices fell upon her like repeated blows and kicks. But still Connie would not give in to the shape-shifter.

'You must help them,' Kullervo urged. 'It is the only way. Only then will you be free of their suffering.'

'I will not do your work for you. I will not become the monster you want me to be,' Connie said through gritted teeth.

'That is what Colin thought at first, but you will—you will.'

The voices left her and for a long time Connie knew no more.

At the Society's temporary command post at the Mastersons' farm, Col was on duty, manning the telephone in the office they had established in the dining room. Keeping Col company, Argand lay curled up asleep in the centre of the polished table, her golden scales gleaming in the reflective surface, small curls of smoke issuing from her nostrils on every out-breath. Col had just thrown the newspapers aside: he could not bear to read the pleading of Connie's parents, who had flown back from the Philippines, urging their daughter to get in touch: it made it sound as if she was callously not phoning just to punish them all.

The Society had seen and heard nothing of Kullervo. Wherever the creature was, he was well hidden, biding his time. Search parties and scouts had combed all likely haunts but no trace had been found and everyone was becoming increasingly short-tempered, frustrated by their powerlessness. They had no idea where he was taking the universal or when he would next strike. Col tried not to think too much about what might be happening to Connie: he knew he could not bear it.

Shirley Masterson, daughter of the house and a companion to weather giants, came into the room, dumping her schoolbag in a corner, startling Argand awake.

'Still here, Col?' she said sharply, swinging her long blonde hair over her shoulder. 'Let off school again?'

Col shrugged, not wanting to start an argument with her. His grandmother had allowed him to stay at the headquarters, knowing that he could not settle into the mundane regularity of a school routine while Connie's fate was still unknown.

'Heard nothing, I suppose?' she went on.

He shook his head.

'Well, perhaps my mentor will know more. He's arriving this evening to help. He has sources of information others don't have.'

Col was intrigued, despite himself. 'Like who?'

Shirley smiled mysteriously, delighted to flaunt her superior knowledge before him. 'I think he has a circle of regular informants—creatures he employs to keep track of us all.'

Col did not like the sound of that, but he supposed it might be useful in the current circumstances.

'I know that he's asked them to keep watch for your mother's campervan,' she continued, putting a callous emphasis on 'your mother', driving it home that it was his parent who was the traitor. Though angered by Shirley's casual cruelty, Col still felt ashamed.

There was a murmur of voices in the hall and more Society members came into the dining room. Dr Brock, haggard with tiredness, led the way. He slumped down into a chair and wiped his misted glasses with a grimy handkerchief. Col had not seen him out of his riding clothes since Sunday and did not think that he had slept. Dr Brock was followed by the stocky figure of Gard, the rock dwarf, one of the Trustees, clad as usual in deepest black. Gard threw back his hood to reveal a face that looked as if it had been chiselled in coal. Each facet gleamed silver as he moved his head. His dark eyes were surrounded by many fine cracks and fissures. This past week had carved new lines into his brow.

'She is being kept inside, you mark my words,' he was saying in a gruff voice. 'I cannot sense her footprint anywhere on the earth.'

'I fear he must have learned not to let her touch the ground,' replied Dr Brock, referring to the rescue they had been able to mount the first time Kullervo had abducted Connie. Thanks to Gard, Kullervo had only been able to hold her then for a few moments, not the days that had now passed since Sunday morning.

Mr and Mrs Masterson came in bearing a tray of sandwiches for their guests, handing out bone china plates and napkins to all who accepted some food. Col took a couple of egg sandwiches, more through habit than desire, and munched miserably on the bread that tasted like cotton wool, glaring back at the family portraits that watched him from the wall. He couldn't remember ever feeling so low.

A car crunched on the gravel outside and, moments later, Mr Coddrington strode into the room, his energy contrasting starkly with the despondent faces that greeted him. The crisis seemed to have galvanized him: he looked positively perky.

'At last I've news,' Mr Coddrington announced. All eyes turned on him, hope rekindled. Shirley hurried to his side to catch some reflected glory. 'The van was seen about an hour ago on the motorway heading in this direction.'

'Heading here!' Dr Brock exclaimed, putting aside his plate of food. 'Whatever for?'

'I don't know that,' Mr Coddrington snapped back, annoyed that his news had not received more fulsome compliments from the gathered members. 'Only Cassandra Lang can tell you that.'

Dr Brock remembered his manners. 'Thank you, Ivor. This is most valuable and welcome news. We must take counsel immediately—let us decamp outside.'

Clutching a forgotten sandwich in one hand, Col trailed out with the others to the barn where the larger mythical creatures were waiting. Windfoal, the unicorn, paced to and fro on the straw, shaking her silver mane fretfully, her gilded horn shining like a flame leaping from her forehead. Storm-Bird, the great crow-like storm chaser, was perched in the rafters, rumbling ominously as his anger built to a peak. Two dragons sat side by side, Morjik, the ancient emerald-skinned Trustee, and Dr Brock's Argot. Their reptilian eyes flickered with a dangerous light. Smoke wound from Morjik's nostrils and at intervals his forked tongue darted out like a whip lashing the air. There was a flash of gold and Col saw that Argand was flitting excitedly around her patient father's head. Other creatures and their companions flooded in through the double door, called in from their training to form a great circle. The barn echoed with the buzz of eager voices and the grunts, squeals, and neighs of the creatures. Col squeezed in beside Skylark who had already positioned himself in the front row by Windfoal on the western side of the barn.

Mr Coddrington and Dr Brock stepped into the centre of the circle. The doctor held up his hand and the room fell silent. He nodded to his colleague, cueing him to speak.

'Trustees and fellow members,' Mr Coddrington began proudly, 'I have just heard that the vehicle belonging to former Society member, Cassandra Lang, is on its way towards Hescombe.' An excited murmur ran around the room. 'It seems that a confrontation is brewing. If they are coming this way, we can assume that Kullervo is not far behind. We must now decide what we can do to stop the shape-shifter and save the unfortunate Miss Lionheart, if that is now possible,' he ended with an unctuous smile at the Trustees.

Then a voice spoke up from the doorway, shattering the silence that had fallen after Mr Coddrington's brief speech.

'It's you, isn't it? You've got her!'

All eyes turned to the speaker. On the threshold stood Godiva Lionheart.

14
Shape-shifter

'What is the meaning of this? Who is she?' Mr Coddrington turned furiously to Dr Brock.

'It's Connie's great-aunt,' Dr Brock explained as he hurried over. 'Godiva, what on earth are you doing here?'

'She can't come in!' shrieked Mr Coddrington, his face white. 'She's not allowed to see.'

His protests went unheeded. Gard the rock dwarf strode by and held out a hand.

'Companion to wood sprites, you are very welcome.'

'I am not a companion to . . .' Godiva shut up abruptly, remembering that she claimed not to be able to see creatures such as Gard. 'What have you done with Connie? Where are you hiding her?'

Dr Brock put an arm around her shoulders. Col expected her to push him away but instead she seemed to sag under the weight. A week's worth of worry had taken its toll on her.

'Look around you, Iva. We don't have her here.'

Godiva raised her eyes.

'You can't pretend any longer you can't see us. You've been hiding yourself for too long,' said Gard.

This angered Godiva. She stood up straight again and shook Dr Brock off. 'I don't want anything to do with . . . all this.' She turned to go.

'But you have to.' Dr Brock took a deep breath. 'Connie's a universal, Iva. Don't you remember what that means? Like Reggie Cony?'

'I don't want to hear this—I don't want to hear any more.'

'But you have to. You're running away because you're scared—not because it's not real. The girl I once knew would never run away but would've faced her fears.'

'That was before the girl you knew saw all her friends slaughtered by that monster. Don't you remember, Francis? George, Ramon, little Michael, Fredrich—all of them gone.'

'Then why are you here?'

231

'I have to help Connie—save her from you.' Godiva's eyes glittered with their old fire. 'I heard the trees in Mallins Wood whispering her name as I came past. I knew you had her in there. She's in danger. I'd've taken the police there myself except I . . .'

'Except you wish to keep your word to the Society not to betray the mythical creatures,' said Gard.

'Exactly,' she confirmed angrily.

'What did the trees say?' asked Eagle-Child, a Native American and Storm-Bird's companion, stepping silently to Godiva's other side.

'They said that she was coming. There's a storm brewing.'

'Mallins Wood—so that's where they are taking her,' Eagle-Child announced to the gathering.

'What are you talking about? Who's taking her where?'

'Iva, Connie's been captured by Kullervo,' Dr Brock said softly. 'I think you know only too well what that means for her.'

'No!' She shook her head in disbelief.

'But what you might not know is that, as a universal, he could use her powers to cause massive destruction. This is no longer about you and your feelings about the Society. This is about human survival.'

Godiva opened her mouth to say something, but then suddenly left the barn. Col could see her sitting on a hay-bale outside, head in her hands.

'Why is he taking her there?' asked Kinga Potowska, Morjik's companion. A forceful woman with iron-grey hair curled in a knot at the nape of her neck, she strode to stand in the centre of the barn, returning the meeting to the pressing matter at hand.

'Road,' growled Morjik.

'That is true,' said Gard, thumping into the circle from the doorway. 'I can feel the earth already groaning under the machines, but tomorrow they start to rend root from soil as should not be done.'

'Kullervo must be thinking of attacking at first light to stop the wood being bulldozed,' added Kira Okona, companion to Windfoal. Her dark skin gleamed in the light as she stepped forward, casting her orange and black cotton wrap over her shoulders.

Dr Brock rubbed his furrowed forehead in thought, casting an anxious look outside. 'Perhaps,' he said at length. 'That may be so. We know that the gorgon is one of his chief followers and that it is her wood the road-builders are set to destroy. Kullervo may think to make a beginning there.'

'So does that mean that the universal has given in?' asked Kinga, giving Dr Brock a sharp look. 'You said she would hold out long.'

'I know, I know,' he said sadly. 'I hoped she would—I thought she would—but can any of us be certain when we consider the power of Kullervo? We understand too little of the bond between the universal and the shape-shifter to make pronouncements on this.'

Indignant that Kinga seemed to be blaming Connie for her weakness, Col spoke up: 'He has the power to make you do his will—I should know: he used it on me.' He glared at Kinga.

'I am sorry, Col, if I angered you,' she said gently, resting a calming hand on his arm. 'Do not misunderstand me. I know Connie would not willingly cause harm to anyone.'

Mr Coddrington, who all this while had been standing in the centre of the circle, disgruntled to have found his big moment punctured by Godiva's arrival, now spoke: 'Surely, we can all agree that we have very little time. We know the gorgon companion, and probably the universal, are headed in this direction. We must assume that the universal is now in Kullervo's power. We must prepare for battle.'

He paused, waiting for the Trustees to give the word.

The Trustees looked at each other in silent debate; each nodded as they reached a mutual decision.

'I fear we must make that assumption,' Kinga said heavily, 'however much it pains us to believe this.'

'I have always warned the Society that universals pose a great—an unacceptable risk to us. They are even worse than renegades.' Mr Coddrington cast a derogatory look at the woman sitting crumpled in the farmyard. 'But no matter: now we have to take action. We must be at the wood before the shape-shifter arrives with his forces.'

'It will be difficult to keep from the sight of humans,' said Eagle-Child. 'The festival-goers, the road builders, the men and women of your media, even the riders of the pageant will all be flocking to the wood tomorrow morning.'

'Yes,' said Dr Brock, 'I would not be surprised if that's why Kullervo has chosen tomorrow. He no doubt wants to wipe out as many people with his first blow as he can. Success at the wood could rally many creatures to his side—creatures that do not care about the deaths of humans.'

'But we cannot be certain of his intentions,' countered Kinga. 'We have spent centuries guarding the secret of the existence of mythical creatures: we must not throw it away rashly. It should only be sacrificed when we have no other choice. I think we should array our larger forces on the moor, a short distance from the wood, but away from the people. We will only use them as a last resort and when we know for certain that Kullervo is there.'

'Your counsel is good,' grunted Gard.

Col listened to the debate, waiting for someone to raise the same suspicions as he had, but they seemed to be coming to a decision to take action without questioning the information on which they were working. It just did not seem right. The meeting was already beginning to break up as the commanders prepared to order their units to take up position. He would have to speak before it was too late.

'Can I say something?' Col said loudly, tugging Kinga's sleeve to get her attention.

'Silence!' she called out to those who had risen to their feet to leave. 'The companion to pegasi wants to speak. Well, Col?' she said more gently.

'It's just that . . .' Col faltered, feeling the attention of the whole room on him, 'it's just that we're reacting just as Kullervo would predict. He's already told me that he's been feeding information bit by bit to the Society somehow. He must know we will send our forces in. Don't you think we might be playing into his hands?'

'What else can you suggest?' asked Dr Brock. 'At least if we act quickly, we might be able to save Connie and stop him—we cannot pass up this chance.'

'I know that, but . . . !' Col could not think of a 'but' beyond his instinct that this was another trap. Kullervo was a master hunter: he knew how to manipulate his prey.

'We will think on what you have said, Col,' said Kinga kindly but with a clear note of dismissal. 'However, until we are wiser on this matter, we must act as we feel is best for those people tomorrow. To your posts, my friends! Francis,' she added in a lower voice, 'if you wouldn't mind, perhaps you could deal with Godiva Lionheart for us?'

'Of course.' Dr Brock was the first out into the yard. Col saw him lead Godiva towards the farmhouse and away from the stampede of creatures that had followed on his heels.

Everyone except Col and Skylark left the barn in haste. Skylark nuzzled his companion comfortingly.

'Something's not right,' Col said fiercely to the empty room, 'it's not right!'

Cassandra parked the van in a lay-by ten miles

from Chartmouth. She climbed into the back and shook Connie's shoulder.

'Time to wake up, Universal,' she said softly. 'You need to get ready.' Connie woke unwillingly, her lids still heavy as she opened them to find a pair of clear blue eyes gazing steadily at her. 'I'll take off your ropes if you promise not to try to leave the van.' Connie nodded. They both knew that she would not get far but Kullervo had ordered that she must not even be allowed to put one foot on the ground.

Cassandra helped Connie climb out of the bunk and then proceeded to wash and dress her like a child.

'I used to do this for Colin, you know,' Cassandra said wistfully, pausing as she brushed Connie's hair.

'Col,' Connie whispered, flinching away from Cassandra's light touch.

'He was Colin then,' Cassandra replied with a rough jerk of the brush, causing Connie's eyes to water. 'I should hate you for what you've done. It's because of you he's turned against me.' The brush clattered to the floor and Cassandra bent to pick it up. 'He would've joined with us if he'd had time to understand what Kullervo can offer—time to complete his training.'

'You're wrong,' said Connie. 'Kullervo was just

using you both. Col would've been burnt out by his bond with him—you'd've lost your son.'

'Ha! What do you know?'

'I know.'

Cassandra frowned and turned away. She then placed a plastic-wrapped sandwich, crisps, and a can of drink on the table in front of Connie.

'Eat,' she said. 'When you've finished, I'll help you put on your flying jacket.'

Connie chewed each mouthful slowly, trying to summon some energy to face the next challenge. The barrage of voices that had battered into her mind had finally fallen silent; she began to recover a little of her strength, enough to start to be curious about where she was and what was going to happen next.

'Are we flying then?' she asked.

Cassandra seemed surprised to hear Connie's voice again. The girl had barely spoken for days, making the task of keeping her a prisoner much easier: she need only think about her as the universal and not as a child of Col's age.

'*You* are flying,' Cassandra said, avoiding her eye. 'Are you ready?'

Connie knew from experience that sooner or later she would have to do what was required of her. She stood up and let Cassandra zip up her jacket. The gorgon companion then slipped the rope loops over Connie's wrists, tying her hands in front of her.

'You should be really grateful he's chosen you,' Cassandra said smoothly, her hands still on Connie's arms, her breath stirring her hair.

'Why should I? I hate him.'

'No you don't—you love him. He's your other self and you know it.'

Connie said nothing, but she recognized that Cassandra had chosen her words well. She let Cassandra steer her to the door. The gorgon companion opened it, letting in a flood of cold night air.

'Wait!' she warned, increasing her grip as Connie made to step down.

Out of the darkness came a midnight blue pegasus. It stopped by the side of the open van.

'Mount,' Kullervo said.

Connie tried to clamber on to the back of the beast, hampered by her weakness and tied hands. She slid back, falling between the pegasus and the door so that her foot would have reached ground had not Cassandra hauled her roughly up by her belt.

'Help her,' Kullervo ordered, angered by this near miss.

Cassandra none too gently pushed Connie up onto his back, making sure that this time Connie's legs were firmly astride before retreating back into the van.

'Hold on with your knees, Universal, and grip my mane: we are going for a little ride.'

Taking advantage of the quiet road, Kullervo galloped down the carriageway and soon he was striding in the air, climbing steeply. Fearfully, Connie looked down at the lights twinkling below and wondered what would happen if she simply slid off. Would such a death be better than the fate that he had in store for her?

'You will not do it,' Kullervo laughed softly. He now had free access to Connie's mind and could hear all her thoughts. 'You love life too much.' Connie knew he was right. She gripped tighter with her knees, her muscles already complaining.

'You are tired, Companion,' said Kullervo, with a hint of tenderness as they dropped through a damp cloud. Since she had become his prisoner, he had come to care for her like a prized possession. Connie could sense how he gloated over her and watched her covetously.

'I am not your companion.'

'Oh, but you are. You have no choice. We were made for each other: our partnership is as inevitable as the sea cleaving to the moon, following it with its tides. I am your moon, Connie.

'You see me as dark and hateful; you do not understand the true potential of our bond. Come, my universal, glimpse what we can be together!'

Connie let out a piercing scream: in mid-flight Kullervo was changing form. The beast she had been sitting on melted away like a cloud dispersed by the wind and she began to tumble to the earth. Kullervo swirled, shapeless, around her, slowing her fall. She struck out with her legs, trying to swim up through this matter as if it were water, but it was taking form once more and she was caught in the beak of a griffin, its lion's tail beating the air behind its pinions as it continued to fly south towards the sea. She felt sick with fright and swung there helplessly, too shocked to feel anything but terror.

Kullervo laughed. 'You do not yet like this game? But have no fear, I will not let you fall. Embrace the changes! Join the dance of the air!' His shape shifted once more and Connie fell from the beak back into the blue-black mist that mingled with the night sky. She closed her eyes tight, desperate to shut out this nightmare. But she was not plummeting to the ground—she was being spun like a twig borne along on the surface of a stream. Realizing she need no longer be afraid of tumbling to earth, she floated free, allowing Kullervo to support her, twist and turn her in the air as his essence regrouped into another form, that of dragon with long whipping tail. He nimbly caught her in his talons, then tossed her to the sky again as he turned into a phoenix with trailing black feathers. Falling to rest on the downy back, Connie sensed the exhilaration that coursed through his being, running into her veins, rekindling her exhausted soul. Kullervo relished his mastery of form, craved to experience all life to the very marrow of each being he became, rejoiced to conquer the secrets of creation by learning to assume its shape.

'So why do you not like us?' Connie asked, confused by this glimpse into his nature. She had not thought that he had delight in anything but destruction.

The joy of the game burst like a soap bubble and the phoenix reverted swiftly to its pegasus form, intent once more on its business.

'Humans are a mistake,' Kullervo said shortly.

The pegasus began to circle round as he descended towards the wood. Connie peered over his neck to see the lights of Hescombe below her.

'What are we doing here?' she asked, not expecting a reply, but to her surprise he was ready with an answer.

'Tomorrow men will start to rip up this forest, but you are going to stop them,' he replied.

'How?' she asked, fearing what would come next.

'You have a choice, Companion. You can aid me by channelling my power so that the work is stopped for good. I had thought that I could shift into a gorgon and we could turn the concrete spreaders to stone—a most fitting end, do you not think?' He gave a rumbling whinny of laughter. 'No? You will not do that? I did not think so. I know you now, Universal: you will not aid me willingly until all else is lost. I must make you see that that point has come.

'If you do not choose to help me today, then you must take the second course of action. Open battle between mythical creatures before the eyes of the world is what I want. The Society will do anything to save you—not only out of concern for you but to stop you from becoming what they fear. You should be sufficient bait to bring them out of hiding.'

'But why do you want this?' Connie gasped as she began to understand his mind.

'It will destroy the Society. They will be forced to kill other mythical creatures in defence of you and these road builders. Think what that will mean! The Society will be exposed for the human-centred sham that it is—prepared to kill us to protect the fellers of trees. Mythical creatures will leave in their droves. They will join me and then I will be strong enough to take on you humans. After that, the battle will be between us and humanity—we stand a far better chance of survival in open warfare than in this game of hide and seek we have been playing for centuries thanks to the Society. And when those two sides are lined up facing each other, I know that you will then join us, as you love the world too much to let it be eradicated by your fellow men. You will then be a willing channel for my power and put an end to all this for good.'

'You're wrong,' said Connie bitterly.

'No, Companion, I am right: I know you better than you know yourself.' The pegasus descended steeply. The tops of the trees were now only a few metres below. 'Prepare yourself!' He gave her only a moment's warning then shifted shape into an eagle, Connie still clinging to his neck as mane turned to feathers in the numb fingers of her bound hands. The eagle spiralled and landed at the top of a tall oak tree.

'Welcome to Merlin's oak,' he cackled.

15
Michaelmas

As grey light grew on the horizon, the sun muffled behind low cloud, Col and Skylark landed on the moor at the place where the forces of the Society had gathered. Wisps of mist curled around the pegasus's legs. Everything was wrapped in this veil of uncertainty, hiding the ranks of creatures from view. All Col could glimpse was the occasional bout of flame from the waiting dragons and the movement of shadowy figures passing to and fro across the rough ground.

'Did you spot us from overhead?' Dr Brock asked as he strode towards them out of the fog.

'No,' Col replied, sliding off Skylark.

'Good, that means Coddrington's giant is

doing a good job. Some mist—but not too much: that's what we asked for. So, Col, why are you here?'

Dr Brock gave Col an anxious look. Amongst his other worries, he had been concerned that Col had not recovered from his ordeal.

'You know you can't fight, don't you?'

Col nodded. 'I don't want to fight,' he said quietly.

'Well, you'd better get yourself off home then.'

Col took a deep breath. 'I think this is a trap. I'm convinced it is. Kullervo's trying to lure you out to rescue Connie. It's the way he thinks. He's a hunter. He used me as the bait to catch her. I'm sure he's trying to do the same again.'

Dr Brock gave his words careful consideration, not wanting Col to think he was dismissing him without due thought. 'But there is an important difference this time. You were no use to him other than as bait, but Connie's another story. He's got what he wanted—he's got Connie. He doesn't need to set any further traps: all he has to do now is work on her until she gives in to him.'

'But we both know that she won't!' Col clenched his fists by his side, angered that everyone seemed so quick to doubt his friend.

'We don't know that for certain,' said Dr Brock. 'You said yourself he had a power to make you do his will.'

'I know, but I trust her. I mean I trust *in* her. I think she won't allow him to take her over as he was able to take me over. I was taken by ambush; she'll fight every inch of the way with him. She won't have given in—not yet.'

'What are you saying, Col?' Something of Col's determined belief in Connie was being transmitted to Dr Brock. Looking at the boy, he felt ashamed that he had himself begun to question his own judgement about Connie in the face of the Trustees' doubts.

'I'm saying that if she hasn't given in—which she hasn't—then Kullervo won't be able to use her powers today. He's here for another reason—he's here to bring all of this out into the open—to force us to fight him.' Col waved his hand at the creatures swathed in the friendly mist.

'Come with me,' Dr Brock said, clapping a hand on Col's back and steering him into the heart of the fog. 'I have a terrible feeling you may be right.'

The Trustees were gathered around a wizen thorn tree that dripped with dew, listening to Col, Skylark, Dr Brock, and Argot. Only Gard's companion, Frederick Coney, was absent: he was now too frail to take active part in Society meetings.

Kira shivered and huddled closer to Windfoal.

'So, Col, you are saying that we are walking into a trap. But what I want to know is what choice do we have? There is no other way: we must use the forces we have to prevent worse harm.'

Col had spent the night thinking about this too.

'It might come to that,' he said, meeting Kira's dark brown eyes steadily, 'but I think we should at least try something else first.'

'What?' grunted Gard, swinging his hammer impatiently at the ground.

'The unexpected. I think we should try to rescue Connie without Kullervo realizing what's happening. If he's got her in the wood, then we need to get in there too, find her, and bring her out.'

'Yes, but how?' asked Kinga, leaning against Morjik's warm shoulder and yawning with fatigue. None of the dragon riders had slept for days, so intensive had been their search for Connie. 'How will you get past his spies?'

'I have an idea about that. All I need is Skylark, Argand, and Godiva Lionheart, if she'll help.'

'Argand? Why do you need the golden dragon?' Kinga asked sharply, her tiredness evaporating as she sprang to defend one of her own companion species.

'She's Connie's companion so will be able to sense her; she's small; she'll be able to go places

Skylark and I can't. And besides, she wants to come.'

A small golden snout peeped out from behind Argot's tail, eyes blinking shyly at the company.

'I don't know about Godiva,' said Dr Brock frowning. 'She wouldn't say what she thought when I left her at the Mastersons. Are you sure you need her?'

'Well, it would be useful to have a wood sprite companion if I'm searching in Mallins Wood for Connie. I could do it without her, but . . .'

'I'll see if I can persuade her. It would be a big step for her if she agrees.'

All that was needed now was the go-ahead from the Trustees. Col saw them exchange doubtful looks. Only Eagle-Child and Storm-Bird seemed convinced as they nodded guardedly at each other.

'Look, just give me until midday—if Kullervo hasn't launched his own attack before then. After that, send in your troops if you must.' There was a new tone to Col's voice this morning. It commanded respect from the adults listening to him. There was a pause and in that moment of quiet, like a shift in the direction of the wind, the balance imperceptibly tipped in his favour.

'You have our permission to try,' said Kinga gravely.

'Not so fast!' Mack Clamworthy strode into the ring. Hearing that his son was in the camp and suspecting he would be thinking of doing something rash to save his friend, Mack had been listening to all that had passed from the far side of the thorn tree. 'I'm not letting my son run off into danger on his own!'

'Then you'll just have to come with me, won't you, Dad?' Col grinned.

Anneena was interrupted at breakfast by a knock at the back door. Her mother opened it to discover Col and Mack standing on the step. Mack was looking awkwardly into the mid-distance but Col seemed untroubled by arriving unannounced at such an early hour.

'Are you feeling better now, Col?' Mrs Nuruddin asked, stepping back to let them in. 'I do hope so. Anneena's been so anxious about you—and now there's Connie to worry about.'

'I'm OK, thanks,' Col said. 'Hi, Anneena.'

'Hi, Col,' she replied, putting down the piece of toast and staring at him in wonder. 'What's up? Not Connie, is it?'

'Sorry, no. It's just that Dad and I, we've changed our minds—at least I have. We want to be in the pageant this morning, if it's not too late.'

'Do we?' exclaimed Mack. This was news to him.

Anneena looked delighted. 'That'd be great. I've got just the costume for you, Col. But I'm not sure about your father.' She looked pensively at the broad-shouldered man towering over Col.

'Well, in that case, perhaps I could just watch . . .' Mack began.

'No, you won't,' Col hissed fiercely. 'If you want to be there, you've got to come in costume.'

Anneena looked at them in puzzlement as they exchanged terse words in an undertone. Finally, Mack nodded and turned back to her.

'OK, darling, I'll take whatever you've got.'

Anneena winced at the 'darling' but let it pass. 'In that case, you'll have to make do with the only man's costume I've got left. Even so, it might be a bit small.'

'Lead on, fair damsel,' Mack said with a mocking bow but Col was too preoccupied even to groan at his father's behaviour.

Ten minutes later, Col clanked back into the kitchen, dressed in a shiny suit of lightweight boy's armour. It had a chinking hauberk that fell to his knees, a gleaming breast-plate and helm, topped by a scarlet plume. Anneena came in from the garden shed carrying a scabbard and a small shield emblazoned with a golden lion, which she handed to him.

'That looks great, Col,' she said, 'a perfect fit. But what are you going to do for a horse? Isn't your friend Rat riding Mags? He's going as a page—or so I thought.'

'I've borrowed a horse—you can't ride a pony in armour. Do you have something I can use as a horsecloth? In the pictures I've seen, these medieval chargers always wore the colours of their knights.'

Anneena was pleased to see Col entering into the spirit of the pageant. 'Yes, you're right. Some of the other riders have them too. I think we've got some material left if you don't mind making do. Shall I put it on your horse for you?'

'No,' Col said quickly, 'that won't be necessary.'

An awkward silence fell between them.

'I'm glad you've changed your mind,' Anneena said after a few moments, 'but it's not the same without Connie.'

'No, it's not. But perhaps she'll turn up today. I've got a feeling she won't miss the pageant.' He cleared his throat. 'What's keeping Dad, I wonder? Perhaps he can't get into his armour?'

'It can't be that,' Anneena said with a smile, 'I didn't give him armour.'

'Dad, hurry up!' Col called out.

There was the sound of a door opening somewhere overhead and the scuff of soft shoes on the stairs. The first thing Col saw was a yellow point of a hat, followed by two red ones, and he could now hear the faint jingling of bells. As Mack turned into the hallway, Col saw that his father was looking both furious and embarrassed. He was wearing the red-and-yellow costume of a medieval court jester.

'I'm not wearing this thing in public,' Mack said angrily as he shuffled into the kitchen.

'I'm sorry,' said Anneena, though she could not suppress a grin, 'but it's all I've got left.'

'There's no time to argue, Dad,' said Col. 'If you still want to come with me, it'll have to do. No one will notice when you're part of the procession.'

'Oh, won't they?' Mack said with deep scepticism.

'Have you borrowed a horse as well, Mr Clamworthy?' Anneena asked pleasantly, changing the subject.

'Yeah, an old nag from Mr Masterson. That was all that was left too,' Mack said gloomily. 'A right pair we'll make.'

'Come on, Dad, we've got to get back to the horses.' Col picked up the sword and shield. 'We'll meet you at the beach, Anneena.'

'We're gathering at nine-thirty,' she called after him. 'You've got an hour.'

The motorbike driven by a jester with a knight riding pillion made an interesting spectacle for the morning commuters as it zoomed through Hescombe back to the farm. A number of cars hooted cheekily, but most drivers just stared open-mouthed, wondering if Mack Clamworthy had finally cracked.

'Utter humiliation,' were Mack's first words as he dismounted by the stables. 'I'll never be able to live this one down.'

'This isn't about you,' Col said unsympathetically as he shook out the bundle of cloth Anneena had given him, 'this is about saving Connie.'

Col fastened the swathes of scarlet at the pegasus's withers and stood back to look at the effect. Skylark's wings were hidden but there were two strange bulges either side of the horse that even the cloth could not camouflage.

'What are you going to do about a saddle?' Mack asked. Col never used one when riding a pegasus.

'Do without, of course,' Col replied. 'I s'pose I could always claim that those are saddle bags under the cloth if anyone asks.'

Mack looked doubtful and Skylark whinnied angrily.

'What is wrong with my wings?' the pegasus asked huffily, nudging Col with his nose.

'Absolutely nothing—it's just that you aren't supposed to have them. You've got to behave like a normal horse, remember.'

Mack guessed what the companions were saying to each other. 'You're expecting him to pass himself off as an ordinary beast, are you? Risky, very risky,' he said, sucking his teeth. But at least it goaded Skylark into submitting to the indignity more willingly.

'Tell your father that he'd be surprised what I can do,' he snorted back to Col.

Mack disappeared into the stable and re-emerged mounted on a tired-looking mare with a dull brown coat. On seeing the stallion, she perked her ears forward and picked up her hoofs, giving a flirtatious flick of her scraggy tail. Col's face cracked into a smile as he sensed Skylark's embarrassment, but they had no time for amorous feelings, welcome or otherwise, just now.

'We'll have to go if we're to reach the beach in time,' Col told his father as he swung onto the pegasus's back. 'I wonder if Dr Brock's got anywhere with that old bat.'

'That old bat,' said Godiva sharply, emerging from the house in time to hear Col's unflattering comment, 'has agreed to do what she can. That old bat has accepted that she is quite mad—you all are—but it seems you require my particular sort of madness to save my great-niece.'

Dr Brock appeared at her elbow and held out a helmet. 'Like old times, Iva?' he said with a roguish smile.

'Not quite—I was a good deal more flexible then.' She crammed herself into his sidecar.

'We all were.'

'Yes.' Godiva crossed her hands on her breast, eyes closed, resigned to her position. 'Start this infernal machine of yours and let's get this over with. Tomorrow, if I'm still alive, you can have me put down as a crazy old woman who hears trees speak.'

As she was driven away, a golden missile shot across the farmyard and circled Col's head twice before landing on the crest of his helm. 'Here, Argand, you'll have to hide,' said Col, lifting a corner of the horse-cloth, but she took no notice of a boy who was not a dragon companion. Instead, she lay still, like a carving, her tail curled round the red plume.

Col swore, but he knew that it was pointless trying to communicate with a creature with which he had no bond. He would just have to hope she would behave herself.

Mack had been thinking the same thing. 'That'll have to do,' Mack said. 'It looks quite convincing. No one would suspect her for what she really is—not if she doesn't move, or breathe fire or something.'

Col took off his helm, resting it in front of him. It was uncomfortable with the added weight pressing down on his brows. He wished now he had never asked for the little dragon's help.

'Let's go then,' Col said with resignation, urging his mount forward.

To show the mare what a real thoroughbred could do, Skylark trotted off smartly, leaving her trailing in his dust some distance behind. Col could feel him pulling forward about to leave the ground but then remembering and checking his urge just in time.

After a couple of miles at this brisk pace, they turned out of the quiet country lanes and onto the busier roads leading into Hescombe. Festival goers were streaming in from all over the country, heading up to the site where the stages had been erected, roof racks crammed full of camping gear. Most car drivers gave the pair of riders ample room as they passed, sparing a friendly wave as they cheered the pageant participants on. But one or two sped by without slowing down, provoking Skylark to unleash a stream of invectives.

'You humans need taking down a peg or two,' he muttered to Col. 'Acting as if you own the place!'

'Not thinking of joining Kullervo, are you, mate?' Col asked sourly. 'That's what he thinks too.'

'Of course not. That wasn't what I meant and you know it.'

'Sorry. I'm just . . .'

'You're just worried, tired, and miserable—I know, Companion. But, if we possibly can, we'll save Connie, I promise you.'

The beach was packed with people and horses by the time they arrived just after nine-thirty, a muddle of spectators, participants, and reporters strewn across the strand at the edge of the iron grey sea. Seagulls wheeled overhead, on the watch to see if the unusual crowd would mean rich pickings later. Anneena was ticking off arrivals on her list with her mother while Jane and Mr Nuruddin wandered amongst those in costume, checking everyone had their gear.

'Hey, Col!' Jane said on seeing him clatter down the slipway onto the firm sand. 'You look great! Amazing helmet! That dragon's so cool! Where did you get it?'

'Oh, it's a family heirloom,' he lied, shifting his shield to hide Argand from her admiring gaze.

Col's entrance, accompanied by the miserable-looking jester, attracted the attention of the news reporters, who were on the lookout for eye-catching costumes, and he found himself surrounded by the last thing he wanted: a swarm of photographers. He tried to keep moving so that Skylark's strange shape and the recumbent dragon were not too closely remarked but this became increasingly hard as they pressed closer. The pegasus was getting jittery, not having been among non-Society people before.

'What's your name, boy?' one man called out as flashes from cameras exploded like shooting stars around them.

'Col Clamworthy,' Col said, trying to calm Skylark's nerves with a reassuring pat on his neck.

'No, no, your pageant name, I mean.'

'He's Sir Galahad,' Jane supplied.

'Put on your helmet, Sir Galahad. Let us get a picture of you in full armour. Tell us why you're joining the protest.'

'Er . . .' said Col, momentarily devoid of ideas, his head full of Kullervo and Connie.

'Move back from the horses there!' Mr Nuruddin called, having noticed the difficulty Col was having with Skylark. Anneena's father stepped forward to wave people away, allowing Col space to get through to join the procession, which was assembling further down the beach. Breaking free of the crowd, Col spotted Rat and turned Skylark towards him.

'A friend,' he told Skylark.

'I know,' Skylark replied. 'I can feel it.'

Col wondered what he meant but there was no time to ask as they were level with Rat, who was dressed in a green tabard and mounted on the back of Mags.

'Hey, Col, wicked costume!' grinned Rat. His eyes fell on the horse that towered many hands above Mags. 'Even wickeder horse. Where did you get him?'

'Borrowed him,' Col replied quickly. He reached down and scratched Mags on his poll, the area between his ears, to let him know that he had not forgotten him. His pony twittered with pleasure.

Mack cantered up behind them, his hat drawn low on his brows, giving him a surly look.

'Hello there, Mack,' Rat said at once, quite unperturbed by his extraordinary appearance. 'I see Anneena conned you into wearing that old thing. We all told her that none of us would be seen dead wearing it.'

'That's exactly how I feel,' Mack muttered.

A whistle sounded at the front of the line and the procession began to move down the beach.

Col recognized the lead rider as Mr Masterson, the farmer's ample frame now draped in threadbare king's robes, a gilt crown on his head. The Society had posted him there to keep watch on the procession and lead a retreat should Kullervo attack. Pacing alongside him was the shaggy-haired drummer from *Krafted*, Zed Bailey, pursued by a pack of photographers.

As the procession left the beach to clatter along the High Street, fear of what was to come sharpened Col's senses, making him alive to every detail of the present. Ahead he could see wisps of chiffon blowing about like tiny flags from the tall headdresses of the ladies, the rich colours shining jewel-like against the grey skies of the blustery day. He spotted the fair hair of Shirley whipping about in the wind as she trotted along just behind her father. Lances bobbed like masts over the heads of the participants. His own armour gleamed with dull splendour in the light, reflecting the roofs and trees in ever changing patterns across its surface. He took no pride in it, but welcomed it as a shell he could retreat behind, taking comfort that no one would guess that this young knight was feeling far from courageous.

'Only the foolish feel no fear,' Skylark commented, following Col's internal debate. 'Companion, do you have a plan?'

'Not really,' Col admitted. 'This was as far as it went. I thought I'd get us up there in disguise and then . . . well . . . improvise.'

Mack must have been wondering the same thing because he spurred his horse alongside his son, his bells jingling at every step, and muttered: 'The first thing we need to do is find out where he's holding her. Do you have any idea?'

Col shook his head. 'That's what I'm hoping Connie's great-aunt can help us with. And as soon as we know where to start looking, we'll let Argand loose. She can sniff Connie out for us.'

'*If* we can—look at all these people! I didn't realize there'd be so many,' Mack said, gesturing at the crowd of spectators lining the road up the hill. Zed was stopping to sign autographs for his fans, gathering up even more followers like the Pied Piper.

The procession was now approaching the edge of Mallins Wood where an even bigger crowd was waiting for them. Over to the left, the festival field was decked with flags. A big stage had been erected at the far end. To the right of the road, a line of dark blue uniforms marked where the police were holding the protesters back from the road builders' machinery. Over their heads, Col could see seven or more bright yellow bulldozers waiting for the signal to begin their work.

A council representative strode up and down behind the police line, appealing ineffectually for the crowd to move back and let them pass. His words were met with jeers and boos.

'Tree killer! Leave the wood alone!' shouted one red-haired woman, shaking her fist at him and trying to break through the police cordon.

'Me ma's giving him what for, isn't she?' Rat grinned proudly, watching his mother being restrained by two burly policemen and a police-woman and half carried away.

'Where's your dad?' Col asked curiously, wondering what the rest of the Ratcliff family were up to.

'He's chained himself to one of those trees. You see him—over there. He's got Wolf with him, figuring no one will want to come near.'

'Too right.'

Rat turned in his saddle to look up at Col, having just remembered something.

'Only person—not counting me, of course—who's ever got on with Wolf is that friend of yours, Connie. Ma said the dog acted real strange around her—turned into a right softie. Will she be here, d'you think? I'd like to see her again.'

'Maybe.' Col scanned the crowd to see if he could spot either Connie or his mother, but so far he had found neither of them. Where would

Connie be, he wondered? If Kullervo wanted to tempt the Society out into the open, where would he put her?

The procession jingled to a halt ten metres from the ranks of machines, police, and protesters. The protesters gave a great cheer. Zed rejoined Mr Masterson at the head of the column. Col could see the mock King Arthur looking apprehensively around, alert for any signs of attack. Zed by contrast was relaxed, joking with those around him as he unrolled a speech written on parchment. He stepped up to a podium and tapped the mike.

'My lords and ladies,' he said archly, nodding at the procession, 'people,' he swept his arm expansively to the crowds, 'we are here today to stand up to those who want to destroy this place of outstanding natural beauty.' A great cheer went up from the crowd. 'I hope everyone here—and I'm speaking to you people driving the machines as well—I hope you're asking yourselves what you want to leave future generations. Do you want to leave a dead land of concrete and tarmac where the only moving things are cars; or a land of trees and green fields, filled with wildlife, open to all of us to enjoy?

'I've been told that amongst the trees at danger today is the very oak under which Merlin is sleeping. If you destroy that, you destroy both our past and our future, because the legend says that he's gonna come back one day. Call me superstitious, but if I were you,' (he pointed at the man from the council; the crowd booed) 'I'd think twice before I tried to bulldoze him.

'But our fight today is not one fought with lances and swords but with your voices and your votes. We call upon the council to allow us, the people, to buy Merlin's Wood from them and create here a safe haven for wildlife.

'So I'm announcing here and now the opening of an appeal to save Merlin's Oak. Save Merlin's Wood!'

A great cheer went up from the crowd, accompanied by the noise of swords banging on shields. Argand gave an alarmed hiss, but fortunately the noise was too great for any but Col to hear her.

During the babble of voices that followed the speech, Dr Brock appeared at Col's side, Godiva Lionheart a few paces behind. Dressed in a severe grey suit she looked out of place among the rainbow colours of the carnival procession. Her eyes flicked to Argand, then looked away.

'Any news?' asked Col.

Godiva cleared her throat as if dredging up the words with great reluctance. 'The place you want is in that direction.' She pointed over Rat's head. 'They say that something odd is happening in the old tree in the oak grove.' Her hands were shaking but she was managing fairly well to hide her distress. Col had not forgotten that Dr Brock had told him that she had once denied her own companion—that she'd let her wood sprite die. Today must have been nearly unbearable for her. He thought it said something good about her attachment to her great-niece that she had sacrificed her self-esteem to help.

Rat was listening in on this cryptic conversation with keen interest. 'You must mean Merlin's Oak, lady. That Connie of yours named it,' he told Col. 'The procession is supposed to get there around midday. That's where we're going to make a stand. We won't be moving until the bulldozers retreat.'

Col swiftly put on his helm, buckling it firmly under his chin, Argand swaying precariously above.

'Don't wait for me,' he said and spurred Skylark forward. He broke from the ranks of the riders in a streak of silver, white, and red, galloping up the line. The crowd gave a great cheer, thinking this was all part of the show. Stirred by a sudden impulse, Col seized a lance from the stunned rider playing Sir Launcelot and charged

267

off into the trees. Mack, as surprised as everyone else by his son's move, sat still for a moment, then kicked his horse in pursuit. This time the crowd laughed as well as cheered.

Anneena, standing at the head of the procession, watched these developments with dismay. Her carefully plotted script was being ruined by the unexpected actions of the Clamworthys.

'What's he up to?' asked Anneena's sister Rupa, who was there to report for her newspaper. A photographer stood beside her, his camera clicking furiously to catch the drama.

'I'm not sure,' Anneena admitted. 'He's been acting weird since Connie went missing—since he went missing himself, in fact. Perhaps it's all got too much for him.'

'In that case,' said Rupa, 'we'd better leave him alone. His dad will look after him.'

Zed sauntered over. 'That was cool. Who are they?'

'Just a couple of local characters,' said Rupa. 'Hadn't we better get on?'

Zed nodded. 'You're right. We're opening the festival in a couple of hours—let's wrap this up.'

King Arthur raised his hand and the procession jingled into life again, following the road around the edge of the wood.

16
Merlin's Oak

The branch Connie clung to felt danger-
ously thin. Her eyes were closed tight as
every time she risked a peek at what was
happening around her, she was overcome with a
wave of fear and her trembling became uncon-
trollable. She could only ever endure heights
when bonded with a flying creature. On her own,
all her dread returned. Clinging on with her
bound hands, she dared not move as every
breath of wind made the branch sway to and fro
with an ominous creak. A kind of paralysis had
struck Connie; her mind could think of nothing
but her terror of heights. She could hear faint
cheers and voices some distance away but did
not realize what they meant. All she knew was

that Kullervo had left her like a flightless fledg-
ling stranded at the top of the oak, staked out
as bait for the first predator to pass by. In this
case, the hunter the shape-shifter hoped to catch
was the Society. While she would like nothing
better than a friendly squadron of dragons to
swoop out of the skies, she knew she should not
wish it as that was exactly what he wanted.

A rustling sounded close by her head and
Connie felt the presence of another creature: not
Kullervo and his allies, hiding below, waiting to
attack anyone who approached the tree on foot
or from the sky, but an earthy nature she had
experienced once before. Opening her eyes a
crack, she saw the wood sprite staring at her
with wonder, its leafy pelt now showing many
more patches of grey skin. It reached out a paw
and touched her shoulder. Immediately, Connie
was swept with the calming ebb and flow of the
tree's sap.

'Universal, you are in danger,' the wood sprite
told her, stroking her shoulder gently. 'You
are too high. There is no way down from here
but one.'

'I know,' replied Connie grimly, 'that of the
acorn—to drop.'

'And there are creatures below; dark creatures
that are hiding in my branches uninvited.'

Connie closed her eyes again for a moment and turned her thoughts to the tree's core, travelling down its stem. On one of the lower branches she felt the smooth touch of the gorgon's hands, grasping the bark. Further down, deep in the roots, there were other creatures hidden, ones she had not yet encountered, sprites of stone. Kullervo had arrayed his forces for an ambush. But where was he? His voice was stilled in her head, yet she knew that he could not be far away. The pieces were set for a battle that she was powerless to stop. It seemed likely that in a short while, the world would never be the same again. The mythical creatures would be forced into the open. They would kill each other in defence of her and the crowds of people in the wood, a sacrifice that would turn many in the mythical world irrevocably against the Society. It would be all her fault. If only she had not been so foolish as to walk into Kullervo's trap! At least she could try to save one creature.

'Hide yourself,' she urged the sprite. 'Danger approaches. Do not go near the creature at the base of your tree. Avoid her eyes.'

The wood sprite snuffed the air. 'Yes, danger does approach.' With a flick of its long tail, the sprite scampered down the trunk and disappeared into a crack.

Having done what she could, Connie grasped the branch more firmly in her hands and waited for the battle to begin.

Once out of sight of the crowd, Col slowed Skylark to a trot.

'We'd better be more careful,' he told the pegasus. 'Kullervo is bound to have set some lookouts. We don't know who or what we'll have to get past.'

'Where are we going?' Skylark asked.

'Merlin's Oak.'

There was a flap of wings and a scratching noise from the top of Col's helm. With a leap that pushed down on his head, Argand took off into the air, flashing gold amongst the branches.

'Off to find the universal,' observed Skylark. 'Let us follow her. She may have sensed her presence.'

Col nodded and together they wound their way through the thickets of trees, chasing the golden spark that darted ahead. Argand appeared to want them to follow her for each time she disappeared from sight she would double back and wait for them to catch her up.

'I think Kullervo will be expecting a full blown assault,' Col told Skylark as they followed their guide. 'He's aware that I've seen his army, so he knows that the Society believes Connie's well defended. If I'm right, I don't think he'll be looking out for a single human on a horse. I'm hoping he'll think we are just strays from the procession and not unleash his attack on us.'

'I hope so too,' Skylark agreed wryly. 'But why not attack at once? What is he waiting for?'

'I think he'll want the road builders to make the first move before he acts to prove to mythical creatures that he *had* to fight us. He's probably waiting for the bulldozers to start rolling—that'll show we didn't stop them tearing down the wood but we did act when he attacked the people. That'll turn many of you away from us humans. It'll destroy the Society— rip it apart. I'm guessing he's got his forces hidden somewhere deeper in the wood, waiting for his signal to strike.'

'Hoping and guessing, Companion, you trust much to luck and your understanding of Kullervo.'

'Well, if there is one thing I can claim to know,' Col said with a shudder, 'it's the mind of Kullervo. He lived in me for many days, remember. He's dark and devious. He's not interested in a straight fight—he wants to trick us into being the bad guys—it'll amuse him to make us hated by you creatures. He'll be taking great pleasure in observing us all perform the parts he's given us. I expect he's somewhere up there, watching the skies for the first squadron of dragons, bursting to bring this all out in front of the cameras.'

The beech trees were giving way to thickets of oak and holly. The dark green glossy spikes of the holly leaves tugged at the horsecloth. Col ripped it free, leaving strands of scarlet waving in the wind. After a hundred metres of heavy going, they broke out into a wide space under the boughs of an old tree with the girth of a bull elephant and bark as wrinkled as elephant skin. A thick, dark-green canopy of leaves, shot through with autumn gold, rustled overhead. It seemed very quiet and still after the bustle and noise of the procession. There was no sign of Connie.

Suddenly, Argand sped back to them, hissing excitedly, before shooting up into the air and out of view.

'What do you think that means?' Col wondered, his heart picking up its pace as he sensed peril near at hand.

'I think it means we are in danger—mortal danger.' Skylark gave a frightened whinny, nostrils flaring, and began to back away. 'I smell that creature.'

Col looked wildly around but could see nothing. He too could now smell something—the acrid scent he associated with the gorgon's cave. It was strong. The gorgon must be very close, but he could see no sign of her. The wood was suspiciously silent, the only sound coming from the leaves whispering to each other in the old oak tree they were under.

Then, with a screech like a whistling kettle, Argand dived out of the sky, colliding with Col's helm, bringing the visor crashing down over his eyes. Col did not need to be a companion to dragons to know what that meant.

'Move!' he urged Skylark.

The pegasus bounded forward. Crash! Out of the branches above them leapt the gorgon, eyes blazing, snake-hair writhing to bite Col. He ducked. She missed him by a hair's breadth and fell to the forest floor, momentarily dazed by her fall. Col had only a second in which to act.

'Don't look at her!' he warned Skylark as he turned his mount to face the gorgon. 'We're going to charge her down.'

With the lance held firmly under his arm, Col crouched low on Skylark's back. He could see very little through his visor. Holding up his tin shield he glimpsed the reflection of the gorgon getting to her feet and raising her face to him.

'Charge!' he yelled, shutting his eyes tightly against her gaze.

Skylark sprang forwards, pounding the turf with heavy hoofs. With a shuddering jolt the lance collided with something hard. Col was thrown by the impact. His armour clanged as he hit the stony ground at the roots of the tree and his helm rolled off into the bracken. Staring up into the canopy above for a few confused moments, Col wondered what had happened. Why was the gorgon not leaping on him as he lay defenceless on the ground? Had he managed to hit her? Rolling painfully over, he risked a look to his right and saw the gorgon slumped at the foot of the tree, her bronze wings crumpled around her and the lance in two pieces by her side. The lance must have thrown her back against the tree when he struck and she was either stunned or . . . or dead?

Skylark galloped back to his companion, bursting through the trees like a white light into the dark shadows under the oak.

'Are you all right?' he asked anxiously, nuzzling Col to see if he was injured.

'Fine—just winded.' Col clambered back to his feet unsteadily and then pulled himself onto the pegasus's back. 'I think this means that we've found Connie. But we'll have to go up to get her.

There's a clearing nearby—we can take off from there.'

Col steered Skylark to the woodland spot where he and Rat had first seen his mother all those weeks ago. On finding the way open before him, Skylark picked up his pace.

'At last!' he rejoiced as he unfurled his wings. The scarlet cloth flapped back over Col's legs as Skylark spiralled upwards.

'Not too high!' Col warned. 'We don't want the people to see, or we might as well have called in the dragons.'

Levelling out, Skylark flew at treetop height, skimming across the forest roof. A flicker of gold flashed ahead and Col cried out:

'There she is!'

Skylark saw Connie clinging to her frail perch with Argand dancing at her side. The dragonet had a piece of rope like a long worm dangling from her jaws. The pegasus kicked towards them, skilfully dodging in and out of branches that stretched up to the sky as if to grasp his legs and prevent him reaching the universal.

'Col!' Connie screamed. 'Skylark! Be careful!'

Skylark swerved down towards her, Col already reaching out to pull her to safety.

'Behind you!' she shrieked.

Col caught a glimpse of dark wings soaring towards him but he was not going to break off their rescue attempt now. He snatched at Connie's outstretched hand as they swooped past; as he did so he clung onto a thick fistful of Skylark's mane to stop them both sliding off. The pegasus climbed up with difficulty because Connie was now dangling over his shoulder, impeding his left wing.

'Try and swing up!' Col shouted at Connie who was hanging on, white faced, by one hand. He could feel her palm beginning to slip out of his grip. 'Grab my belt.' Connie flailed about in the air trying to grasp hold of something, pulled on the scarlet cloth but it ripped.

At that moment, a midnight blue eagle dropped out of the sky like an arrow flying to its target, talons stretched out to tear at the pegasus who had had the audacity to slip under its guard. One talon raked across Skylark's hindquarters, leaving a bright red trail against the white flesh. The pegasus reared in pain, Col struggled to retain his seat—and Connie's hand slid from his grasp.

'Connie!' Col almost flung himself after her as he watched his friend fall backwards towards the trees, her arms and legs thrashing helplessly in the air.

But then something strange seemed to be happening to her: her descent was slowed, she became wrapped in a blue mist and swirled this way and that like an autumn leaf carried on the breeze. She disappeared from view into the trees.

'We must land!' Col shouted urgently.

Skylark turned and prepared to descend. But before he had got far, a blue-black pegasus burst out of the trees and came charging towards them, nostrils flaring and his fiery eyes blazing at them with hatred. His wings swept great gusts of air down onto the branches below, driving flurries of brown leaves up into the sky as if they had been struck by a tornado.

'You think you have been so clever, boy,' Kullervo sneered at Col, his detested voice ringing through Col's mind as he forced entry again, trespassing on the bond between pegasus and rider. Col crumpled forward onto Skylark's neck, disabled by an intense pain in his temples. 'You forget—I know you too well to be caught out by any trick of yours.'

But this time, Col was not alone: Skylark too could hear the voice and whinnied angrily.

'Boy? He is no boy of yours!' Skylark declared, stamping out the voice that had infiltrated his bond with Col.

'Die then, if you will, horseboy!' Kullervo screamed as he quit Col's mind, his counterfeit presence no match for the real thing. 'There is no universal to save you now!'

His mind emptied of Kullervo's polluting presence and his pain receding, Col turned in his seat to see the pegasus striding through the air towards them, his ebony hoofs raised to strike, flecks of foam flying from his open mouth. Col knew then that Kullervo would not rest until both he and Skylark were dead. But having passed through so much anxiety today, brought face to face with the worst, Col was now beyond fear. He and Skylark had trained for just such an extremity: it was time to test if they had learnt their lesson well.

'Thessalonian roll!' he commanded and Skylark swerved hard to the right.

Kullervo abandoned Connie at the foot of the tree once he had carried her safely to ground. He was burning with anger, eager to return to punish the pegasus and rider, so he called on the stone sprites hiding in the roots of the tree to keep Connie there for him. His task would not take long; he would be back to deal with her, he had told them. On his call, grey fungal growths extruded from the soil, dividing and curling into shapes like the emaciated hands of a corpse.

Driven by an unerring instinct for warm flesh, they gripped her ankles, pinching spitefully, anchoring her to the spot. Before Connie managed to raise her shield, she caught a glimpse of the cold nature of the creature that held her, sensing how it spent its days gnawing insatiably through the inner chambers of the earth. It hated warm blood and flesh and with its touch tried to freeze her to be like itself.

Caught unprepared, Connie found the cold had crept to her ankles before she realized: it was like standing in a pool of iced water, numbing all sensation. Grappling for her shield, she repelled the attack forcefully, driving the cold back into the earth so that frosted particles now glistened on the mossy stones under her feet. The inner assault beaten, and desperate to return to help her friends, Connie reached down to prise herself free, only to have her hand grasped by a third fist thrust up out of the flinty soil.

This was how Mack found her when he crashed his way through the trees, having left his horse back amongst the beeches. He had been following the trail of tattered scarlet cloth left by Skylark but got more than he bargained for when he stumbled upon Connie.

'What the hell!' he exclaimed, staring with horror at Connie, the stone hands, and the spread-eagled gorgon. 'What's been going on here?'

'Don't come any nearer,' Connie shouted. 'There are stone sprites everywhere in the roots of this tree.'

He halted in the very act of running to her side.

'How can I free you?' he asked, looking desperately about for inspiration.

'Don't worry about me; worry about Col and Skylark. They're fighting Kullervo up there!'

Further words were interrupted by someone else stumbling into the space at the foot of the tree. Connie looked round to see a woman sprinting across to the fallen gorgon, but she stopped short on seeing them. It was Cassandra.

17
Stone Sprites

'You evil snake!' Mack shouted at his ex-wife. 'You'll pay for what you've done!' He took a step towards her, but she was undaunted, her sole aim to reach her fallen companion. She dodged past him and ran towards the trunk. Mack lurched after her.

'Don't!' Connie yelled, but too late: a crop of stony fingers burst through the soil like the spears of winter wheat, grasping the ankles of both Cassandra and Mack.

'Let go!' Cassandra screamed at them. 'I'm on your side!' But stone sprites did not listen to humans who were not their companions; they hated pounding feet and the heat of human touch and did not care for 'sides'.

'Get off!' yelled Mack, trying to fight the fingers which had gripped his shoes. 'What are they doing?' he asked, now panic-stricken as he felt their cold creep up his body. He turned to Connie, his eyes wide with alarm. Cassandra moaned.

'It's their touch—they are trying to make you as cold as they are. They only like corpses, not living bodies.' Connie did not want to explain that she could hold the sprites off with her shield for herself but was unable to aid them at this distance.

Mack, infuriated by his powerlessness, rounded on the only object to hand on which he could vent his anger. 'You . . . you stupid cow! Don't you know that your precious Kullervo is trying to kill our son up there!' He jerked his head to the sky above but the screen of leaves hid all that was happening from them.

His words were like a slap in the face for Cassandra. She stopped trying to reach out to the gorgon and now stared frantically up. 'No! It can't be true! He promised he wouldn't hurt my young!'

'Ha! You believed the promises of that shape-shifting liar! You're even dumber than you look, Cassie. Aargh!' Mack's last cry had nothing to do with her but the cold that had crept to his waist, pinching his stomach in its grip.

'If I'm so dumb, why are you also standing here being turned to ice, huh? Not such a big man now, are you?' Though Cassandra was suffering, she seemed to derive vindictive pleasure from the fact that Mack was enduring the same pain and was not above taunting him with it.

'Will you both shut up!' Connie said with uncharacteristic anger, driven to distraction by the bickering of the pair. Her back was aching as the stone sprite pulled on her wrist to bend her closer to the ground. 'You're both about to die if I can't think of a way to help you—and I can't think if you're both arguing with each other. So just be quiet!'

They wheeled round to look at her in surprise, torn from their private feuding by her blunt words.

'These things kill?' Mack asked hesitantly.

Connie nodded curtly, biting her bottom lip as she tried to remember something from her reading that would help. But she had learned so little, barely scratched the surface of what she needed to know as a universal. If only she had been allowed to continue her training properly!

Cassandra had fallen very quiet. 'I want you to understand, Mack, I never wanted Colin to get hurt,' she muttered, barely audibly, to Mack.

'What?'

'I had to save the gorgon; Kullervo was the only one who'd help us. What good was the Society wringing its hands when she was about to be crushed?' Cassandra stopped. A horse screamed overhead. 'What was that?'

'Skylark!' shrieked Connie, feeling the pegasus's pain as if it were her own. Frantically, she redoubled her efforts to free herself.

'Skylark?' echoed Cassandra. 'It's true then? They're fighting him up there?'

'Of course, it's true. Kullervo likes killing—that's all he likes. It looks to me as if you've got to decide if your loyalty lies with her,' Mack nodded stiffly at the gorgon, 'or with our boy.'

'I . . . I can't choose,' whispered Cassandra, tears streaming down her pale cheeks.

Mack sighed, but with difficulty as the cold had now reached his lungs and he was struggling to breathe.

'Perhaps you won't have time to choose. But at least it looks as if your gorgon will pull through,' he said in a hoarse whisper. A snake-lock was beginning to stir.

'That's good,' Cassandra said huskily. 'She's the last of her kind. I did it for her.'

'I know.'

Cassandra looked over at Mack with new respect. 'You knew?'

'Of course I did. But that doesn't mean I think you were right.'

Connie had not been listening to this exchange but had sunk deep into the earth to plead with the stone sprites. They had recognized her, but refused to relent. Instead they gnawed at the edge of her shield, attempting to lure her to join them.

'Darkness, silence, emptiness—these are what we offer you!' they called to her.

Chilled by their words and their hunger for oblivion, Connie gave up in disgust. She groped her way to the surface, reaching out to the tree roots to guide her back. The living energy of the oak flowed like a healing spring through her. She heard the wood sprite in her mind again.

'Companion, you are sad.'

'Yes, these people will die—will be felled—unless I can help them,' she told it. Connie opened her eyes to hear the leaves whispering overhead and to see the lower branches swaying: the tree itself was disturbed by the evil taking place in its shelter.

'That must not be,' the leaves whispered.

Connie felt something move at her feet. Fearing to see yet more stone fingers reaching out to grip her, she looked down. A root was breaking through the earth and slowly sliding towards the hand that grasped her wrist. It was like watching the film of the growth of many seasons speeded up so that it happened in a few moments. Two more earthy tendrils were winding towards the fingers clasped around her legs. The roots twisted themselves around the hands, seeking out minute cracks in their surface. Once any weakness was found, the tendrils burrowed in and began to split the stone apart. She could feel the rock creaking as it resisted the inexorable pressure of the tree, but suddenly the hands cracked apart with an explosion that sent clouds of dust into the air. She was free.

Connie leapt away from the ground where stone sprites lurked and then looked back to see how the other captives were faring. Tree roots had just freed Mack and he was now pulling Cassandra clear as the last hand holding her was destroyed. Clouds of choking dust floated on the breeze, leaving them all covered in a thin film of the white grit as if they had been fighting each other with flour.

'Right,' Mack gasped, taking deep breaths into his starved lungs. 'What are we going to do to save Col?'

Connie reached out in thought for a moment, trying to sense what was happening above them. She could feel Kullervo's hate spilling out across the skies like a dark miasma. The pursuit was still on.

'We need a weapon to use against him,' she said. 'Kullervo's still hunting them.'

'You defeated him last time,' Mack said looking at her with new-found confidence. 'Simple—you can do whatever you did then again.'

'I can't—not unless he turns his anger on me and at the moment it's directed at Col and Skylark. I've no power myself; I can only use the power of others.'

Silence fell. The three of them turned to the gorgon.

Skylark came out of his swerve to see that his sudden move had wrong-footed Kullervo. The dark pegasus had crashed his hoofs into the topmost branches of a beech, sending showers of splinters into the air. Skylark had gained some ground but did not know what to do with it.

'Where shall we go?' he asked his companion.

'We must draw him away from Connie and towards help,' Col replied. 'Let's head for the moor.'

'What about the procession—they'll see us!'

'I really don't care. My plan's failed: the Society will have to come into the open now.'

Skylark kicked north but even he, one of the swiftest of his kind, was too slow to dream of outpacing Kullervo. Their enemy had shifted shape to that of a weather giant. He loomed in front of them, cutting off their escape—a storm cloud crowned with a thorny wreath of lightning that flickered with savage barbs.

'Not good,' Col muttered.

The weather giant opened his dark mouth and howled at them, blowing Skylark back in the gale so that the pegasus was standing in mid-air on his hind legs, wings flapping desperately to stop himself tumbling backwards. Col flung his arms around Skylark's neck, clinging to stay on.

'Hold tight—Athenian dive!' Skylark panted. Retracting his wings abruptly, the pegasus allowed the wind to flip him right over then he fell head-first towards the ground, twisting and turning like a sycamore seed. Once out of the slipstream of the wind, Skylark unfurled his wings and struggled to convert the spiralling plunge to a controlled glide. Col could do nothing as all his energy was absorbed in trying to stay on the horse's back. Finally, Skylark's wings took control and his spinning slowed. He pulled out of the dive, but not before he had crashed his knees into the branches of a pine tree and scored his underbelly with deep gashes.

His mount injured, Col looked desperately for a place to run.

'We'll have to return to the clearing and land—try to lose him on the ground!' Col said.

Skylark did not reply as he fought his pain. He turned to head back the way they had come. But they had not lost Kullervo so easily: a dragon with scales glistening like wet slate emerged from the storm cloud, sucking the dark matter up in a long tail behind it as Kullervo took his new shape. Thwack! With almost lazy ease, the dragon's tail curled round and hit Col squarely on his back, gouging into the chainmail like a knife through butter. Col was catapulted over Skylark's head and fell between his striding hoofs, narrowly missing being struck. He landed with a splintering crash in the branches at the top of the old oak. The impact of his fall smashed the frail bough Connie had clung to and he slid down to rest at a fork in the trunk, winded, bruised, and bleeding from numerous cuts.

The dragon's tail whipped round for a second blow and hit Skylark's right wing. Col caught a glimpse of Skylark tumbling out of the sky in a sickening repetition of what had happened to the kestrel, his broken limb trailing helplessly as he plunged from sight. One enemy down, Kullervo turned to concentrate all his malice on Col.

Cassandra and Connie followed the line of a thick tree root to reach the gorgon in safety. Kneeling beside the creature, Cassandra gently stroked her snake-hair: more of them were moving now as their host fought her way back to consciousness.

'Get out of the way, Mack,' Cassandra called over to him briskly, 'she won't be in a good mood when she wakes up.'

'Yeah, too right,' Mack said, backing away. 'It would be just my luck to escape freezing to death only to be turned to stone by your friend here.'

Cassandra bent her head over the gorgon, closed her eyes and pressed her hand against the creature's forehead, summoning her back. The snake-locks slithered towards Cassandra's curtain of hair, winding around her ringlets, enmeshing themselves in an embrace with each blonde strand. At the same moment, the blue eyes of Cassandra and the dark eyes of the gorgon snapped open and stared deep into each other. A perfect connection had been made and Cassandra was now immune to the killing power of the gaze. They stayed like this for some minutes, Connie fretting at every second that passed, worrying about Col, but knowing that this could not be hurried. Dazed and angry as the gorgon would be on waking, it was by no means certain that she would agree to help them against Kullervo, not even to save the offspring of her companion. Finally, the snake-locks unwound themselves and the pair broke off their silent communion.

Cassandra turned to Connie. 'I've pleaded with her to save my hatchling. She . . . she didn't want to at first but I think she now understands how important it is to me. She said she'll help. But you must bond with her as you saw me do.'

'OK,' said Connie bravely. 'But how are we to get up there together? Can she carry me?'

Cassandra shook her head. 'Her wings are for gliding only. She will climb: you'll have to do the same.'

'Right.' But it was far from 'right' as Connie quailed at the thought of leaving the ground again.

Mack, who had been listening some metres away with his hands clasped firmly over his eyes, called over to Connie.

'I'll help you climb, Connie. Just hurry up will you!'

Connie knew he was right: she must hesitate no longer. 'So do we bond or climb first?' she asked Cassandra.

'Climb.'

Cassandra helped the gorgon to stand up. A large black bruise on the creature's scaly chest showed where Col's lance had struck. Wincing with pain, the gorgon turned to the tree as if to embrace it.

'Wait!' Connie cried, hurrying forward. 'We must ask permission from the oak.' Concentrating for a moment, she rapidly sought out the wood sprite. It was not far away, watching events as they unfolded beneath its boughs.

'Climb,' it said and bounded up the trunk ahead of them.

Connie nodded to the gorgon and the creature began to ascend, winding herself around the branches, not climbing but slithering up the tree.

'Is she gone?' Mack called out.

'She's gone,' Cassandra confirmed.

'Right then, here you go,' he said to Connie, 'I'll give you a leg up.' He cradled Connie's foot in his cupped hands and hoisted her up to the lowest branch. Connie swung her leg over and looked up, bewildered by the criss-crossing black boughs amid green and yellow leaves above. Which route should she choose? The gorgon was already high, gliding smoothly through the leaves, barely disturbing them with her passage. Connie reached up to the nearest branch on a fork in the trunk to the left but heard a creaking squeak to her right. The wood sprite was sitting on a higher branch, chattering urgently at her, clearly telling her that her choice was bad. She reached her hand out towards the limb it was sitting on and it ceased squeaking and bounded up to the next level. The branch she should move to next, however, was too far for her to reach by stretching. How could she possibly make this climb?

Then Mack pulled himself up onto the bough beside her.

'All right, darling,' he said cheerfully, seeing her terrified face. 'I told you I'd lend a hand. Lean out and I'll make sure you don't fall. Can't go losing our universal after all the hassle we've had saving you, can we?'

For the second time that morning, Col lay on his back looking up, but on this occasion the prospect was much grimmer. His vision was filled by a blue-black dragon slowly gliding down towards him out of the grey skies, its eyes contemplating him with cold joy. Would it burn him or bite him, Col wondered vaguely? His only hope now was that the end would come swiftly.

A flash of gold streaked across his sight and

the progress of the dragon was halted, distracted by a new nuisance. A tiny creature was darting around its head, too fast to be properly seen, like a fly worrying a bull. The dragon raised a claw to swat it away but then bellowed in pain. A searing stream of fire had shot from the creature's mouth and burnt the dragon's snout. Furious at this attack, the dragon drew deep on its stores of fire and spouted a blast of flames at the creature, catching it with the full force of its blaze. The creature just danced in the flames, taunting the beast. The dragon drew back its long neck to inhale deeply, then rammed it forward, jaws open wide, breathing a second river of white-hot fire over the strange creature, the tips of the flames scorching the branch near to Col's head, sending up a cloud of sparks. The only reply the creature made was to return its own small puff of fire, singeing the dragon's forked tongue.

'Argand!' Col said in wonder, both terrified and impressed by the dragonet's audacity.

'Col!'

He heard a shout below. It sounded like his father but he could not tear his eyes away from the unequal combat overhead.

'I'm here!' he shouted back.

'We're coming for you. Just hang on! Don't look down—the gorgon's with us.'

Col did not need to be told twice. He clung to the tree, his knuckles white, watching the dragon being driven into madness by the persistence of the tiny attacker. But suddenly the dragon disappeared, dissolving into dark blue mist, leaving Argand flying in a bewildering cloud.

'Watch out!' Col called out quite uselessly as the dragonet would not listen to him. 'He'll take shape again!'

The mist spun itself around Argand, reshaping into the cruel beak, sleek head, wings, and lion's claws of a griffin. With a swipe of a talon, Kullervo knocked the dragonet from the sky, sending her spinning into the treetops like a shuttlecock. With a grating caw, the griffin turned back to its main quarry.

18
Choices

Hauling herself onto a branch two-thirds of the way up the tree, Connie could now see Col's armour shining above her head. The sparse leaf cover at the summit of the wind-ravaged oak no longer obscured the fight in the air. She could also see the flash of gold dancing around the black jaws of the dragon and realized that Argand was doing all she could to buy some time for her.

'This is far enough,' she called down to Mack, waiting on the branch below. 'Stay there—I'll summon the gorgon.' Connie looked anxiously around, wondering where the creature had concealed herself.

'You have to drum on the branch,' Mack

shouted, seeing her hesitation, 'at least, that's what Cassie used to do.'

Connie nodded and, gripping the branch with her knees, began to thump on the bark with her fists. Almost immediately, a bronze body unwound itself from a broad limb jutting out from the trunk, and slid along the branch to her. Connie tried to restrain her urge to flinch as the creature approached, but she could not help wondering, even if it were too late to ask such questions, if the creature could be trusted? To whom would the gorgon be loyal: Kullervo or Cassandra? It would be so easy for her to use her gaze to immobilize Connie, kill Col and Mack, finishing Kullervo's task for him and earning his gratitude. Would that be her choice?

The gorgon reached out a hand and touched Connie's forehead with her dry fingers. What would come, would come, Connie thought fatalistically, and bowed her head forward, eyes closed. She felt snakes sliding over her shoulders, up her neck, and twisting themselves in her dark hair, their skin whispering against her head and their soft voices hissing in her ears. Her bond with the gorgon cracked out of its shell. She felt herself begin to elongate, twisting and turning in a new skin, shedding her old one, which now seemed absurdly irrelevant to the serpentine world she was embracing. Sliding forward, every part of her in contact with this world, snuffing its scent, feeling each feature of its surface ripple under her, she plunged deeper. At the heart of the gorgon lay a core of adamant quarried from the bones of the earth. Here lived the power to sear through flesh and turn it to stone, fossilizing in an instant what normally took the earth eons to achieve. She felt the beautiful simplicity of petrifying enemies so that she could then glide over them with no danger. Connie slithered to greet this power, to touch it . . .

Her eyes opened with a suddenness that took her by surprise. She found she was staring deep into the black irises of the gorgon, seeing her own face reflected in them. The gorgon's lips were curled in a cruel smile, as through their bond she could now hear Connie's doubts and fears.

'You will help, won't you?' Connie pleaded.

'Perhaps,' the gorgon replied elusively, her deepest thoughts sliding beyond Connie's grasp as the snake-locks released their hold and she parted from the universal.

There was an explosive crack overhead and Connie looked up to see Argand falling in a shower of golden sparks through the twigs of a nearby tree, squealing with indignation. It was time. Clinging to the trunk, Connie pulled herself to her feet and the gorgon slid to the far side, winding herself once more around a thick bough.

'Kullervo!' Connie called out to the dark presence that was now never far from her mind. She had to goad him, deflect his attention away from Col. 'You coward—picking on a boy and a dragonet! So brave, so very brave, when you know they don't have powers to match you!'

The griffin hovered above the boy, its talons stretched out to pluck him from the branch. Connie could sense that he was listening to her.

'Why don't you pick on someone your own size for once?' she called out.

The boy could wait. He was going nowhere. Kullervo turned towards Connie, nimbly gliding down to land on the end of the branch she was balanced on, bowing it so it creaked in protest.

'So the universal thinks she is my match, does she?' he screeched, taking a step towards her. 'What has cowardice to do with me? A feeble human idea. I rip and tear whom I will. Even the universal. Perhaps you need a mark in your flesh to remind you *whose you are*?' He emphasized each word with a flick of his lion's tail.

Connie reached behind her, groping the far side of the trunk in search of the fingers of the gorgon but found only rough bark. The griffin was now only a metre away. Kullervo paused to contemplate her, his eyes greedily devouring her fear.

'You tremble before me and yet you think you are my equal, Companion.' He raised a claw and gently stroked her cheek with its razor-edged tip. 'Where shall I put my mark? Perhaps here? I would like you to remember me each time you look in a mirror.' Connie flattened herself against the trunk, her knees buckling, her hands still fluttering behind her in a last desperate attempt to find the gorgon. But the creature must have reneged on her promise because Connie's fingers met no answering touch.

'You can mark me, but I'll never be yours,' Connie replied in a whisper, her heart failing.

'As I have told you, Companion, you already are mine,' countered the griffin and he raised his foreleg to strike her.

At that moment, Connie's fingers were grasped in a strong fist and she felt a rush of cold fire blaze up her arm, mounting through her neck to her eyes. Her head jerked back and she stared straight into the slit-like pupils of Kullervo, meeting his disdainful look with a new and completely unexpected power. His talons froze in the air a hair's breadth from her face. She could see rage and confusion in his eyes now as he realized that she had tricked him. Pressing the attack further, Connie forced the paralysis deeper into her adversary. Caught by the skin of stone in which she had encased him, he was unable to shape-shift. She could feel the gorgon urging her on: her decision made to protect Cassandra's hatchling, she was now fighting as if for her own young. Heaviness was overcoming the griffin's wings and he began to sway, no longer able to maintain his balance on the narrow branch. Connie paused, holding him there with her gaze, knowing that if she pursued the attack further it would cause him to topple to the ground, trapping the immortal part of Kullervo in a tomb of stone.

Mack, who had been watching the combat with horrified fascination, was now distracted by the sound of drums and horns approaching.

'Connie, the procession's coming!' he called up. 'Whatever you've got to do, you'd better do it fast!'

His words melded in Connie's head with the urging from the gorgon to kill, their voices weaving round each other like vipers in a nest. Confused as to what she should do, Connie gazed into Kullervo's fierce eyes glaring in outrage at her. Did he not deserve death? Deserve to be stamped out for being the vicious creature he had proved himself to be? Should she not be revenged on him for all the pain he had put her through? Why should she show pity? He had showed no pity towards her. Her mind filled with bitter anger against him and the temptation grew to complete her conquest.

Then, like a match flaring in the darkness, she had a fleeting recollection of how they had flown together, dancing in the air for one wild moment of exhilarating companionship. She then knew that, try as she might, she could not hurt her companion. He was part of her and she was part of him. The light grew stronger as she remembered how he had saved her life today by catching her as she fell. She could not murder him in cold blood. Godiva had once killed her companion and destroyed part of herself in the process—she would not be like that.

'Go!' she ordered him, closing her eyes and freeing her hand from the gorgon's grip. 'Go, or I'll not spare you again. We're even now.'

With a screech and a bound from the branch that made it oscillate violently, almost unseating Connie, the griffin shot into the sky and sped away over the treetops, screaming his hatred of her mercy to the heavens. Connie collapsed with exhaustion against the trunk, her head bowed.

'You let him go!' Mack protested, his voice laden with accusation. 'You had him and you let him go!'

'Shut up, Dad!' Col intervened from above. 'You don't understand.'

'Too right, I don't,' Mack fumed.

Connie looked up at Col and saw that he was watching her with a pitying expression on his face.

'You made the right choice, Connie,' he said to her. 'Whatever he's done to you, to us, you mustn't become like him.'

'But I . . . I couldn't do it, Col,' she said, her voice choked. 'I can't kill my companion.'

Just then the blare of police megaphones, cheering voices, miscellaneous musical instruments erupted into the space under the oak's boughs.

'Save Merlin's Oak! Save Merlin's Oak!' chanted the protesters.

Looking down, Connie saw the pale ovals of upturned faces. She glanced about her, wondering what had become of the gorgon. The creature had slithered further up the tree and was lying camouflaged in a thick spray of lemon-coloured leaves. Some of the crowd below, however, had spotted the vivid red and yellow costume of the jester and a babble of voices built as more and more people pressed into the confined space. The man from the council, with his bodyguard of police, pushed through to the front and looked up. He seemed to regard the presence in the oak tree of Mack Clamworthy, dressed as a belled jester, as the final insult. Incensed, he grabbed a megaphone and bellowed up the tree:

'Get out of that tree! That tree is scheduled for clearance today. You are trespassing on council property.'

The crowd jeered but then gave a cheer as Mack waved two fingers at him.

'Come and get me then!' he shouted.

'Mr Clamworthy,' Connie called down to him, 'it might not be such a bad idea to get down. And I wouldn't mind a ladder.'

There was a shrill scream from below. 'Connie!' It was Anneena. She had just spotted her friend half-hidden in the branches above.

'Hello, Anneena,' Connie shouted back. 'I'm a bit stuck. So's Col.'

The rest of the crowd now noticed the girl straddling a bough.

'Who's that?' exclaimed the council man.

Godiva Lionheart shouldered her way through the press. 'There are children up there. Do something useful for once—get your men to fetch a rope and a ladder.'

Rupa pushed her way over to Anneena. 'What's happening?' she asked.

'It's Connie. Look, she's up there. She says Col is even higher.'

Mr and Mrs Nuruddin now joined their two daughters.

'We need the fire brigade,' Anneena's father announced. He collared the closest policeman and entered into an earnest discussion, resulting in the use of a police radio to summon help.

'Hang on, Connie!' Rupa shouted up.

'I'm not exactly going to do anything else, am I?' Connie called back.

Zed made his way to the front with his entourage of photographers and news crews. He was grinning broadly.

'This is really wild. Who are they?' Zed asked Rupa, removing his sunglasses to take a closer look at the inhabitants of the tree.

'You're not going to believe this, but you are looking at a jester, a missing schoolgirl and, somewhere higher up, Sir Galahad.'

'Schoolgirl? What schoolgirl?'

'Connie Lionheart.'

The name began to buzz around the circle of reporters. Two of them even climbed up to get a closer view until they were threatened in no uncertain terms by Mack if they tried to get too near. He was mindful of the gorgon curled around a branch only a few metres above. Forced back to the ground, the reporters began to shout up questions.

'What you doing up there, Connie love?'

'How long have you been here?'

Connie looked up to Col. 'What shall I say?' she mouthed to him.

'Improvise,' he said with a pained grin.

'I've ... er ... I've been up here all week,' Connie lied. 'I've come to give my support to the protest—Save Merlin's Oak! Save Merlin's Oak!'

'Yeah, you heard the girl,' shouted Zed. 'Save Merlin's Oak!'

The call was taken up by the protesters who began to chant it again, drowning out further questions from the reporters, much to Connie's relief.

There was a commotion below as police forced the spectators and horses back, allowing a team of yellow helmeted firemen through to the tree. Two of them were carrying an aluminium ladder, which they placed against the trunk. Before they could reach Mack, however, he had swung down and dropped to the ground.

'Don't need help, thanks,' he said.

His escape was prevented by a policeman who

placed a restraining hand on his shoulder.

'You'd better come along with me, sir,' the officer said. 'We've got a few questions for you that you'll have to answer down at the station.'

Mack shrugged. 'Fine, but not till my son's down safely.'

The policeman hesitated.

'Hey, man, have a heart!' said Zed, slapping Mack on the back.

Faced with a barrage of cameras, the officer nodded.

Having climbed as high as they could by ladder, two firemen were now making rapid progress from branch to branch towards Connie. She looked anxiously over to the gorgon, but the creature had not stirred, her head well hidden in the folds of her wings.

'Col,' Connie called up softly so only he could hear, 'do you think you can make it down to us? I don't think it would be a good idea for them to come any higher, do you?'

'I can't, Connie,' Col replied, 'there's something wrong with my leg. I think it might be broken.'

To Connie's alarm, the gorgon began to move. She unfurled herself and slithered higher up the tree.

'Don't look!' Connie called out in warning. 'She's coming.'

'It's all right, love,' one of the firemen shouted, thinking she was panicking, 'we're almost with you.'

The gorgon climbed to the very top of the tree, spread her wings to their full extent so they surrounded her like a butterfly, and leapt into the air. Lifted by the wind, she slipped away on the air current accompanied by a flurry of dead leaves. She glided into the distance, fluttering down like a bronze seed and out of sight into Snake Hollow.

'Here you are, love, take my hand.' Tearing her eyes away from the horizon, Connie held out her arm and found it grasped in the reassuring clasp of the nearest fireman. He clipped a harness around her, to which he had attached a rope. The other fireman climbed to join them, looked up and whistled.

'How did your friend get up there?' he marvelled. 'Got wings as well as armour, has he?'

'He thinks he's broken his leg,' Connie said quickly.

'We'll need the stretcher then. Hang on, son.'

Connie was lowered to the ground dangling like a spider on the end of a thread. Once her feet touched ground, she was immediately wrapped in blankets and bundled away by a police-woman.

310

'But Col!' she protested.

'As soon as there's news, I'll let you know,' the policewoman said, dragging on her reluctant arm. 'But I think I'd better return you to your parents, don't you?'

'My parents are here?'

'Of course. They're coming up from town now. Your great-aunt is here somewhere already.'

Godiva was the last person Connie wanted to see right now. She tried to slip away but the police officer had a firm grip on her. Connie caught sight of Col's father. 'Mack—tell the others I'm down,' she shouted. 'They've got to know. And Argand and Skylark—you've got to find them—see that they're all right.'

The policewoman clearly thought she was raving. 'Calm down, love. What you need is a nice cup of tea and a rest. All your protester friends are safe,' she added, clearly thinking that Argand and Skylark were nicknames for some of the ecowarriors. 'You've got to come with me.'

19
New Member

The policewoman guided Connie out of the wood and over to a police van parked in front of the bulldozers which sprawled like yellow crocodiles on a river bank, teeth-edged jaws gaping open. A dozen or so road-workers were sitting with their feet up in the cabs of the idle machines. A few of them looked up from their newspapers curiously but then seeing nothing more than a bedraggled girl and her escort, returned to the sports pages.

Connie sat on the back step of the van holding a mug of tea from a police flask in her shaking hand. The shock of all she had gone through over the past week was beginning to hit—the forced entry into her mind made by Kullervo and his followers, the days spent lying tied up on the top bunk, the last few perilous hours at the summit of the oak. And now she was going to have to give some kind of explanation to her parents and great-aunt, but what that would be she could not even begin to imagine in her numbed state. One thing of which she was certain: whatever she said would not stop Godiva telling her parents to impose the severest punishment she could think up. Connie's suffering was not over.

A police car came up the hill on the tail of an ambulance with lights flashing and siren blaring. The ambulance turned into the picnic spot and disappeared from view, but the second vehicle continued up the hill to where Connie was waiting. The moment of reckoning had come. She stood up, letting the blanket fall to her feet, and took a deep breath. The rear doors opened and her father and mother got out, then her great-uncle. There was a momentary pause as the three of them looked over at her silently, her father's face grey with the strain of the past few days, her mother's tear-stained, her great-uncle's eyes full of pain. All Connie's made-up words of explanation died on her lips and she burst into tears. It was the best thing she could have done because it immediately released an outpouring of emotion from her mother that swept over her like a storm.

'Darling, where have you been?' her mother cried, sweeping her into a tight hug as if she never wanted to let go of her again. Her usually immaculate clothes were rumpled and had clearly been slept in. 'Do you realize what you've put us through? We were beginning to think that all sorts of horrible things might have happened to you when we didn't hear from you.'

Her father put his arms around both his wife and daughter. Connie could smell his reassuring scent—she felt secure in his strong embrace. 'Now, now, she's safe,' he said with unusual softness. 'Let's not talk about this now. Let's just be thankful that she's back with us.'

Uncle Hugh came over to stand awkwardly beside the family huddle.

'Are you all right, Connie?' he asked uncertainly.

'I'm so sorry,' Connie said, brushing the tears from her eyes with the back of a grubby hand. 'I wish it'd all never happened,' she added truthfully.

'I'm sorry I didn't realize how bad it had got,' he said gruffly. 'I let you down.'

This was what Connie feared: that he would blame himself.

'No, no, it's all my fault. I know I shouldn't've run away.'

The policewoman returned with Godiva Lionheart. Connie thought her great-aunt looked dazed. Godiva walked up to her. She said nothing but patted Connie on the back.

'What? Y-you're not going to tell me off?' Connie stammered.

Godiva shook her head.

Hugh approached his sister and took her arm. 'Are you all right?' he asked in a low voice.

The policewoman gave a discreet cough. 'I think we'd better get Connie away before the media get here. I'll need to ask her a few questions later, but for now I suggest you take her back home.'

It was a very subdued party in the police car for the short journey back to Lionheart Lodge where Connie's parents had been staying over the last few terrible days. There did not seem to be a safe topic of conversation. Uncle Hugh began to ask about the procession as a way of lightening the mood but fell silent when it was clear that Connie did not feel like talking. The police driver sensed the awkward atmosphere and tried to help by switching on the radio. Unfortunately, the local news station was running continual coverage of the exciting events up at Mallins Wood:

'. . . a most extraordinary day, you'll agree, Steve,' the reporter burbled to the studio. 'First

315

the stand-off between the protesters and the construction team and now this.' The policeman moved to switch it off, but Connie intervened:

'No, leave it, please!'

'Yes, and now I can see them winching the boy down. A local lad, according to the procession's organizers, Col Clamworthy. He arrived here this morning dressed as Sir Galahad. You may remember, Steve, I reported how he left the others, waving a lance over his head. Look, here he comes—but I can't see how badly injured he is. Two firemen are lowering him to the ground. We had no idea that he'd gone on such a dangerous quest when he galloped off. Quite how he got up so high is anyone's guess . . .'

'Is there any news of the girl they brought down earlier?' the studio presenter asked in a voice that suggested he was lapping up the drama.

'Connie Lionheart, the missing girl? She's already made a name for herself as an environmental protester over that tanker incident at New Year. Too bad the police didn't think to look earlier at the obvious place where all the ecowarriors in the country were congregating, ha, ha,' the reporter laughed heartily making Connie wince. 'From what she said when she was found, she had been up the tree all week as a kind of protest—extraordinary dedication for one so young.'

'And how is the campaign to save Mallins Wood going now the appeal to buy it has been launched?'

'Zed Bailey told me earlier that he's been bowled over by the response. He only launched the appeal a matter of hours ago but the website has already been inundated with messages of support and cash pledges from people all over the country. Of course, the dramatic coverage of the rescue of the missing girl and her friend has helped give it publicity they could not have dreamed of. And yes, the boy is down. Sir Galahad is once more on the earth and in the care of the emergency services.'

'Thank you, Mike. If any of our listeners would like to make a pledge, you can log on to the Save Merlin's Oak website, check our site and follow the link. And now, stay tuned for *Krafted*'s first live appearance at the Hescombe Music Festival . . .'

The car pulled up on the Abbey Close. Walking down the path, flanked by her parents, Connie took a last look up at the sky and wondered what was happening up on the moors. Had her message got through in time to stop them coming to rescue her? What would Kullervo's forces do now that their leader had fled? Confused and abandoned, would some of

317

them try to attack, or would they just melt away, biding their time for a more favourable occasion? From what the reporter had said, everything seemed quite normal in the wood, apart, that is, from the assortment of medieval characters, horses, reporters, and emergency services all milling around the foot of Merlin's Oak. It looked as if the attack had been postponed. The Society had survived this crisis—just.

'Now, darling,' her mother said as she ran a hot foaming bath for her, 'take off those clothes and have a nice relaxing soak.' As Connie discarded her brown leather flying suit, her mother picked it up gingerly. 'Godiva mentioned your strange taste in clothes, but I'm pleased to see that it has stopped you getting too scratched whilst you've been perched up that tree,' she said with a hint of approval at the once despised garment.

'And,' Connie said with a yawn as she stepped into the bath, 'at least I'm not on national TV wearing bells and armour.'

'What's that?'

'Nothing.'

Connie's mother stepped softly out of the room as her daughter lay back in the bubbles to let the warm water wash away both the grime and the bad memories.

***

The fire crew wrapped Col up like a very large papoose for the journey down the tree. His leg was aching, his back screaming with pain where the dragon's tail had caught him, and the rest of him a network of minor injuries, but he didn't care. All he cared about was Skylark, last seen tumbling through the trees not far from the clearing where they had taken off. As soon as he bumped to the ground, he looked frantically around for his father and spotted him in the company of a stern-faced policeman.

'Dad,' Col shouted, 'Dad!'

The crowd fell back, allowing Mack to reach his son's stretcher. He knelt down beside him and took Col's hand.

'It's all right, son,' Mack said out loud. Then, quietly, he added, 'No need to worry—I've called off our forces—just in time too. The dragons were about to set off. I had some difficulty though: my guard here was very suspicious—thought I was talking to some ecowarrior reinforcements or something.'

Col was only half listening to him, desperate to get an answer to the only question in which he was interested. 'But Skylark? How is he?'

'I don't know, Col,' Mack said with a shake of

his head. 'Captain Graves and some volunteers are leaving now to search the wood for both him and Argand. I'd go myself but apparently I'm under arrest.' He grimaced. 'They seem to think I put you and Connie up to climbing that tree. Your gran's on her way to the hospital—she'll meet you there.'

The paramedics ushered Mack back and picked up the stretcher. Col felt his frustration building: he could not bear to be carried away like this not knowing. Skylark could be lying injured somewhere close by. He might even be dying. He could be dead.

'Col! Col! It's me, Rat!' The familiar sharp face bobbed up by the side of the stretcher. 'I've come to tell you that I've got something of yours. Don't worry, I'll look after it for you!'

'What?' Col asked in confusion as Rat was pushed back by a policeman. 'What've you got?'

'I've got your . . .' But the doors of the ambulance were slammed shut and Col did not hear the answer.

Mrs Clamworthy wheeled Col out of hospital later that day to the waiting taxi. He had spent many hours in Accident and Emergency having his right leg encased in plaster from the ankle to the thigh, the cut on his back dressed, and his other injuries cleaned up. The nurse who dealt with his back marvelled over the extent of his injuries.

'You tell me you didn't fall?' she said doubtfully as she dabbed his wound with disinfectant. 'But this is the strangest cut I've seen in a long time—all lacerated as if you've been hit by a saw. And your costume—completely shredded! Very strange.'

'Yeah, weird,' agreed Col, deciding that blank incomprehension was his best defence.

Mrs Clamworthy helped Col slide into the back of the taxi.

'Right, home and bed for you, young man,' she said firmly.

'No way. Not till I find out what's happened to Skylark.'

'But there's no word of him, Col dear, as I told you,' Mrs Clamworthy said in a low voice, glancing nervously over at the driver.

'Then we're going back to the wood. I'm not giving up just because I've taken a bit of a battering.'

'A bit of a battering!' Mrs Clamworthy exclaimed, forgetting to keep her voice down in her indignation. 'You've a broken leg and stitches in your back. You're lucky to be alive.'

'But I am alive and I have to find out if Skylark is too.'

Mrs Clamworthy sighed. She too had a companion and could not in all honesty have said she would not have been demanding the same thing if it had been her friend at risk.

'All right, Col, but only for an hour—no more. Then it's . . .'

'Yes, I know: home and bed.'

The picnic spot was quiet when the taxi turned into it as the festival was now in full swing and everyone had gone to listen to the bands on the main stage. Col could hear the music booming from the speaker system. Lights arced in the sky, dancing on the clouds.

'What exactly do you think you're going to do?' his grandmother asked him in an exasperated tone as Col began to hobble on his crutches over to Rat's bus. 'Too much of that and you'll split your stitches!'

Col knocked on the door with a crutch but there was no reply except a torrent of furious barking from Wolf.

'I'm going to the clearing,' he told his grandmother, swinging himself around. 'It's where he fell.'

Mrs Clamworthy's face lightened as she saw someone approaching through the trees, a cane tucked under one arm. 'Look, here's Captain Graves. He'll be able to give you the latest and stop you doing anything rash.'

'Col, my boy, delighted you're up and about!' barked Captain Graves, his neat moustache twitching with a smile on seeing his pupil. 'Actually, I'm pleased to see you for another reason. We've got a bit of a situation on our hands.'

'Skylark?' Col asked anxiously.

'He's . . . er . . . well, you'd better come and see for yourself.'

'But, Michael, Col's injured!' Mrs Clamworthy protested. 'He's got a broken leg. He can't go hopping off without causing himself more damage.'

'Half a mo.' Captain Graves gave a piercing whistle and Mags trotted out of the trees. 'Intelligent animal, this,' he said with approval. 'You can still sit on a pony, can't you, my boy?'

'Yeah,' Col replied. Captain Graves helped Col onto Mags's back, his leg sticking out awkwardly in its plaster.

'Off we go.' Captain Graves took the pony's halter. 'Are you coming, Lavinia?'

Mrs Clamworthy, who had long since decided she was not going to let her grandson out of her sight again that day, followed them along the woodland track that led to the clearing.

'Skylark's all right, isn't he, Captain?' Col asked hopefully.

'He'll be all right now. We could've done with the universal to help Windfoal heal him but apparently she's incommunicado at the moment. No, the problem is that it wasn't us who found him.'

'And Argand—the golden dragon?'

'She's been found too. Tough as old boots are dragons—even young ones. Her pride rather than her body was injured—at least, that's what Dr Brock says.'

'So, who did find Skylark?' Col asked, though he thought he could guess the answer.

'You'll see.'

Mags stepped out of the lengthening evening shadows into the clearing. There was a nip in the air. Col shivered in the breeze that drove drifts of seed heads across the open ground like snowflakes. On the far side, in the shelter of the large chestnut tree, he could see a huddle of people gathered around something on the ground. He could sense a presence and the hairs on the back of his neck began to tingle: it was Skylark. Urging Mags through the waist-high bracken, he dismounted heavily onto his good leg, swearing softly as his wounds protested, and collapsed beside his friend, throwing his arms around his neck and burying his head in his mane. Instantly, their connection was re-forged. Col and Skylark rejoiced to be together again after they both had feared the other to be dead. Skylark's right wing was broken but he had managed to control his tumble with his left and landed heavily, spraining his right foreleg. He had been fortunate: the wing had been set in a splint and his other injuries cleaned and dressed, even before the Society had found him.

'Who did this?' Col wondered. He looked up and saw Rat grinning down at him.

'That's an amazing beast you've got there, Col Clamworthy,' Rat laughed. 'I told you I'd look after it for you.'

Col could see Dr Brock and Captain Graves exchange a worried look. This was a major problem—a mythical creature had been exposed to an outsider and there was no way of hiding the truth from him. They could not even pretend it was some elaborate costume as the boy had tended Skylark and knew all too well that he was made of flesh, blood, and bone.

'And I suppose you're going to tell me now that that dragon on your helmet was real too,' Rat continued. Dr Brock stuffed something deeper inside his jacket.

'Um . . .' said Col.

'Don't fret yourself, Col,' Rat said, 'I won't tell anyone your little secret. I see things like this all the time. Me dad thinks I'm mad but I've seen the little people in the trees and rivers.'

Col looked up at Dr Brock. Surely Rat must have the gift? How else would he have seen all these things? Skylark had sensed something in him already when they had first met. Dr Brock nodded, understanding Col's unspoken question.

'Thanks, Rat, thanks for looking after Skylark,' Col said. 'Would you mind not telling anyone about this?'

'No worries! I've already said I won't.'

'And would you be interested in meeting some more friends of mine—some people who'd like to find out more about you?' Rat looked suspicious. 'Not to do anything to you,' Col added quickly, 'but to see if you might want to join our Society?'

'Is that where you got this winged horse from?'

'Sort of. I didn't get him—I don't own him—he's a friend and a member of the Society too.'

Rat shrugged. 'You're cracked, Col Clamworthy, but it sounds as if it might be a laugh. I'll meet your friends.'

'Now, Col, I really insist that you come home with me,' Mrs Clamworthy broke in. 'Sitting on the damp ground—riding horses—you'll be back in hospital in traction if you're not careful.'

'You'd better do as the lady says,' said Rat with a respectful nod to Col's grandmother. He had always been scrupulously polite to her whenever he had visited Col's home, having a healthy fear of matriarchs. He helped pull Col to his feet and gave him his shoulder to lean on as Col hopped back to Mags. 'There was a dragon, wasn't there?' he said quietly in Col's ear. 'And I know—I have to keep quiet about that too, don't I?' Col floundered for an answer but Rat cut him short by giving him a wink. 'Don't worry: no one would believe me even if I did tell them,' he said. 'They're so used to hearing my stories they just think I'm cracked. It's good to know that you're cracked too.'

20
Hescombe

A tense silence reigned at the breakfast table at Lionheart Lodge. For once, Godiva was completely innocent—she had been very quiet since returning from Mallins Wood. The protagonists in this scene were Connie and her parents. The feelings of relief that had let Connie off any explanations the previous evening had been replaced this morning by a determination on the part of her parents to 'get to the bottom of things', but they were being met with evasive answers from their daughter. She neither wanted to explain clearly where she had been nor give reasons for her abrupt departure from her great-aunt's home.

'But if it wasn't so very bad, as you maintain,

Connie,' said her mother with a hint of asperity in her voice, 'why on earth did you run away? You can't tell me you were so worried about a few trees you put us through all this agony.'

Connie looked down at her cereal, which was sagging into the milk untouched. She had no appetite.

'I don't think you realize what a fuss you've caused,' her father said angrily. 'You've had the police of half the country out looking for you, national appeals—you can't even begin to imagine what your mother and I have suffered—and you have the gall to sit there without giving us a single word of credible explanation.'

What could she say? Connie thought miserably. They were right to be cross with her. Everyone would be cross with her—even the Society members who knew the truth—because she had foolishly wandered into a trap. She now saw that she should have gone to someone first for advice—Evelyn, for example—and saved everyone a lot of heartache and danger. Of course, she had not meant to be away so long. Of course, she had meant to return at once with Col and apologize for disappearing for a weekend, accepting the inevitable punishment handed out by Godiva. She had not meant it to end like this.

From the other side of the table, Godiva

was watching her niece closely. Hugh was absent-mindedly buttering and re-buttering the same piece of toast, deeply uncomfortable.

Godiva suddenly spoke up. 'Beryl, Gordon, have you asked yourself whether Connie is able to give you a "credible explanation" as you put it?' Connie flinched, sure that her great-aunt was about to begin another diatribe about the madness induced by the Society. 'It looks to me as though she doesn't really know why she did what she did, but she does seem sorry for it.' Connie's jaw dropped—Godiva, defending her! 'But I can tell you a few things that I know now: she's not happy here, she's happy in Hescombe with her friends. Your daughter is not . . . well, not entirely normal, but that's not always a bad thing.'

Beryl and Gordon looked at each other in astonishment. Hugh put his toast down and stared at his sister. Slowly, his face broke into a grin.

'If you are not going to take her back with you to Manila . . . ' continued Godiva.

Beryl tutted. 'That isn't possible, Godiva, what would we do about schools for a girl like Connie? And we can't afford to give up our jobs without having new ones to come back to.'

'I know. As I was saying, if you aren't taking her back to Manila, then I'm afraid I cannot take her back here where I know she'll be miserable.

There is only one answer: she'll have to go back to Evelyn's. I know she'll have her. As for school, well, after all, she originally had a place at Chartmouth. I'm sure it's just a question of having a quiet word with the headteacher.'

'But what about you?' asked Gordon. 'I thought you were weaning her off her Society-thing.'

'I'm afraid I won't be doing that any more.'

'Why ever not?'

Godiva smiled at Connie. 'I'm going to Brazil.'

'You're what!' exclaimed Gordon.

'You heard me. I'm joining a team trying to save the Amazonian rainforest.'

Gordon choked on his coffee.

Hugh clapped his hands. 'Good for you, Iva. Whatever persuaded you?'

'I've decided it's time I made up for past mistakes. I'm sorry, Connie, that I've been so hard on you but I think you of all people know what I was running from.'

Connie nodded. 'Yes, I do. I think I'd run from him myself if I had the choice.'

'What's all this?' spluttered Connie's father. 'Who's she talking about?'

'Our family inheritance,' said Godiva briskly. 'Now, what are you going to do about your daughter?'

331

'Well, I . . .' Gordon turned to Hugh. 'Are you going to Brazil too?'

'No, I don't think so,' said Hugh with a fond smile at his sister. 'I don't think she'll need me any more.'

'So, can Connie stay with you here?'

'Oh no,' said Godiva, 'I'm going to shut up Lionheart Lodge—let the garden run wild for a while.'

'It's too big a place for me on my own,' agreed Hugh. 'You'll have to send her back to Shaker Row.'

Gordon and Beryl both looked doubtful.

'But what about that man—the biker-jester man? He's to blame for half of what went on yesterday according to the papers,' Beryl said with an anxious glance at her daughter.

'Oh no,' said Connie, 'that's all wrong. As I told the policewoman last night, he was trying to help me down but I got up too high.' She felt cheerful about this half lie, knowing that the whole business was absolutely not Mack Clamworthy's fault.

'And I've been thinking,' said Hugh. 'I'd like to be nearer the sea. A friend of mine, Horace Little—you know, Godiva, the man who took Connie out with his granddaughter?—he and I, well, we've been putting together a little scheme to set up a boat together—he likes swimming apparently, must be mad—so I was thinking of getting a little cottage somewhere on the coast not too far from Evelyn. Connie's brother could come and stay during his holidays if he liked. What do you think, Connie?'

'I think it's a dream come true,' Connie said, smiling at him through glistening eyes. She could not believe this turn of events: it was as if her great-aunt and uncle had waved a magic wand and made all obstacles to her happiness disappear. She felt like leaping across the table and hugging them.

'Well, I suppose you could help Evelyn keep an eye on Connie for us,' said Gordon, beginning to see the benefits of this scheme. 'Monitor developments. Make sure she's not getting into anything dangerous again.'

'That's settled then,' said Hugh. 'Now, how about some toast, Connie?'

'Yes, I'd like that,' she replied. 'But perhaps with a bit less butter.'

After lunch, Connie approached her parents as they were setting off to fetch her brother Simon from his school. They were planning for the whole family to spend some time together before they all had to return to their normal lives.

'Would it be OK if I called on Col?' she asked. 'He's at home with a broken leg and I really want to see if he's all right.'

Her parents exchanged looks. 'I suppose if you go back to Hescombe we can't stop you seeing people in that Society of yours, can we?' her father said severely.

'It would be difficult not to see them,' agreed Connie humbly.

He sighed. 'All right then. But I need hardly remind you that your great-uncle will be keeping a close eye on what you get up to from now on.'

With a gleeful nod, Connie dashed out to the shed and pulled out the bike. Cycling past the wood, she saw that the fields were still teeming with festival-goers and the bulldozers had retreated back down the hill. Not a tree had yet been felled.

Free-wheeling down the hill into Hescombe, she sang at the top of her voice, rattled into Col's road and dumped her bike at the gate. As she paused to knock at the kitchen door, she heard a babble of voices inside and realized that they must have a houseful at the moment. No one heard her tap so she pushed the door and entered. The room fell silent when the people inside saw her standing in the doorway. Dr Brock, Evelyn, Mack, Mrs Clamworthy, and the

Trustees, Kira Okona, Kinga Potowska, and Eagle-Child, were all clustered around Col, who sat enthroned in an armchair by the stove, plastered leg up on a footstool. Mack, as usual, was the first to recover from her abrupt appearance.

'Hey now, if it isn't our universal! Come on in, darling.'

'Connie, we're delighted to see you!' Mrs Clamworthy exclaimed.

'But a bit surprised,' added Dr Brock. 'We thought you'd been taken away for good by your parents.'

She shook her head shyly in front of all these watching eyes. 'No, and it's better than that.' She knelt beside Col. 'I'm back.'

'You're what?' he burst out.

Evelyn swooped down and gave her a hug. 'That's great, Connie!'

'I'm back—back in Hescombe, going to Chartmouth Secondary School—I'm back.'

'And the Society?' Dr Brock asked quickly. A golden snout peeped out of his jacket pocket and sniffed the air.

'We haven't worked out the finer details yet,' Connie admitted, reaching to take Argand from him.

'But that's good enough for now!' Col said happily as Connie cradled Argand and scratched the

335

dragonet's neck, causing her to shiver with pleasure. 'So, I'll see you at school next week then?'

'Absolutely,' Connie beamed.

The following Wednesday, with the seagulls calling raucously outside, welcoming her back to Hescombe, Connie put on her new uniform in her bedroom in the attic. Tying her school tie in the mirror, Connie smiled at herself. Yes, it was going to be OK.

Her parents escorted her to the bus stop leaving her in the capable hands of Anneena and Jane.

'It's so good to have you back where you belong,' said Anneena, giving her a hug. 'Has your great-aunt really gone off to Brazil?'

'Yeah.' Connie's smile stretched from ear to ear at the thought. Godiva had been so happy as she set off on her voyage.

'Did you hear about the wood, Connie?' Jane asked. 'Zed Bailey was on the TV this morning.'

Connie shook her head. 'No, what's happened now?'

'Well, the road scheme has been stopped in its tracks and there's going to be a further public inquiry,' Jane said with a triumphant smile. 'Thanks to the outcry over Merlin's Oak.'

'They're now calling it a site of unique cultural importance!' Anneena butted in proudly. 'And the appeal's going through the roof. It seems that your story got on the American news last Saturday and we've been inundated with pledges from Merlin enthusiasts from all over.'

'So what'll they do about the road, do you think?' Connie asked, trying to ignore the reference to her fame in the States.

'Oh, it'll be built, of course. Axoil is too powerful to be stopped,' Anneena said grimacing. 'They still want a road for their tankers. But they'll have to bypass the wood and take a less direct route.'

'It's not all good news: it'll mean that a lot of farmland will have to be sacrificed,' Jane added.

'Oh no.' Connie began to imagine the new casualties this would cause—the meadow dwellers and other animals. She wished there didn't have to be any road at all but in that she knew she was out of step with the fast changing pace of modern life.

'Don't worry too much, Connie: it's probably the best we could hope for,' Anneena concluded. 'We may not have got everything we wanted—but we got enough to save the wood.'

The bus was already drawing up when they spotted Col swinging along on his crutches as quickly as he could towards the stop, a heavy bag over his shoulder. Jane ran to relieve him of his burden while Anneena held the bus for him. He hobbled on board and sat down next to Connie.

'So, finally all the team's here then?' he said with a grin at the three girls. 'Are you OK with being a late arrival with me at Chartmouth, Connie?' he asked her.

'I wouldn't have it any other way,' she said firmly. 'As you once told me, we share many things.'

'Yeah, like life and death situations,' he said softly so Anneena and Jane could not hear. 'I haven't thanked you for coming for me.'

'And I haven't thanked you for coming for me.'

'I suppose that makes us even.' His words recalled Connie's last words to Kullervo. 'He'll be back, won't he?'

'I'm afraid so. We've only bought ourselves a little breathing space. But next time, I'm going to be better prepared.'

'And so will I.'

They sat in silence for a few minutes. Watching the streets of Hescombe pass, Connie pondered the change that had come over her in the last week, how Kullervo had forced a door open in her mind and claimed her as his companion. Would she ever be able to sever that link? She felt

338

guilty about the decision she had made in the wood. She was no use to anyone if she couldn't bring herself to destroy Kullervo when she had him in her power. He was still out to eradicate humanity from the earth. If she couldn't stop him, who would be able to do so? Turning from these gloomy thoughts, she thought of another question she wanted answering.

'And your mother?' Connie asked Col hesitantly, sensing she was trespassing on some very private territory for him.

'I don't know.' He looked out of the window. Rat was waiting by the roadside at the picnic spot. The bus pulled over to pick him up. 'She's disappeared again. I don't know what she'll do now: thrown out of the Society and not best mates with Kullervo any more. But I expect she'll turn up again some day.'

Connie said nothing as she waited for Rat to board the bus. She was not sure she could yet forgive Col's mother for keeping her captive all those days. She hoped she would not have to see Cassandra again and, she added to herself, she would not be too upset if she never saw the gorgon again either.

'Present for you,' Rat said, squeezing onto the seat next to Col. He threw a handful of gleaming chestnuts in Connie's lap. 'Hand them round—

there'll be plenty more where they came from, thanks to you lot.'

The bus climbed out of Hescombe, taking the winding road that led around the edge of the wood, leaving the secrets of the trees untouched.

JULIA GOLDING grew up on the edge of Epping Forest. After
reading English at Cambridge, she joined the Foreign Office and
served in Poland. Her work as a diplomat took her from the high
point of town twinning in the Tatra Mountains to the low of
inspecting the bottom of a Silesian coal mine.

On leaving Poland, she joined Oxfam as a lobbyist on conflict
issues, campaigning at the United Nations and with governments
to lessen the impact of war on civilians living in war zones. She
now works as a freelance writer.

Married with three children, she lives in Oxford. *The Gorgon's
Gaze* is the second part of the glorious 'Companions Quartet'. The
first part is called *Secret of the Sirens*.